HOLLYWOOD GEMS

CHRISTINA MIANO

This is a work of fiction. Names, characters, places and
incidents are the product of the authors imagination or are used
fictitiously. Any resemblance to actual events, locales or persons
living or dead is purely coincidental.

Printed in the United States of America

First Printing, 2016

ISBN 978-0692574157

Biederman Books
2150 Portola Avenue, Suite D305
Livermore, CA 94551

Dedicated To My Sisters:

Antonia, Denise and Allison Miano

&

To Michelle Lucas-Rice:

A little piece of you is in Mia, Dee, Frankie and Me

CHAPTER ONE

I usually take the steps to my apartment two by two. I actually have to psyche myself up to start the journey because I live in a third floor walk-up, and these floors are not normal floors. This is San Francisco I'm talking about, and you're looking at about fifteen steps a flight. Once, when I was sitting on the bottom step for an unusually long amount of time, my downstairs neighbor, Charlie, came out his front door with a boom box and started playing the *Rocky* theme to help motivate me. I should fess up early on that there have been times when I've had too much to drink and I've actually started to crawl up. I'm admitting this now in case it happens later on so you won't be too surprised. As long as I'm admitting to things, I should probably tell you there have been times when I've started to crawl sober.

I'm having one of those days where my energy level is so low that I'm sitting on the bottom step trying to think of a way to get to the third floor without using the stairs. Could I straddle the banister and shimmy up? Could I go outside and scale the building using the windows as steps? Could I warp myself there like Spock? I'm a Trekkie; I think of warping often. I've been sitting here so long that I'm starting to nod off when Charlie comes through the front doors. He's looking at me in a really pathetic way, and for some reason I'm not bothered at all that he pities me.

Charlie is the kind of neighbor you dream of having. He's on the first floor so noise is never a problem, and we both purchased our apartments so we know the value of taking care of our homes, inside and out. As far as I'm concerned, his good looks only add to our property value. He's a little over six feet tall with dark, wavy hair that he's constantly running his fingers through. His eyes are a deep blue and he has an amazingly boyish grin. You would think after I've gone on about him as I have that there would be feelings between us, but I assure you there are none.

In fact, I promise you this story will not end up with me ignoring the neighbor who is so perfect for me just to get together with him in the end after I realize he is the one. He's not the one for me, and I'm not the one for him. I can't give you specific reasons why; it just is what it is. You know how you can't fight chemistry when you feel it with someone? Well, the same goes when you don't feel it.

"So John left?" Charlie asks.

I'm a little confused, and I guess my expression speaks volumes because he repeats it.

"Left where?" I ask.

"Well, I thought you two were on the outs but you didn't tell me he was moving today."

Probably for the first time since I've lived here, I take the steps three by three, and when I reach my locked apartment door I realize I've left all my things, including my purse with the keys in it, on the bottom of the steps.

"John, open up, I'm home." I think even at this early point, I know what I'm saying is wishful thinking. I say it again anyway and again and again until Charlie appears at the top of the stairs with my bags. I'm so grateful I don't have to run back down and get them that I almost forget what is about to happen to me. He drops them on the ground and says he'll be right back. Charlie happens to be the only one I know who could care less about the stairs and has no idea why everyone makes such a big deal about going up and down them. Keep in mind; this is coming from someone who lives on the first floor.

As I ease my key into the lock, I am already tearing up. I know what is about to happen. I can't turn the knob because when the door is open, I'll have to face what is inside and whatever that is, there will be no going back. So instead I'm just standing here, with the key inserted completely into the lock and my hand turned on the knob. Just a small push is all it would take, but I just can't do it. Charlie reappears with a bottle of Wild Turkey and some lemons.

"Wild Turkey?" I ask.

"It's all I had."

"But where do you even get a bottle of Wild Turkey? I mean, where did it come from?"

Charlie just shrugs and looks at me as if I've gone mad. I admit I'm often like this. If there is a crisis going on around me I will look for something completely unrelated and ask questions about it. Actually I'm the one who says the things that everybody wishes they had the guts to say. My friend Frankie calls me a 90/10er. Ninety percent of people don't like me at all after meeting me but the good news is the other ten percent love me to death. Is this good? She claims to be a 10/90er but only because she is an ass-kissing wimp.

Is that good? I mean, if she knows this about herself, wouldn't she take all the steps necessary to change it? She's an events planner, though, so you can see why she spends so much time kissing so many asses. I wish Frankie were here now. She would know what to do, and she would open the door for me. Charlie's no help at all as he is just standing there with the bottle of Wild Turkey and the lemons.

I push open the door, just gently at first so I can kind of peek in. It wasn't like I was expecting to see John sitting on the couch or anything but I could never have been prepared for what comes next. I was cleaned out. I mean really cleaned out. There is almost nothing left in my apartment. My television that had once sat inside a beautiful armoire is sitting on a cardboard box, and the phone is just lying on the ground. I immediately notice that the message light is blinking. I pretty much skid to the ground and hit the play button.

"Pick up, Mia. Mia, it's me. Pick up. Fine then."

That was my mother, and even though I swear to her that I do not screen my calls, she insists on screaming into my machine as if I was here. She actually gets upset. Every time I call her back it takes me about 20 minutes to explain to her that I wasn't even home and then I have to go into where I was and give her exact details until she believes me.

I listen to the next message. "Mia, your cell phone is off. Where are you? Michelle has been using my toothbrush again, I just know it, and Natas is sitting right in front of me just staring at me, like he's judging me. Please call me back."

That was Frankie. She has been my closest friend for all of my

4

life. Michelle is her roommate and Frankie, aside from hating her, is always accusing her of using her things. Not to her face, of course, because remember she is the 10/90er. Oh, and Natas is her dog. It is Satan spelled backward. I feel like skipping over this whole my-boyfriend-moved-out-and-took-all-my-stuff-without-telling-me just so I can call her back and tell her that her dog can't judge her.

That was it; no other messages. I rummage through my purse for my cell phone and power it on as I start walking from room to room and trying to itemize what is gone. I'm trying to visualize what the place looked like just this morning before I left. My last stop is the bedroom, and it's pretty much like the rest of the place, just a few scattered things. The mattress and the headboard are gone, but the box spring remains.

"What is that? Who does that?" I didn't even realize I was speaking out loud until Charlie makes a little noise and I remember he is still here. The little noise he made was really a sucking in of his breath. He wasn't paying attention to me at all; he was busy pulling a yellow Post-it off the closet door. I recognize John's handwriting on it. No way is this happening. No way is my life becoming an episode of "Sex and the City." He must have just placed it there to remind himself of something and forgotten about it, that had to be what it was.

"What is it?" I ask.

"You sure?" Charlie asks me back.

"Of course I'm sure, what the hell does it say?"

But Charlie won't read it to me. He just hands it over and watches me. I read it myself, check my cell phone, tap favorites, hit Frankie, and pray she answers. She picks up on the first ring and goes into an immediate tirade.

"Okay, Michelle has definitely been using my toothbrush because I put one of my hairs on it, just a little bit so I would know if anyone had moved it. Do you think she's brushing her teeth with it or do you think she would really put it in the toilet like they do in movies? And right after I left you that message about Natas, he went into the kitchen and peed right on the floor. The back door is open and everything and he pees right on the kitchen floor instead. I just knew he was sitting there judging me. That's why he did that, to tell me what he thinks."

"Frankie, you need to come over. NOW!"

"Mia, I've been thinking a lot about those stairs lately. I've come to the conclusion that I just don't want to climb them. You really should look for a new place. Remember when you were dating that guy Wally and he said part of the reason he was breaking up with you was because he hated going up the stairs to your place?"

"John moved out. He took all my stuff and left me a Post-it note. COME NOW!"

I hang up the phone. Two seconds later it rings and it's Frankie calling me back.

"Did John really leave you or are you just trying to get me to climb the stairs and come over to your place?"

I hang up again. Unbelievable! What Charlie had said about John and me being on the outs was true. We had been together for six months before he moved into my place, and that was about three months ago. I thought everything had been going really well between us. We both had jobs we loved, we both were reality show addicts, he liked the burnt French fries and I liked the soft ones—you know, all the important things were in place.

John works as a documentary filmmaker and he had been trying desperately since before we were even a "we" to get funding for a film he wants to make. He was always so optimistic, and every time a rejection letter arrived, he never let it get him down. The documentary he is interested in making would take him to Africa for almost a year, and although he talked about us going together, I just never imagined it happening. I guess after so many rejections, I didn't think it would ever materialize for him.

Well it did happen for him about two weeks ago. The assumption was that I was going, too. It really blew up when I tried to make the argument that I wasn't leaving San Francisco, my job, my clients, my family and my friends to go to Africa for a year when he would be working the entire time. I tried to convince him that we could make it work, that I would come visit for weeks at a time and we would talk, text message and Skype every day.

John kept being his optimistic self and telling me that I'd saved up enough money to travel for a year and that it would be an adventure. I could rent my apartment and I didn't have to give up my job, just take a hiatus. It wasn't until last week that I made it clear I was absolutely not going with him. We hardly talked after that and every time we set out to discuss the situation it would turn into a huge argument and John would usually end up storming out of the apartment. There were times I considered the dramatic slamming door exit myself, but I'm too smart: I knew that if I did that I'd have to eventually climb back up the stairs after I cooled off.

Speaking of the stairs, Frankie is practically on her knees as she comes through the door. Her face is bright red, and she's begging Charlie to get her a paper bag so she can breathe into it. Frankie can be a bit dramatic, but it's one of the reasons I love her so much. She can really turn nothing at all into something huge. She is also a hypochondriac, and the combination can be downright hysterical at times.

Normally I would have been laughing really hard, and I know that is what Frankie is attempting to get me to do, but I just don't have any laughter in me at the moment. After she starts begging for water in a really dry, whiny voice, I tell her to cut it out. She knows I'm serious as I hand her the Post-it note. The look on her face tells me what I need to know, that John is not coming back. There isn't going to be any second chance, no returning of property, no make-up sex. No returning of property? I really want my stuff back. Charlie, Frankie and I start walking around the apartment again and writing down all the things that are missing. It ends up being a fairly long list.

"Where do you think he put all your stuff? And why would he take all of your big pieces of furniture when he's going to Africa for a year?" Charlie asks.

He has a really good point. What John had done just didn't

make any sense. Why would he take all these things when he very well couldn't drag it all with him to Africa?

Frankie chimes in immediately and says, "Spite."

"What do you mean, spite?" I knew that John and I had been having a rough time of it over the last week or so, but the great relationship we had had for the last nine months would never lead him to do something this outrageous just to hurt me or get revenge on me.

"I mean, spite." Frankie says while breaking my chain of thought. "He had figured you were going with him, you said you wouldn't go so he was pissed off. I mean, really pissed off. You have to be pissed off to take all of somebody's shit when you don't even have a place to put it. He probably had to rent a storage space or something. He must have been really upset with you to want to make all those trips up and down the stairs with all that heavy furniture." Frankie says this as if she has it all figured out already.

"Frank," I say, "enough with the stair comments for tonight, okay?"

We both look at one another and really start laughing. It feels good to laugh right now. Charlie is looking at us like we are insane.

"Women," he says and starts walking out the door.

Frankie screams after him to leave the Wild Turkey. He looks around to put it on the table by the front door where John and I normally drop the keys and mail until he realizes that the table is now gone. He ends up just putting it on the floor.

"Don't forget the lemons, too," she adds.

Charlie drops the lemons on the floor, says, "Maybe he sold all your stuff," and makes his exit out the door.

The thought had never even entered my mind. There were a lot of questions that I wanted to ask Charlie, like how he even knew John left, but they could wait until later. It wouldn't make a difference now. I am just so relieved that Frankie is here with me. I really need someone to dissect this, and she is the perfect person to go over every detail and analyze it until it almost doesn't exist. Could he have really sold my things? If he did, Frankie is right: John wasn't just mad, he was completely pissed off and had done it out of spite.

I spend the next couple of hours saying all my thoughts out loud and crying while Frankie listens and offers advice. She reassures me that I did the right thing and that I would have been miserable in Africa. She also insists that I never could have known John was going to steal all my furniture, and she is right. I could never have predicted this. I just don't know what hurts more, his leaving like he did or his leaving and taking all my things.

Aside from having to redecorate my place, I would now have to start over in the romance department. I am not ready for all that again and I certainly don't want to play the dating game or get swiping cramps from Tinder. I thought at 27 years old that I had finally settled down with somebody and that we were really building something. Although I know I am attractive and I do get my fair share of men hitting on me, I just don't have the patience to deal with getting to know someone through a series of uncomfortable, awkward dates just to realize it's not going to work.

I'm not one of those women who lack self-esteem. I'm not conceited or vain, but I just don't do the whole "Does my butt look big?" thing. I never have. I've always been fairly happy with my body and myself. I know I'm a rare breed considering some of my friends go on and on. I feel the majority of my features, like my brown eyes and my small nose are just regular, but I do have some features that stand out and I emphasize them as best I can. I have very full lips and long, brown, naturally curly hair and I've been a size six for as long as I can remember. That's a lot to work with.

By the time Frankie and I have downed about a half a bottle of Wild Turkey I really start crying. We're going back over the list of things that have been taken and some of them are truly irreplaceable. I had hand painted the armoire in the living room and several other things in the house. One of my beautiful wooden chests with all of my grandmother's handmade quilts is gone. And these are just the things we already noticed. Frankie keeps trying to subtly prepare me for things I'm going to find missing as the days and the weeks go by.

Because my furniture is gone, Frankie and I have made ourselves comfortable in a little corner on the carpet by the kitchen. We are both lying on the floor talking when I notice Bob's bowl is empty. Bob is my cat. Bobcat, get it? Anyway, with all the madness going on I have forgotten to feed him. Oh shit, where is my cat?

"Frankie," I ask, "have you seen Bob since you've been here?"

She shakes her head no and both of us start calling Bob's name along with a couple of here, Kitty Kitties. Bob is a no-show.

Frankie looks at me and says, "That fucker stole your cat!"

CHAPTER TWO

Thankfully the next week is a busy one for me. I have a strange but amazing job that came about because of my artistic side. I've always been really creative. Since I was very little I've been making things with my hands. I went through the whole beading stage in college where I would endlessly torture my friends and family by making them wear strange pieces of jewelry that I had put together. Inevitably all their birthday and Christmas gifts were my handmade jewelry. I must admit there were some nice pieces, but after about a year or so Frankie told me, enough already. She was the only one to admit to me that although everyone loved my things, they all had beaded jewelry pieces coming out of their ears. She also told me they were planning a beading intervention for me but instead decided she would be the chosen spokesperson to let me know it had to stop.

I had a good job at a start up company after I graduated from college, but it felt like just a paycheck and not something permanent. It did enable me to put a down payment on this apartment and pay my mortgage every month, but I was always looking for more and wanting to do something else. During that time I tried my hand at a new craft. I was taking colored jewel pieces and adorning my Levi's, T-shirts, pillowcases, Bob's cat bed, you name it. I would do anything like my initials, names or a cute little saying. Frankie had given me a black silk jacket of hers and I had written *Frankie* in cursive on the back in pink jewels. Frankie wore it to a meeting with one of her celebrity clients she was planning a party for and the rest, as they say, is history. The celebrity had fallen in love with Frankie's jacket and wanted me to do her baby's name on a stroller. My greatest job yet was doing the initials of a very famous movie star on his Rolls-Royce, but this time he had me do it in real diamonds. It looked fabulous and the referrals have been endless. I have a website where I accept orders directly and then I have my high profile clientele.

Because I've been so purposely wrapped up in my work it's hard to believe it's been almost a week since John left and I haven't heard a word from him. It wasn't as if I thought I would; I suppose I was just hoping he would offer up some type of explanation. As the days have gone on, I keep finding little things that disturb me. For example, my curling iron is gone and so are all of my body products, although he chose to leave all my clothes and all of the kitchen things.

I put some sheets on top of the box spring and tried to sleep on it the first night, but it was crazy uncomfortable. I finally decided to just sleep on the floor and that's where I've been ever since.

Today I am going to buy myself a new mattress and a headboard before I go to an appointment I have scheduled for later. Frankie is coming with me and we're going to make this mattress-buying experiment a fresh start.

I have to admit I've been terribly depressed and aside from going to my work appointments and picking up new supplies, I haven't gone out with my friends or returned any of their calls. The only time I'm not thinking about John is when I'm working. I really get lost in what I do and the longer the assignment lately, the better for me. I think the thing I'm struggling with the most is that I can't decide whether I'm really sad to be losing John or whether it's just when something ends, no matter what it is that's ending, you feel a loss and have to give yourself time to adjust.

Frankie told me she called Dee to update her on what has been going on. Frankie and I met Dee in college at San Francisco State. We were all liberal art majors and the three of us have stayed the best of friends. We have our regularly scheduled girls' night out once a week. Dee is outrageous, and Frankie and I have nicknamed her the Warrior of Optimism because she can cure anything or turn any bad situation into something good. Neither of us has ever seen her depressed or upset about anything. She finds the best in the worst, and nothing ever seems to get her down. She got fired from her job, but it was all right with Dee because it just meant a better job was out there for her and if she hadn't been let go, the other opportunity would have passed her by. She totaled her car, but it was all right with Dee because nobody was hurt and it just meant she could use the insurance money to buy herself a newer car. Anyway, you get my point.

I'm supposed to meet Frankie in front of Mambo Mattresses at noon, and she is late. I'm not too keen on the whole Mambo Mattress thing to begin with, but Dee said they have the best prices and you can haggle with them to go even lower. Mambo Mattress is in a very seedy part of San Francisco and I'm starting to feel a little bit uncomfortable. I lean against the wall on the side of the entrance and start biting my cuticles and eventually start pacing back and forth. Frankie calls it my CAN, for my creepy, anxious, nervous routine. She makes acronyms for everything.

Actually, I wasn't even aware I was doing it until she called my attention to it several years ago, and I still can't stop. There was a time when I tried to stop just the pacing and my whole nervous routine consisted of only biting my cuticles. When they started to bleed, I did them a favor and started pacing again.

Just when I think I've waited long enough and I'm about to leave, I see Frankie's car pull up with Dee in the front seat. The window is down and Dee is scream singing a Jay-Z song while Frankie tries unsuccessfully to parallel park. They finally have to switch places so Dee can park the car. When they get out, Dee immediately comes over and wraps me in one of her bear hugs. I'm hoping that whatever her antidote is, it will make me feel better when we're done embracing. It works temporarily, but only because when you're in Dee's presence you just naturally feel better. Frankie and I both secretly think she is forever the optimist because she is so damn good looking. She is the stereotypical blonde-haired, blue-eyed beauty with full, pouty lips and legs up to you know where. Frankie is more like me, but she has red, straight hair.

Dee breaks my whole trancelike state from her hug and says, "Frankie told me the whole story, Mia, and you know what?"

"What?" I say.

"Fuck him, that's what." Dee says this with such confidence I almost believe for a second that all I have to do is say "fuck him" in my head and I will be cured.

"He's gone because he wasn't the right one for you." Dee continues with the same air of confidence. "He's making room for the right one to come along, and to be honest, Mia, your furniture was shit and you needed new stuff anyway." With that, Dee puts her arm around my shoulder and the three of us head into Mambo Mattresses.

By the time our shopping spree is over I really do feel elated. I've managed to purchase a new mattress, a leather couch set with a coffee table, a dining room table and a headboard with a dresser to match. Most of it Dee picked out but I was grateful seeing as she really does have the best taste out of the three of us. I probably spent more money than I should have, but I've been earning so much lately and just stuffing it into the bank. Besides my mortgage payment and an occasional new piece of clothing, I'm just not a big spender. Don't get me wrong, I do buy designer clothing and shoes, and the three of us always go to the trendy, more expensive places to eat and dance. I've just never had this kind of money before and I don't want to squander it, so it's nice to stash it away and watch it add up.

My biggest job to date was the Rolls-Royce, and that person just happened to refer me to another famous person who lives in San Francisco. A lot of the Hollywood jobs I do are people coming to visit San Francisco for one thing or another, and so the job is usually very time sensitive. Sometimes I have a week or two, but on other occasions I've been limited to two or three days and I have to make sure my work is great. One person actually had his personal assistant drive his Mercedes to San Francisco from Los Angeles, and the personal assistant stayed in a hotel while I did the work. There are others who have their clothing or accessories shipped to me, and I do the job and ship the pieces back. It's nice to have those side jobs, which I can do in the comfort of my own home.

I know you're wondering about any strange requests from famous people, right? I can't mention any names, but I really don't see the harm in telling you the crazy things I've done for people or even some of the outrageous things that I've been asked to do and gracefully declined. Okay, the craziest one I accepted? I once did a woman's underwear, and on the front she wanted me to write in green jewels the name of her cookie. Well, we call it cookie; you can call it whatever you want. I accepted this job only because I had to find out what she named it. Appropriately enough, it was Gina. The craziest one I turned down? A man offered me a large sum of money to write in jewels on his, well, his jewels, to be quite blunt. Aside from the compromising position that would put me in (and I do mean compromising), I declined because I just couldn't think of any type of adhesive small enough to stick the jewels on without ripping the jewels off afterward, if you know what I'm saying.

The client I'm going to meet today in San Francisco did about four amazing movies in a row and then disappeared for a couple of years. Her name is Andrea Snowden, and the word is she has a drug or drinking problem, but nobody knows for sure. Apparently after being out of sight for so many years, she has just finished wrapping up a new film that is supposed to be phenomenal. Maybe she'll make a comeback. Who knows? All I know is that she wants me to meet her at her home to show her my portfolio, and then, as she says, "we can talk business."

CHAPTER THREE

Upon arriving at Andrea's house I feel immediately overwhelmed. She is amazing, even more willowy, wide eyed and blonde in person than in her movies, but that's not just it. I've been to a couple of movie star homes and this one takes the cake. It's not really the size of the home; it's the decorating and construction. There are all of the normal things you might find in a mansion this size, like the tennis courts and the large pool with a guesthouse, but as Andrea leads me out to the back I'm amazed. The outside of the home looks as if it's lived in. There is a bed with a canopy that is draped in billowy, white fabric and there is furniture you would normally see inside set up all around the backyard. Andrea tells me she can't stand to be without fresh air so she has made the outside her living space. It's fantastic and eccentric and innovative all at once. I immediately like her.

We sit down and Andrea starts to look at my portfolio. I'm delighted by all of her ooohs and aaahs. She asks me several questions while she flips through the book, and I'm eager to answer them all and find out what she has in mind. After she is done, she gently closes my portfolio and lays her hands in her lap. She does something completely unexpected and starts to cry, silently at first and eventually long, slow sobs. I get up to approach her, but she motions for me to sit back down. She starts to speak slowly and deliberately as if she has made this speech several times before and she wants to make sure I completely understand her.

Andrea Snowden has cancer. Not only does she have cancer,

but she has decided not to fight it any more. All the rumors about drugs and drinking were just that, rumors. She left show business and came to San Francisco to get away from it all and to heal. She went through chemotherapy, and her cancer had been in remission for a very short time. It was then that she made her last movie. Now her cancer is back and she has been told that without more treatment she does not have very much longer to live. She does not want to endure another round of chemotherapy and has chosen to live out the remainder of her life here at home in San Francisco surrounded by the things she loves. Andrea Snowden asks me if I will decorate her casket.

Her request is overwhelming, and I'm grateful she continues to talk because I don't know how to respond to her yet. She wants me to use jewels on her casket and to create pictures of all her friends and lovers, of the roles she's played in movies and of her many pets. It is to be a collage of her life that she can be buried in and take those things with her in some way. She's requesting I use real jewels, and I'm disgusted with myself for a minute thinking of how much this is going to cost and all the money I am going to make. Can I profit from this? Can I really profit from someone's illness and last dying wish?

I think Andrea reads my mind, because she tells me I have to accept payment for my work and she wouldn't have it any other way. She would also like for me to come and help her pick out a casket because I will know what material and which shape will be the easiest to work with. I find myself agreeing to go with her and accepting the job.

Perhaps looking back on it I should have asked for some time to think about it, but I desperately wanted to help her even after knowing her for such a short period of time. You had to be there to feel the effect she had on me; I suppose she probably has that effect on most everyone and that is why she is a movie star.

Our meeting comes to a close and after I run a few errands, I meet up with Frankie and Dee for dinner and drinks. I haven't decided yet if I'm going to share what happened today with them. I feel hesitant at first as if I would be betraying Andrea's trust, but these are my two best friends and I really feel as though I need to talk to somebody about the situation. I know for sure I can count on Frankie to keep this confidential, and I am banking on Dee to tell me what she really thinks, to give it to me straight. I wait until Frankie and Dee are in the middle of discussing something and then I just blurt it out.

"Andrea Snowden is dying of cancer and she wants me to do a collage of her life with jewels on her casket." There, I have done it. It is like ripping off a BAND-AID: one swipe and I have said it.

"Oh, and she wants me to come with her tomorrow to pick out the casket." I add that on at the end for dramatic effect.

Dee is the first to pipe in. "I'm sorry; did you just say you were going casket shopping with Andrea Snowden?"

Frankie immediately follows with, "Holy shit! How can she be dying of cancer? I just saw the previews for her new movie that's coming out and she looks incredible!"

"Well," I start, "first off, I did just say I am going casket shopping with Andrea Snowden tomorrow and secondly, she looks so good in that movie preview because her cancer was in remission when she filmed it."

"For some reason," I add, "I really took an immediate liking to her and I want to do this for her. I know it's an odd request and I usually turn the odd ones down, but this has meaning for me and I think it will be a good thing."

"Listen," says Frankie, "I'm all about your exploring different job opportunities, but you have to really think about this one. You're going to form a relationship with this woman while you're doing a job for her, and do you really want to do that when you know that she is dying?"

I do. There isn't anything for me to think about or consider. I want to do this. It has become more important to me than anything else right now. Maybe I just need a distraction from my life for a while or maybe you recognize a kindred spirit in someone like I did in Andrea today. Either way, my mind is made up, and I tell the girls so.

"Frankie," Dee says, "you meet people every day and you never know when they're going to die. If for some magical reason you were to find out Mia or I would be gone by next year, would you stop being friends with us because that would make it easier for you? You wouldn't. Mia, I think this is a great opportunity for you careerwise and spiritually. Let me know if you need any help."

Frankie responds with, "Leave it to the Warrior of Optimism to find the good out of this situation. I support you, too, Mia, but you're definitely not going to get any referrals out of a dead woman."

It's probably not the way I would have chosen to close the topic, but I was just grateful I had told them, they supported me and we could move on.

Our next subject is Frankie's undying love for Charlie. I forgot to mention that earlier, you'll have to excuse me but I was going through a crisis at the time. Ever since Charlie purchased the apartment below me in our building Frankie has had a huge crush on him. Dee and I often spend a large portion of our girls' night out listening to Frankie go on and on about Charlie. Even though he's not my type, I can see why Frankie has a thing for him.

When he first moved in I used to have to give Frankie a daily Charlie Update, or a CHUP, as she likes to call them. There are too many acronyms; sometimes it's hard to keep up. Whenever I mention Frankie's undying love (by the way, those are her words to describe it, not mine) to Charlie, he just blushes and tries to change the subject. I have no idea if he likes her or not. He's so sweet and shy it's hard to get anything out of him, and Frankie is so sweet and shy she would never make the first move. So, there you have it. Dee and I just help Frankie pick apart and analyze every little thing he says or does when she is around, and that seems to satisfy her for now.

Dee, on the other hand, has a love life like a soap opera. She's constantly involved in these really tumultuous, dramatic relationships that always end very bitterly and with the other person getting hurt. Dee always comes out unscathed and unfazed. As soon as one relationship ends, it seems only days pass before another one starts up. She has no prerequisites for the men she dates, which makes for a wide array of personalities and looks. There was Canon, who claimed to be an actor but couldn't name a single thing he had ever acted in; Adair, the musician who played bass in a band that nobody had ever heard of; and Carlo, who might have been in the Mafia but disappeared and Dee claims he is the one who got away: just to name a few, of course.

After dinner the girls and I hug one another good-bye, and they make me promise to call them as soon as I'm done casket shopping. That does sound pretty creepy. I end up walking the couple of blocks home so I can get some fresh air. I'm strangely looking forward to tomorrow and spending time with Andrea. I really have no idea what is in store, I just know that I want to get to know her better. Sometimes when the jobs I do are of a personal nature, the better I know the client the better the final product. When I reach the front of my building I see Charlie sitting outside on the front stoop having a cigarette, so I sit down beside him. It's complete silence for a while except for the noise of the city, and I start to cry. I can't tell if my tears are for John's leaving or for Andrea who is dying. Charlie doesn't say a word; he just grabs my hand and sits with me for a while longer. When we get up to go inside I tell him I was coming home from dinner with Frankie. He smiles, and as he closes his front door I could swear there was a blush on his face.

CHAPTER FOUR

Every morning when I wake up I usually check my e-mail and my schedule first thing. As I'm scanning through I come across an e-mail address I don't recognize, but the title catches my attention. I open it up.

> To: GemItUp@Yahoo.com
> From: ShyGuySF12@hotmail.com
> Topic: Frankie's E-Mail address?
>
> Hi Mia. I was wondering if I could have Frankie's e-mail address? I was thinking I could ask her out for coffee sometime?
>
> Thanks,
> Charlie

Oh, this was just too much. I couldn't wait to respond so I immediately start a new e-mail. I only ever click respond when I'm messaging clients so they can look back at the chain in reference. With family and friends I hate to have every e-mail we've ever written attached.

> To: ShyGuySF22@hotmail.com
> From: GemItUp@Yahoo.com
> Topic: Are you kidding me?

Where do I start on criticizing your e-mail? Where, oh where do I start? Okay, I know… how about the fact that I could practically spit on your front door from mine and you send me an e-mail instead of coming over? Secondly, ShyGuy? ShyGuy? What is that? Very creepy. And thirdly, you see Frankie all the time, you can ask her out in person, you chicken shit. Oh, and don't do coffee, it's too… something.

Mia –

I'm almost in tears laughing at my oh so witty response and I know Frankie is going to be ecstatic about the whole idea that he even wants to ask her out, so I call her to let her know. As soon as she answers the phone I tell her that I have a CHUP and she's already freaking out just hearing that word.

"Well, I was checking my e-mail this morning and he sent me a message asking for your e-mail so he could ask you for coffee sometime." I'm so smug as I say this like I'm responsible for it happening. "And" I add, "His screen name is ShyGuy. Can you believe that? ShyGuy."

Frankie starts screaming at the top of her lungs. I think she might be hyperventilating for real this time. When she finally comes up for air, she wants to know if I've responded.

"Of course I responded." I continue by reading her the e-mail I sent back to him. I start whooping and laughing at what I think is my sarcastically cute e-mail until I notice there is complete silence on the other end of the phone.

"Frankie," I say, "Did you pass out?"

"I can't believe you did that. What were you thinking? After all this time I've been just waiting for him to show some kind of sign and you blew it for me." I can tell that Frankie is really upset. "Now he'll never ask me out. Any chance I had is gone after that. The reason he e-mailed you instead of asking you and the reason his screen name is ShyGuy, IS BECAUSE HE'S SHY, STUPID!" And with that she has hung up on me.

Oh my God, did she just call me stupid? I am stupid. I didn't even realize what I was doing. How could I have done that to her? I was so caught up in how cute I thought my response was that I forgot I might be ruining any chance Frankie might have with Charlie.

My phone rings again and seeing as I am stupid, I don't even look to see who it is before I answer; I just pick up and start talking.

"Frankie, oh my God, I'm so sorry. I'll fix it, I promise. Just give me a chance."

"What did you do to Frankie now?" It is my mother's nasally, accusing voice. It's absolutely unmistakable in any situation.

"Hello, Mom. Oh, I didn't do anything to Frankie, just a little joke." I am trying to douse the flame on this. The last thing I'm going to do is let the Queen of Guilt make me feel even guiltier than I already do.

"Well, it sure didn't sound like it was nothing and it certainly didn't sound as if you were joking. Did John give you the message that I called the other day? He didn't mention anything about the lasagna I sent home with you and I thought that was rather rude. I mean, a woman slaves over homemade lasagna for half the day, the least he can do is say thank you."

In my mind, I'm debating whether or not I should tell her about John now or wait until it's a more convenient time. I decide there will never be a convenient time and as long as my best friend hates me, I might as well receive my punishment in the form of my mother.

"John is gone, Mom. He up and moved out while I was at work and he took all of my things with him." That was easier than I thought it would be. I really feel relief at having told her.

"What do you mean he's gone? He took your stuff? Surely you told him he could have it." This is her response?

"You're right, Mom, I did tell him he could have all my things and move them out in the middle of the day while I was at work so I could come home to a completely empty apartment and a Post-it note as my Dear John letter. I can't believe I forgot I told him it was okay until right now." I'm seething with anger.

"Well, did he mention anything about the lasagna before he left? Did he even try it?"

"Yes, Mom. In fact, that's what the Post-it note said. It said, 'I'm leaving you, Mia, and stealing your cat, but please tell your mom I loved the lasagna.'"

"You know, Mia, I really don't like this tone of voice you've taken. I understand you must be upset but there's no need to get an acid tongue with me."

"You're right, Mom, and I should probably go. I'm already late for an appointment and I'm just too upset right now to talk about John."

"All right, dear. Remember when you come on Sunday to bring back my lasagna dish."

I hang up.

I wasn't expecting my mother to lavish me with love and all the it's-all-rights I could handle, but I was expecting her to care just a little.

I should know by now she's just not that way. She's not like Frankie's mom, Bessie, who will just scoop you up in her pudgy arms and bake you warm cookies with milk. Come to think of it, I could use a dose of Bessie right now.

I'm really not late for my appointment. I actually have a couple of hours to kill before I'm supposed to meet Andrea, so I take some time to research her film roles online. As soon as I Google her I'm surprised at the amount of matches that come up. She only has five movies to her name, but there are over 1,000,000 results. There are numerous fan clubs dedicated to her and several early reviews on her new movie. I decide to click the first listing that comes up, and I'm sad to read the word is out on her cancer. I'm not sure at this early point if she leaked it or if somebody else did. I can't imagine how hard that must be. I could never handle the invasion of privacy that celebrities deal with.

There have been times when a celebrity has been asked by the press or paparazzi who made the custom-designed whatever it is they currently have and the celebrity will say the name of my company. I'm grateful for the exposure, but I've actually had people follow up and call me and ask about my dealings with that specific person. What was she wearing? How much did you charge? And on and on and on. One reporter even had the nerve to ask me how a particular celebrity smelled. I said he smelled like a celebrity and left it at that. I usually won't return the call if a reporter leaves a message. I don't need publicity that badly, and I certainly don't want to be quoted in a tabloid as "a friend of so-and-so."

I print out some of the more interesting pictures and data I have found on Andrea. I want to create an idea with her, and using photos is probably the best way to achieve that. I also want to confirm the details with her in case I decide to use any of the facts in her collage. One quote really catches my attention and sticks in my head. It reads, "When you find true love and you're faced with a decision, love will always make the decision for you." I want to know what and whom she was referring to. I also want to make that part of her casket collage if she really did say it.

I'm almost done printing when I hear the infamous ding of my e-mail. I practically fly across the room to my computer, hoping it's Frankie saying she forgives me. Or maybe Charlie laughing off my e-mail and still wanting Frankie's info. It's neither. It's my e-mail I sent to Charlie and the topic is Host Unknown. Could I be this lucky? Apparently I had written my response to ShyGuySF22 instead of ShyGuySF12, and as luck would have it, there is no ShyGuySF22.

I immediately whip out two e-mails, one to Frankie explaining my good fortune and writing the line "Sorry, I'm stupid" about 500 times, and the other to Charlie. I keep it simple and just write Frankie's e-mail address and phone number. Now I really am going to be late.

CHAPTER FIVE

I'm meeting Andrea at a funeral home she has picked out. She's not there when I arrive, so I go into my usual creepy, anxious, nervous routine and start biting my cuticles and pacing back and forth. I decide to go inside just to make sure I haven't missed her. When I step through the glass doors, there is a humongous wooden desk and a man standing behind it that I'm not quite sure isn't dead himself.

"May I help you?" He asks in a very soothing, comforting voice. I'm assuming that comes with years of practice dealing with the bereaved.

What do I say? "Oh, don't mind me. I'm just meeting a friend here so we can casket shop"? I opt for something a little subtler.

"Not just yet, thank you. I'm waiting to meet someone first." That seems to do the trick. He gives me a polite smile and goes back to standing like a cadaver.

I'm so grateful when Andrea finally arrives that I almost hug her. Instead, I gently shake her hand and admire how she looks the picture of grace and femininity. It's only been one day since I saw her last, but it seems she looks paler and thinner than before. And I don't know if it's because I know she's sick now, but I notice there are dark, puffy circles under her eyes I didn't see before. Her presence still commands attention, and Lurch immediately springs to life behind his large, wooden desk when we walk through the door.

"Ms. Snowden, it is a pleasure to make your acquaintance. May I offer you a beverage? Take your coat?" Wow, Lurch surely didn't treat me that way. He's certainly not scoring any points since the woman is dying.

"No, thank you," Andrea replies. "We would just like to see the caskets you have to offer."

Lurch leads us down a long, grim hallway. I am thoroughly freaked out by the whole situation. I keep wondering what it would be like if I just let out a loud, long scream. I begin to bite my cuticles again, and I have to physically force my hand out of my mouth to stop. I don't know why, but I'm nervous. I look over at Andrea and she gives me the sweetest smile. It's then I realize Andrea probably needs me as much for support as for actually picking out the casket. Maybe the whole reason she asked me to come with her was just a guise so she would have someone to go through this with. I know she is famous, but I didn't see a sign of any other person when I went to meet her at her house.

Lurch finally leads us into a room where we start looking at all the different caskets on display. I thought maybe we would be looking through a catalog or something, but obviously I'm wrong. The caskets are all spread out in this one very large room. Andrea and I go up to each of them one by one and examine them inside and out. They range from literally just a pine box with no lining all the way up to a glossy mahogany lined with pure silk. It's unbelievable. The only thing separating someone from burying the dead in a beautiful casket is tens of thousands of dollars. It's becoming depressing, if you want me to be honest, and I let Andrea know any one of them will work. I don't see a problem with the gems adhering to any of the finishes. I suddenly want to run out of here as fast as I can. I don't know if Andrea senses the way I'm feeling, but she looks at Lurch and points to the most expensive casket and we start walking back out to the front.

I tell her I want to wait outside while she settles the bill. When I open the front door the fresh air hits me like a ton of bricks and I take long, slow, deep breaths, in and then out. I'm slowly starting to relax and feel like myself again. One's own mortality is a tough thing to face. I feel the need to cleanse myself and maybe go buy some vitamins, have a smoothie, something. Andrea steps out of the front doors. She looks satisfied.

"Thank you for coming with me, Mia. I know that must have been uncomfortable for you, but I appreciate your company and advice."

She's still the class act, even after casket shopping. I have to hand it to this woman.

"No. I'm sorry about that at the end there. I didn't think I would react that way. I apologize." I'm being really sincere here. I don't know why I'm getting so worked up over someone who is still a stranger to me. It must be the extraordinary circumstances.

"Will I do the work here?" I'm already freaking out at the thought of it. I'm hoping something else can be worked out. I don't care if I have to drag the casket myself up my three flights of stairs and do the work in my house. Anything is better than here.

Andrea starts to laugh, noticing the complete fear in my eyes.

"No such luck, kiddo. I've asked them to deliver it to my home, so you can work on it there. It will be arriving tomorrow and I'm hoping you can start right away. Unfortunately, this really is a time-sensitive issue for me."

The seriousness of what is happening sets in for me again, and the lightness that had entered our conversation went just as quickly as it had come.

"Call me when the casket arrives and I will make you my first priority." I say this while giving her a hug good-bye. I feel this experience has taken us beyond the hand-shaking point, and besides, I really need a hug to hide the tears that are starting to well up in my eyes. I hand her the things I've printed off the Internet and she promises to go through them tonight so we can start to put our collage plan into place.

After we say our good-byes, I take an Uber to visit to my friends at the jewelers' store. I have made small gem purchases from Vincenzio and Dominic in the past, but after the Rolls-Royce deal they really started to take me seriously. Dee referred me to them saying they were the best, and since Dee always seems to know the best, I have used them for all of my real gem purchases.

Their store is called Pappas Brothers. Their father had been Greek and their mother had been Sicilian, so they ended up with the strangest combination of very Italian-sounding first names and a very Greek-sounding last name. Perhaps more interesting than their names, is that both brothers are gay. They are these very machismo, stereotypical Italian men: hairy chests with thick, gold necklaces and shirts unbuttoned practically to their navels. They talk very loudly and gesture with their hands a lot but also have a lot of soft mannerisms that you would find in a stereotypical gay man as well. They are a walking contradiction, which is a riot. I look forward to my visits there, and besides it being a necessity for my work today, I thought it would also help to change my mood.

"How do you like that, Dom, it's our friend Mia." I hear Vincenzio saying this as soon as I walk in the front door.

"Are you fuckin' kiddin' me? Ah, you're right, there's our girl right there."

When I first met Dom I was shocked by his use of the word fuck, but you get used to it fast and even come to realize that he can't seem to help it.

Both Dee and Frankie tell me they can always tell when I've made a recent visit to the Pappas Brothers because I sound like a truck driver for about a day afterward. It's contagious. You should really try it sometime; it's very liberating.

"I got a big job for you gentlemen." I'm saying this with a huge smile on my face as the first half of my day starts to slowly fade away. I begin to explain the details of my next job as Dom and Enzo's faces start lighting up. This will be the largest job I've ever done, and I'm sure that I ever will do. We're looking at hundreds of thousands of dollars in gemstones in varying colors and sizes. I want them to be prepared, so I make a general estimate of what I will need to get started and place the first part of my order. Dom and Enzo agree to let me pay when the gems arrive. The price always varies for large jobs after I have estimated how many hours it will take, and there are set prices on some of the smaller items I do consistently like clothing and strollers.

"Why would somebody pay so mucha for something they gonna get buried in, huh? You tella me, Enzo, why somebody is gonna do this? Famous people are fuckin' crazy I tell youse."

Enzo thinks for a little bit and says, "We no judge nobody, eh. It's a her money and she wanna make us a money with a her money. We no judge nobody."

Nicely put if I do say so myself.

I'm walking home again. It seems I've been walking a lot lately. I do own a car, but it's so hard to find a parking space in the city that when I find a good one, it takes a special occasion to get me to move it. I normally take an Uber or taxi everywhere except on nights like tonight. As I pass the coffee shop down the street from my apartment, I'm debating on whether or not I want to skip dinner altogether and get a smoothie instead. The coffee shop windows are tinted, but I spy Charlie inside, I recognize him immediately. I try to stay hidden while pushing my face as close to the glass as I can get without looking obvious. He is sitting at a table with his face toward the window and there is someone with him. Now I'm looking so hard my entire face is smashed up against the window. IT'S FRANKIE! I'm so excited I think I have let out a yelp. I walk very fast past the window to make sure they don't see me, and it's as if I'm walking on air. I'm so happy I practically do cartwheels the rest of the way home.

When I get into my apartment I settle myself on the floor in front of the television with four pairs of jeans and two strollers. I'm going to do some work and watch "Survivor" while I eat my frozen dinner. My furniture is being delivered the day after tomorrow and I can't wait. I mentioned before that I'm a reality show junkie and I DVR everything. I think John intentionally didn't take my DVR and my television because that's the one thing that would have made me hunt him down. I know I'm subconsciously waiting for Frankie to call me. Hopefully she has forgiven me. If she hasn't, she will when she realizes she needs to tell me all the details of her night when she gets home. Frankie and I have both agreed in the past that if we don't have one another to share things with, it's almost as if they didn't happen. Sharing things with Frankie makes them more real for me, and I don't have to hold anything back. Sometimes when we're with other people they tell us it's like we have our own language. John used to say that he'd given up on trying to figure out what we were talking about because he couldn't understand us anyway.

On my slow, relaxing nights like tonight, Bob used to come and cuddle up beside John and me on the couch. I am just now realizing how much I miss Bob. At first he was an unwanted present from Dee when she was dating a guy who worked at an animal shelter. They were going to have to put the cat to sleep if somebody didn't adopt him. Frankie's roommate Michelle is allergic to cats and Dee can't have pets where she lives, so I got guilted into taking him. Dee's boyfriend kept telling me the cat wouldn't adjust well if I changed his name from Mittens to Bob. I didn't even want a cat and there was no way I was going to own a cat named Mittens. I told

Dee's boyfriend the cat's options were death or being named Bob. He let it go after that.

I have finished both of the strollers, "Survivor" and half of a "Keeping Up With the Kardashians" episode when Frankie finally calls. I decide not to tell her I saw her and Charlie because I don't want to steal any of her thunder.

"Oh my God! Mia, are you sitting down?" she asks.

"On the floor, yes, but I'm sitting down. What's up?" I can just hear the excitement in her voice already.

"I just went out with Charlie. We went and had coffee at the place down the street from your house, and you wouldn't believe how romantic he is when you're alone with him. He brought me a bunch of wildflowers and held my hand for a little while."

"Oh, Frankie, I am so happy for you. So, what did you guys talk about? Were you nervous?"

"We talked about our jobs a lot. I told him some of my funnier celebrity stories and he told me about some of the marketing campaigns he has done. I didn't even know he was in advertising, did you?"

"Of course I knew that." Oh God, how shallow am I? I had no idea what Charlie's job was up until this moment. "Did you set a time when you would see him again?" I try to change the subject quickly.

"No, not yet, but he said he would call me tomorrow and guess what?"

"He gave you a *Rocky* CD?"

38

"What? No. He has really bad breath."

She does not even sound disappointed. I think she is kidding.

"Was it from the coffee? I mean, was it halitosis bad or just strong coffee bad?"

"Oh, it was halitosis bad. Like sweaty feet wrapped in bacon all day bad."

That analogy was too much for me. How could this be? Frankie had been waiting forever for a date with Charlie.

"All right, Frankie, tell me this: Was it deal breaker bad?"

There are certain things Frankie and I refer to as deal breakers when it comes to relationships. Our list is nowhere near perfection and we add to it quite often, we have even been known to subtract on the rare occasion. Some of the things on the top of our list are cheating, porn/drug addicts, guys that still live with their mothers and anybody that works at a fast food restaurant. That last one is because Frankie dated somebody that was a student but had a part-time job at Wendy's and she gained ten pounds in a month.

"I'm not sure yet. I guess we'll have to try it again and see if it's still the same. Maybe I caught him on a bad night. Maybe he was as nervous as I was and his mouth was really dry. I don't know, I just feel like I can still smell it on me."

"Eeeew," I say. "Are you sure you're not being overly dramatic, Frankie? You do tend to go overboard."

"Are you kidding me? I'm afraid when he calls me I might get a whiff of it through the phone." We both start laughing at that.

I am surprised Frankie is taking this so well but like she said, it would have to wait until her next opportunity to kiss him before a decision can be made. I apologize again, we say our good-byes and I go to bed on the floor.

CHAPTER SIX

Andrea calls me the next morning to let me know the casket has arrived. I usually start very large projects by drawing out the design and making a template. Then I trace that over to the object I will be decorating. I do this by using something similar to an X-Acto knife but with a much blunter tip. The idea is to get the initial indentation on the object so I can follow the lines with the jewels. You can see how this process leaves absolutely no room for error, and both the pattern and the transfer have to be done perfectly. If I screw up, I either have to redesign a little to fix it or worst-case scenario, I have to purchase a new item. Thankfully so far I've only had to do a little redesigning.

Since my first order of gems won't be ready to pick up from the Pappas Brothers until tomorrow, I'm going over to Andrea's house to work on the collage design with her. She told me she has already chosen the pictures and the sayings she wants to use. I normally dress very professionally when I have my first client meeting in order to set a good impression. I have a wide array of suits in varying colors depending on the season. When I go to do the actual work, I like to wear jeans and a T-shirt or sometimes even sweats because the majority of the time I'm sitting and bent over in strange positions trying to attach the gems. Seeing the change in my dress usually surprises a lot of my clients, and I end up feeling uncomfortable for a moment and then I explain the reason for my sloppy wardrobe. I have yet to think of a way to resolve this.

I arrive at Andrea's house a little past noon wearing my most casual and newest lululemon outfit. I know I'm not starting the real work until tomorrow, but I thought I would get her used to the idea of my new dress style today. Andrea answers the door herself and immediately proceeds to tell me how adorable I look. I knew there was a reason I liked this woman.

Andrea seems to light up, almost, as she takes my hand and leads me into her house. When we arrive in her foyer I smell something funny, almost like patchouli. It is patchouli. There is a woman half running, half skipping around the living room and she is holding incense in her hand and waving the lighted stick around. She's dressed in a brightly colored sari, wearing anklets and bracelets with little bells all over them so when she dances around they make tinkling noises. Andrea introduces me to this woman, whose name is Antonia, and then she excuses herself for a minute. Alone with Antonia, I have an overt look of confusion on my face. Antonia begins to explain to me she is in the process of cleansing Andrea's home of any bad karma or negative spirits so Andrea can make her final voyage home in a safe haven. I've never even thought of something like this before, but then again I've never been told I don't have very much longer to live, so who knows what I would do. Either way, Andrea seems to be very happy with Antonia's presence so who I am to say anything. I just smile at Antonia as she goes about her business. She retreats to a corner of the room and starts chanting in another language as thankfully, Andrea reappears.

We go out to her backyard and sit at a table where she has laid out all of her photographs and information she wants on the casket collage.

"You'll be safe here," she says with a giggle. "Antonia has already finished the backyard. I hope you'll excuse me while I help her finish the rest of the house. You can get started with these things here." She smiles and disappears back into the house.

The photographs and movie memorabilia she has amassed overwhelm me. Of course she's a movie star, but there are pictures of her in the most beautiful evening gowns, posing with some real legends. There are some playbills of work she did Off Broadway when she was younger and she looks just beautiful. I feel so privileged she has allowed me into this most private part of her life. I feel as if it is a blessing I can do this for her. I notice there are no pictures of children or people who look like they might be her parents and I start to wonder if she has any family.

"Hi. So, all that stuff is pretty amazing, huh?" It's a man's voice and I practically jump out of my chair. I had no idea anyone else was here and I certainly wasn't expecting anyone to come up behind me.

"Sorry, didn't mean to scare you. I just had to get out of that house; the patchouli smell is giving me a headache."

Holy shit! Holy shit! Holy shit! It's Joe Barrick, commonly referred to as just J.B. At least that's how they refer to him in all the tabloids and on "TMZ." He's this amazing actor who currently grosses 20 million a film and he's standing right in front of me in all his greatness. He seems a little smaller than on film, but he's much better looking if that's even possible. He's got these hazel-green eyes,

43

and it looks like you could just get lost in them, and his smile. Holy shit, his smile: those are the whitest, straightest teeth I have ever seen and these beautiful heart-shaped lips. My next thought is that all of these traits are probably why he is considered a modern-day Casanova. He is always being photographed with the hottest model or the new "it" actress. I still can't believe that he is right here, talking to me. Holy shit! I think for a second I might have just said that out loud, but I can tell by the look on his face I haven't spoken at all. I'm a crazy person. He must think I'm a crazy, mute person. I can't speak. I'm actually trying to talk to him and a strange, elongated croaking noise comes out of my throat.

"I'm Joe, by the way. You must be the person who Andrea has hired to decorate the casket." I know this is rhetorical and I'm grateful because I couldn't answer him even if I wanted to. Instead, I just stick out my trembling hand for him to shake. He's acting as if everything is normal and as far as his world goes, my reaction to meeting him is probably something he comes across every day. He takes my hand and gives it a very gentle shake while placing his other hand on top of mine. Oh, I just love when men do that. I just love it. Holy shit, I can't believe he just did one of my favorite things. I fumble for my water and take a huge gulp because my throat feels like sandpaper and I'm finding it hard to swallow. I finally feel like I might be able to get my name out, so I take my best shot.

"Mia." Okay, so far so good. I was just testing the waters. "My name is Mia."

"Well, it's very nice to meet you, Mia. I think what you're doing here is a wonderful thing. I have a few friends of mine who you have done some work for, and I've always been a fan of yours."

HE KNOWS ME? I mean he knows of me. That's amazing. I can't believe this is happening to me. I feel something a little wet on my chin and raise my hand up to feel what it is. I'm drooling. Oh my God! Do you think he saw that? Now I'm a crazy, mute, croaking, drooling person. This has got to be the single, worst experience of my entire life. I don't get it: I've done so many jobs for celebrities before and I've never had this type of reaction. He's just staring at me. Was it my turn to talk? If he's just staring at me there's no way he missed the drool.

"Thank you." That's all I can manage. He has to talk now because I just can't do it. I'm really not afraid of embarrassing myself anymore at this point because aside from peeing in my pants, there's not much else I can do. I want to crawl under the table and die. I can't believe I thought that woman Antonia was weird. I'm a freak show compared to her. I pull my hand out of my mouth before my cuticles draw blood, I take a deep breath in, and then I exhale slowly. I've got to pull it together.

"Do you live in San Francisco, Joe, or are you just here visiting?" I feel like my lips are sticking to my teeth and I'm making this sucking sound while I talk. I'm not even sure he understood what I just said. I just keep looking up at him and making the sucking sound. I can't stop doing it. I feel like Jim Carrey from "In Living Color" when he played Fire Marshall Bill. Is that how I look?

"I'm just here visiting Andrea. I got the news yesterday and drove up really early this morning. I can't believe I've never been to San Francisco before. I guess I just haven't had a reason to come until now. I'm sure you know she doesn't have any family, so I figured she could use a friend."

I thought that might be the case. It explains why there aren't any in the pictures. At least I'm beginning to regain partial control of myself, but unfortunately with that comes the realization that I'm sweating profusely. You know when you can sense the perspiration on your brow and upper lip area? I excuse myself to Joe and tell him I need to use the restroom, and right as I'm about to stand up I feel a bead of sweat drop from the side of my forehead all the way down my cheek. It falls. Where did it go? I look down and it's sitting on one of Andrea's pictures. I look up and Joe is looking at it, too. Maybe he's just looking down to see what I was looking at. This is so wrong on so many levels that it doesn't even matter anymore: I'm done for. I get up and start to walk away when Joe asks me something.

"Pardon?" I say.

"Do you mind if I sit down and join you?"

"No, please, help yourself."

Help yourself? What does that even mean? That doesn't even remotely apply to this situation at all. We're not eating. Help yourself to a what? So that's it. You never get a second chance to make a first impression. Let's just sum up how that went again, shall we? I am a crazy, mute, croaking, drooling, sweaty pig. When I get to the bathroom I lock the door behind me and collapse on the floor.

I pull my phone out of my pocket and call Frankie. I really need to talk to someone right now. It's her voice mail, just my luck. I leave her a message and I start whispering the events that have just taken place. I decide to turn on the water to make sure nobody can hear me, but now Frankie probably won't be able to hear my message over the water. I hang up and look in the mirror. It's not half as bad as I thought it would be. I readjust my ponytail, take some toilet paper and blot my face and underarms, flush the toilet, wash my hands and walk out of the bathroom with my head held up high. Who am I kidding?

When I get back outside Joe is sitting in a lounge chair and he's leafing through one of Andrea's playbills. He looks up when he hears me approaching. I smile at him and sit back down. I can already feel the heat rising up my neck and to my cheeks, but I have forbidden myself to lose control again.

"Listen, Mia, I was thinking maybe you might want to take me sightseeing. You know, let the local tourist traps rip me off, grab a bite to eat. What do you say?"

Is he kidding? Did he not see the sweat? The drool? Is he asking me out on a date? Who cares, I'm going to accept. I might have to pop a hydrant and hose off in the middle of it but I'm going to go.

"I'd love that, Joe." Just saying his name sounds wonderful. "When were you thinking of doing this?"

"How about tonight?" he asks.

"Tonight sounds perfect." I can't believe I'm telling him tonight sounds perfect. I have to buy new clothes. I have to get a haircut. I have to shave my legs.

"Don't forget to leave me your address. I'll pick you up around six?"

"Six works for me." All of a sudden I'm this confident person acting like I'm making a date with the mailman. I pull out one of my business cards and write my home address on the back. As I'm handing it to Joe, Andrea walks out into the backyard, looking just radiant.

"Are you ready to start?" she says.

And I am.

CHAPTER SEVEN

For the second time in two weeks I'm running up my front stairs three by three. As soon as my front door is open I start ripping off my clothes. It's five o'clock, and I've got only an hour to get ready. On my best day it takes me longer. I start running the bath water while throwing things out of my closet in an attempt to try and find something to wear. I would normally just get into the shower but I have to shave my legs. If you're a woman with sensitive skin like me, then you know they need an appropriate amount of time to soak before you can start shaving. The shower doesn't give me this opportunity so I have to run a bath, lie on my back and wash my hair under the tap while my legs are soaking. It's almost acrobatic, but sometimes you've got to do what you've got to do. I could just wear pants tonight, but it's really beautiful outside. This is one of those warm and amazing San Francisco evenings every local takes advantage of. Plus, I'm trying to avoid another situation where I'm dripping with sweat, and so I'd like to dress light.

I'm out of the bath by five twenty-five, which is record timing. Now I have to decide what I'm going to wear before I put on my makeup. If I'm wearing something I can button, then makeup goes on first so I don't get any on my clothes. If I'm wearing something that goes over my head, makeup has to come last or I will smear it all over my clothes while putting it on. Then I have to make a quasi-bib to avoid any drips or powder falling. If men only knew what we go through. These are huge decision points and have only come about by a lot of trial and error.

I'm thinking white linen shorts because they'll keep me cool, but the second I sit down they will be completely wrinkled. I'd like to wear something with a heel, but if we're going to be walking around a lot I should go for a flat so my feet don't start to hurt. Five thirty-two. I've just wasted seven minutes thinking. I put on a pair of black capri pants, a white halter-top that shows off my tan and some black Manolo sandals. Fuck the foot pain, Joe Barrick is worth it. I'm back in the bathroom for hair and makeup by five thirty-seven. I need to be completed by five fifty-two because of the eight-minute mandatory cooldown period. That's where you have to sit and relax, take deep breaths, think good thoughts, spray on perfume and eat a breath mint. It used to be only five minutes, but one time one of my dates was three minutes early so I changed it.

I make my quasi-bib by putting a hand towel around my neck and holding the ends together with a hair clip. I'm putting on my makeup with my right hand and holding the blow dryer to my head with my left hand. Something has got to give so in order of importance I shut the blow dryer off. My hair I can put up; my face I can't hide. Wonder of all wonders, I am done at exactly five fifty-three. I'm off by a minute, but hopefully Joe will be a little late. I haven't even had time to call Frankie because I've been so rushed. I did get a message from her when I was still at Andrea's, and the entire message was her laughing hysterically. I guess the water running didn't drown out what I said on her voice mail. Sometimes when you've been best friends long enough, you're allowed to laugh first and console later, like when you see someone fall and you lose it in a fit of giggles before you can even ask if they're okay.

Joe rings my buzzer at five minutes after six. I hit the intercom button and tell him I'll be right down. I should have been waiting outside for him. Now he's going to be standing in front of the glass doors watching me walk down three flights of stairs in four inch heels. You just can't do that gracefully. I should have thought of this during my mandatory cooldown period. I grip the handrail and make my descent without a hitch. When I walk outside Joe gives me a kiss on the cheek and tells me I look lovely. It's so surreal that I feel as if it's not even really happening to me. He looks amazing in a pair of jeans and a black T-shirt.

We decide to stay in my neighborhood and window-shop a little before we get dinner. I live in a place called North Beach that some people refer to as Little Italy. It has the most amazing restaurants, cafés and also a wide array of stores. I'm grateful the conversation is flowing easily, and we both talk about how we got involved in the businesses we're in and how we got our big break. Talking to him is effortless. It just feels so casual and comfortable. While we're walking and talking it just seems like a normal date, until we stop for a moment or I look up at him and I remember I'm with Joe Barrick. It doesn't take long for people to start to recognize him, and I feel a little bit strange when somebody comes up and asks him for his autograph. He is so polite about it and even agrees to take a picture with her.

We settle on a small Italian café and after the young female hostess is done freaking out, she seats us in a corner booth in the back. It's very quiet, and there are candles on the table, giving it a romantic ambience. I'm still not sure if this is a date or not, but I'm starting to see what all those other gorgeous women see in Joe. Aside from the good looks, he is really charming and attentive. He looks you straight on when you're talking to him and really listens to what you have to say. Even though there are people coming up to him all the time just to say hello, ask for an autograph, or give him a compliment, he acts like you're the only one in the room. I feel as if the entire earth has been swallowed up and it's just us two. The only other time I can ever remember feeling this way is when I was a little girl and my father would take me on special outings with just the two of us.

The topic of relationships eventually comes up and Joe sort of implies that he is single. My face must have a funny expression on it because he starts to explain about all the tabloid photographs before I even have a chance to ask. He tells me that a lot of times when you're making a movie with someone, you become good friends from working long hours and it's not uncommon you end up hanging out together to get a bite to eat, etc., on your downtime. The latest tabloid report was of him shopping for expensive jewelry with another woman and there was even a photograph. His brother had called him laughing and asking what Joe and his brother's wife had gotten him for his birthday because that's who the woman was, his sister-in-law.

I tell him about my latest relationship disaster. I find myself opening up to the point where I even admit the guy had stolen all of my things. Joe is very sympathetic without being condescending. He laughs in all of the right places. Joe Barrick might be too good to be true.

Dinner is done along with an entire bottle of red wine and a half-eaten plate of tiramisu. When the waitress drops off the famous black leather check holder and places it right between us on the edge of the table, I don't know what to do. It's been almost a year since I have been on a date and I don't know the proper protocol. Would I be insulting him if I grab it? I don't really want to pay. It has nothing to do with the money; it is more an old-fashioned state of mind for me as far as dates go. I'm all for women's lib, but I enjoy the door being opened for me and the man picking up the tab on the first date. Wait. Is this a date? Maybe I should pay. The manager of the restaurant, who had come up to our table earlier in the night to meet Joe, is walking back toward us. He says the meal is on the house and he hopes we had enjoyed our dinner. We thank him. I almost hug him with relief.

The next part of the night is still a little blurry to me. I know we got up from the table, and Joe took my hand. I remember it felt soft and big with my small hand inside of it. Plus, I was a little tipsy from the wine and his hand was helping me to keep my balance with the strappy sandals. We walked outside and I noticed it had become dark while we were inside eating dinner, and the next thing I knew, I was practically blinded by flashes of light. There were three paparazzi taking photograph after photograph of us. Joe did his best to try to shield me from the cameras, but I was like a deer in headlights. He wrapped his arm around me and asked me which way back to my house. I pointed him in the right direction, and we started running down the street with these crazy people following us. I had a moment of clarity and realized I didn't want to be followed by them to where I lived. A cab with its light on started to drive by; I put my fingers in my mouth and did my loudest whistle until the driver came to a stop. Joe opened the door, we jumped in, and the taxi took off, leaving the paparazzi still snapping pictures in the street.

"Where to?" The cab driver asks.

I'm still trying to catch my breath. The light buzz from the wine has been replaced by complete soberness in a matter of minutes. I look over at Joe, and he seems upset.

"Please take us to Coit Tower." It was the only place I could think of.

Joe and I ride the entire way in silence. At one point I feel him grab my hand again and even though I am feeling confused, I let him take it. When we arrive at Coit Tower I ask the cab driver if he would be willing to wait, and he agrees. Joe and I step out of the car and into the front of the tower. It looks almost like a circular driveway with an observation deck. Even though it isn't very crowded tonight, I take him around to the back. One of Dee's old boyfriends used to work here, and he had showed us a semisecret place you can access when you go around to the back of the tower. It's a beautiful lawn area with the same view as the front, but you can also see inside the building. The first floor has all glass windows, and there's a mural of San Francisco inside. We stop to appreciate the art and eventually end up sitting on the grass. We still haven't spoken.

"I'm so sorry." Joe breaks the silence. "I have no idea how they knew I was there. I don't even know how anyone knows I'm in San Francisco. The only person I told was my agent."

"It's not your fault; please don't blame yourself. I was just a little bit startled, that's all. I'm fine now."

"I just wanted us to have a chance to have a nice night, you know. I wanted you to get to know me, Joe Barrick, not the J.B. that is in the movies or splashed on every tabloid cover. I'm just sick of it, the whole thing. I want a normal life back, with a normal relationship. Andrea always says, 'Fame at what price?' and she's so right."

"But you love what you do, right? I just always assumed movie stars knew the sacrifices they had to make for fame and fortune. Those people following you seem like a small price to pay for what you get in return." I wasn't trying to be insensitive but I think at 20 million a film you can stand a couple of blinding lights flashing at you when you go out in public.

"It's a complete invasion of my privacy." Joe says this very loudly; he's apparently upset at not only what I had said but also the whole situation. "I'll gladly pose for a picture or sign an autograph but these people want to know what I eat, where I grocery shop. Hell, they dig through my garbage and set up camp outside of my home. Where do you draw the line? They've run people off the road in their cars and they ruin lives."

I was trying to take in everything he said. I have to admit I'm guilty myself of buying a tabloid or two when the cover catches my eye. It's also the first thing I go to when I'm waiting in line at the grocery checkout stand. Frankie reads every Blog and subscribes to every entertainment magazine out there, and even though she says it's purely business related, I know better.

"Okay, Joe, here's what I think. You might not care and you might not want to listen but I'm here right now with you stuck in this situation, and I'm going to give you my perspective." I sound so confident. I'm at my best in high-stress situations. Perhaps when I first met Joe I should have lit a lounge chair on fire in Andrea's backyard and we could have avoided the whole sweat, drool situation entirely. "I'm guessing you make movies because you love to act, the money is fabulous, and you are entertaining people for a while. You know, letting them forget about their worries and disappear into something for a couple of hours. Well, I'm also guessing that's the same reason the paparazzi do what they do. They probably love the rush of getting the first or the best picture, it pays them pretty well, and they supply a form of entertainment people can disappear into for a while and fantasize about as well. You can't set boundaries for them besides what the law has in place, so it would seem you only have two choices: either deal with it the best way you know how or complain about it and be miserable. If you look at all the other things the fame and money has afforded you to be able to do, I'm sure you wouldn't want to give it back."

"You're wrong," Joe says quietly. "If I knew then what I know

56

now, I would give every cent back to be just a normal person again."

"Well, that's not one of your choices, Joe."

"I think I like you, Mia. I really think I like you." Joe grabs my hand again as he says this, and I turn away to look toward the view so he can't see the heat rising again on my neck and the smile that has appeared on my face. I'm beginning to think I can get used to this whole hand-holding business.

CHAPTER EIGHT

The next morning I keep drifting in and out of sleep. I had basically been like this all night. I would bolt upright not knowing if last night was a dream or not. I even pinched myself a couple of times just to make sure. I hear the home phone ringing and roll over to take a look at the clock. Seven thirty a.m. Who the hell would call me this early? My phone is nowhere to be found. I'm usually a very organized person but for some reason I misplace both my phones all of the time. Maybe it's because I have no furniture? Thankfully that will be arriving this morning. I end up crawling along the floor and following its ring. I finally find it behind the cardboard box the television is on top of and while I'm there I happen to notice one of Bob's squeaky toys. I ignore the phone, pick up the squeaky toy in my hands, and all of a sudden I'm crying. I have no idea where this is even coming from. I'm not even supposed to like that stupid cat.

I hear my machine click on, then the beep, and then a very long, loud, "MMMMMMMMMMMMIIIIIIIIIIIIIIIIIIIAAAAAAAAAAAAA!"

I know instantly that it's Frankie's voice. Jesus, what is her problem?

"I CAN'T BELIEVE YOU WENT OUT WITH J.B. AND DIDN'T EVEN TELL ME. You have to call me right away, this is incredible."

It really was incredible. I mean it is incredible. I should have called her last night when I got home, but I was just too tired and I kind of wanted to just snuggle up and fall asleep with his smell still on me. Did I mention that last night? That he smelled terrific? When the cab dropped us off back at my building, I walked him to his car. He took my face in his hands and gave me a long; weak-in-the-knees kiss good-bye. If I imagine hard enough, I can still feel his hands on my face. WAIT! How did Frankie know I went out with J.B.? I didn't tell her. I grab the phone and press one on my speed dial. I feel like the phone is ringing in slow motion.

"MMMMMMMMMMMIIIIIIIIIIIIIIIIIIIAAAAAAAAAAAAAA!" Here we go again.

"Frankie, shut up and calm down. How did you know I went out with J.B. last night?

"What do you mean how do I know? All of San Francisco knows. You're in the paper!"

"I'm what?" I can't believe this. This is insane. "What paper, Frankie? And are there any pictures on the internet?"

"Nothing on the internet yet, just The *Chronicle*, Datebook section. You look so pretty. I told you those Manolo's were a good investment. Just look at you with your bad self in those sexy, strappy sandals."

"I have to go. I need to go get the paper. I'm sorry; I'll give you all the details later today, okay?" I don't even wait for her to respond; I just hang up. I'm already wearing sweats so I put on my flip-flops and a Giants cap and start my way down the steps. I look up, and I can see through the front glass doors there are paparazzi out there. Holy shit! This is a nightmare. They're already taking pictures of me through the glass. How do they know where I live? I run up the stairs and back to the safety of my apartment. What to do? What to do? What to do? I know. I grab the phone and dial Charlie's number.

"Hello." He answers like I've woken him up which I probably have.

"Charlie, it's Mia. Listen, I know this sounds weird but you have to go to the corner and get me the *Chronicle*, okay?"

"Mia, why are you whispering?" I had no idea I was.

"Oh, I didn't know I was. Sorry. Will you go, Charlie, please?"

"Fine, give me a minute."

We hang up and I sit down on the floor and wait, biting my cuticles. In hindsight I should have warned him about the paparazzi, but it was too late now. I'm guessing since they are already parked outside my apartment, the pictures from last night will hit the internet any moment now. I hear a knock on my door and practically slide across the floor to open it. Charlie is standing there with the paper and he's rubbing his eyes. I notice he's breathing sort of heavy from running up the stairs, and I try to get in close to him to see if his breath smells bad. I can't detect anything, but he looks like he thinks I'm going to kiss him.

"What the hell is going on here, Mia? Who are all those people?"

"They're paparazzi. I went out with J.B. last night and somehow they found out where I live. Frankie called me and told me our picture was in the paper this morning."

"Jesus, you went out with J.B. How did this all happen?"

"I met him at Andrea Snowden's house yesterday and he asked me to show him the sights; it was no big deal." But it was a big deal, to me. I was already falling for him after just one date.

"By the way, how did your date go with Frankie?" I'm trying to change the subject while I flip through the paper and find the Datebook section.

"It went good. I had a great time. Did she say anything to you about...?"

"I GOT IT!" I didn't mean to interrupt him, but I am so grateful I have finally found it. And there it is, a picture of Joe and me walking out of the restaurant. I hadn't noticed the cameras yet and we both just look really happy with smiles on our faces. The caption reads: *Joe Barrick "J.B." and Mia Roman of "Gem It Up."* There is a short story on how J.B. was in town visiting a sick friend. These people are good. I have no idea how they found out who I was, but they did it in record time. All in all, the article is not bad and the picture is really flattering. Frankie was right about the shoes. I notice Charlie is leaning over me reading the article, too, and once again, I lean in and take a good sniff. Nothing. What was Frankie talking about? Charlie looks at me like I am crazy, and I just smile and pretend like I'm not done reading yet.

"I have to get to work, Mia. Are you sure you're okay?"

"I'm fine, really. Go ahead and go. Thank you so much for getting the paper for me. I really appreciate it."

I walk Charlie to the door, lock it, and take a seat back on the floor so I can read the article once more. My door buzzer goes off and as I'm walking over to the intercom I'm hoping it isn't the paparazzi.

I press the button. "Hello. Who is it?"

"Mambo Mattresses. We're here with your new furniture."

I buzz them up and open the front door. A young man appears on my landing holding a clipboard. He has short, blonde, spiky hair sticking out of his baseball hat, which is turned to the side. He keeps puckering his lips like he's going to start rapping.

"Excuse me," I say. "Are there still photographers outside with cameras?"

"Yo, lady, I don't know what you talking 'bout. There's nobody outside but us movers."

I think the lesson I have learned already from this whole experience is that you should never judge anybody. The mover is probably the second person besides Charlie to think that I am crazy today.

"Yo, lady, 'dis where you live? Cuz nobody tole us 'bout no stairs or nothin."

He looks like Vanilla Ice. I have to do everything I can to keep myself from cracking up in front of him. I half-expect him to start doing the running man.

"Yes, this is where I live. I apologize about the stairs; they were here already when I moved in." My attempt at lightening the conversation doesn't work, and once again, I know this guy thinks I'm crazy.

"Ain't no way we gonna be able to move all this stuff up these

62

stairs. Take us all damn day. Yo, can I use your phone? Mine is downstairs and ain't no way I'm going back to get it. I gotta go call Vito, cuz this is some shit."

I hand him my phone and start humming *Ice, Ice Baby* under my breath. It figures a guy named Vito would be in charge of the movers at Mambo Mattresses. I go inside my bedroom and start clearing the floor to make room for my new furniture when I hear Vanilla calling my name.

"You got somebody on the phone for you, lady. Says his name is Joe or somethin' like that.

I grab the phone.

"Hello. Joe?"

"Hi, Mia. Was that your son?" My son? How old does he think I am?

"Um, no. That's the mover. He's here to deliver some furniture I ordered."

"Oh. It's just weird that he answered your phone."

"Yeah, I don't know why he did that. He's a little strange, and I think he answered it because he was talking on it when you called. Anyway, how are you?"

"Hey, lady?" Vanilla interrupts our conversation. He's just standing in the living room staring at me. I'm so excited that Joe called I didn't even notice.

"Joe, can you hold on for one moment?" I don't wait for an answer; I just muffle the phone in my hand and look up at Vanilla.

"Vito says we gotta move your stuff in and he don't care 'bout no stairs, so we're gonna get started."

"Okay, thanks." I keep looking at him to see if he has anything more to add. He just looks away and starts downstairs.

"Sorry, Joe. Where were we?"

"I wanted to know if you had seen this morning's paper?" There was apprehension in his voice as if he thought the article might upset me.

"I've already seen it and I'm fine with it, really. It was a nice article and the picture wasn't bad at all. I can't believe how fast they found out who I was and what my business is." I know I sound sincere because I really do mean it.

"Well, I have some other news, and I thought I should let you know about it right away. My PR rep just called me and said US Magazine has picked up the story and they're going to run it. They called her to see if she had any comment, and of course she called me to confirm and see if there was anything I wanted to say."

"What does that mean they're going to run the story?" I ask. "There is no story; we just went out to dinner." This can't be my fifteen minutes of fame. I won't let it be. If anything is going to put me in a magazine, I want it to be my work, not this.

"We know there's no story, but you saw what they were like last night: they'll run anything to make the magazine sell. It's not just them, Mia, it's all of the media outlets. If I don't make any comment at all, they will just run assumptions and try to get quotes from your friends and maybe people who work at the restaurant."

"Isn't there any way you can make them stop? Even if you give

64

them a comment they're still going to skew the story. I don't think you should say anything."

"I can't make them stop, Mia. But I can refuse to give a comment. Sometimes the less said the better. We'll just have to wait it out and go from there. On the brighter side, I have a black tie event that I've been invited to tonight if you'd like to come along. I could sure use the company, and I had a really great time with you last night."

I really want to accept this invitation. I want to spend more time with Joe so badly, but I'm just not used to this media attention. Do I want to invite more of it?

"Joe, I appreciate the offer, but I think this might be just a little too much for me. I don't think I can handle this. I didn't tell you before, but this morning when I went downstairs to go get the paper, there were paparazzi standing outside my door." I am saying the exact opposite of what I really want to say. I want to scream out that there is nothing more in the world that I want to do at this moment than be with him, smell him again, and feel his hand holding mine.

"Please think about it, Mia. I don't want you to do something you can't handle, but can I just say something in the hopes of it possibly changing your mind?"

"Of course, I would really love for you to change my mind."

"I wanted to tell you that last night was more real to me than any date I've had in years. I didn't have to watch what I said or put up any false pretenses. You allowed me to just be Joe, and do you want to know why?"

Did I want to know why? Hell, yes I wanted to know why, and I can't believe he just called it a date.

"Yes, I want to know. Why?" I say this in almost a whisper.

"Because you're real. Everything about you is real and kind and fun and beautiful. If you would rather stay out of the public eye, then come over to Andrea's and we'll all hang out and make dinner. Come on, what do you say?"

"Yes." That's what I say. "That sounds perfect! I'll bring the wine and dessert. I'm actually coming over there after the movers are done to begin working on the casket, so I'll see you early this afternoon anyway."

It was a done deal. My second "date" with Joe in two days. Speaking of the movers, where were they? I had gone into my bedroom to avoid the noise and forgotten all about Vanilla Ice. I walk into the living room and there they are, three of them. They all look exactly the same. So much so that it's hard to tell which one Vanilla is. It would probably help if they were standing up. The three of them are lying on the floor panting.

"Hey, lady, you got a bag or somethin' we can breathe into? I've been deliverin' furniture for a coupla years now and I ain't never seen no stairs like that before."

CHAPTER NINE

The rest of the morning flies by pretty quickly. I call Frankie back and get her up to speed. I also let her know that I smelled Charlie's breath twice, and both times I got nothing. She seemed pretty relieved. The movers finish by about noon. I feel so guilty that I end up treating them to Chinese food and a six-pack of beer. As it turns out, moving is just their side job. They have a rap group called The White Boys, but they just haven't had their big break yet. Vanilla (whose real name is Uriah) loves my work, and I'm going to do some jackets for them for free. He says they might even use my stair experience in one of their songs.

When everyone has left my apartment, I go over to my new couch and take a seat. It's wonderful. I have to remind myself to thank Dee and Frankie for encouraging me to buy new furniture. The living room looks so nice that if I didn't have a busy day ahead of me, I would probably just sit here, open up all the blinds, order in more food, and watch my reality shows all day. Come to think of it, I haven't had a day like that in some time. Lately, since my workload has been so heavy, I've taken to scheduling one day a month on my calendar as a "me" day. I don't do any work, I make no plans for that day, and I always start it off by sleeping in. Sometimes I go shopping and treat myself to some new clothes and a nice lunch out. Last month Frankie and Dee started scheduling "me" days, too, and we spend them together.

I walk backward through the hallway into my bedroom so I can stare at the living room a bit more. When I finally turn around and look inside my room, it's really beautiful. I love my new headboard and the mattress. It's double padded and it's called the Rosebud. How do you like that? I put on fresh sheets while Vanilla and his friends were finishing up in the living room, and I can smell the fabric softener. I start to feel like I'm in a commercial, so I jump on to my bed and lie on my back. I'm really happy right now. I feel like there should be opera music playing in the background and fresh laundry hanging from the line outside blowing in the breeze. My commercial is abruptly interrupted by the realization that I have a very full day ahead, and I still haven't even decided what to wear yet.

The idea is casual cute, which as you ladies know, is one of the hardest looks to achieve. It is a brutal job to look absolutely marvelous while making people believe you put no time at all into your appearance. Makeup is essential, but not too much or you look overdone; remember the idea is to look effortlessly amazing. I usually go for mascara with no liner or shadow, pink blusher to give myself a more youthful glow, and may I recommend Spite lipglass by M•A•C, which is truly the best neutral you can get.

I'm doing a ponytail for my hair, but I'm going for middle placement instead of low: this way little strands will start to fall out and voila, casual cute. Jeans. Boyfriend style for sure, but not too frayed or ripped, and not so loose that you lose your figure in them. I have one pair of jeans that are in this shape, and I cherish them like my gems. I only wear them on special occasions that call for this particular look. White cotton button-down shirt. It has to be crisp and dry cleaned and a little oversized so you can unbutton it and wear a white tank underneath. Wife beater style is the sexiest. The button placement is the most important part because it has to be low enough to show the tank clinging to your skin, but high enough that you don't see waistband.

Now for the shoes. If it's wintertime, I say go for a black Louboutin boot with that signature red sole and a black leather motorcycle jacket. If it's summertime, like it is now, I suggest some light colored wedges to show off your tan without stealing the show. I'm going for the nude Jimmy Choo's with the raffia heel. They are perfect because it gives you a little added height while blending in with the rest of the outfit. And ladies, for the love of God: no open toes unless you've had a pedicure. All right, time to go.

I stop off at the Pappas Brothers' and pick up my first order. Since Andrea and I finalized the collage yesterday afternoon, I now have enough information to place another order for the rest of the gems. Thankfully Andrea paid me for the estimate I had made on materials yesterday or the Pappas Brothers would have cleaned out my entire savings account. I'm still having a hard time grasping this big of a job and the amount of money involved. I was thinking that Andrea is spending more money on jewels than most people will probably make in a lifetime. Then I remember that her lifetime is going to be over very shortly. I ask them if I could return any gems that I don't use and they agree on the condition that I only go through them from now on. I agree. I wasn't planning on ever using anybody else anyway. I thank Dominic and Vincenzio, and I am about to walk out of the store when Dom stops me.

"Mia, we gotta present for youse."

"For me? But why?"

"You justa become our best fucking client." He says this while taking my arm and leading me outside. There is a beautiful black stretch limousine parked in front.

"You thinka me and Enzo gonna let you walk around by yourself with all those jewels? You fuckin' crazy." He's laughing this big belly laugh, and I turn around and hug him. The limousine driver comes out of the car and opens the door for me.

"You take her wherever she wants to go, eh?" Dominic tells the limousine driver and then winks at me. I mouth the words thank you as the door is being closed. I can see him standing on the street smiling, and I'm thankful for the tinted windows because I'm beginning to cry and I don't want him to see. Man, I'm like a waterworks lately with the tears.

I ask the driver if he knows where San Mateo is, and he nods.

"I'd like to go there first, please." He nods again. San Mateo is about twenty-five miles south of San Francisco, and I just happen to know that one of the best Italian bakeries in the world is on Thirty-seventh Avenue. It's called Romolo's, and they make the best cannoli that money can buy. Romolo and his wife have owned this bakery for over 30 years. When I was little my father would take me to their bakery, and I would get a scoop of bubble gum ice cream that Romolo made himself. Now I want to share these desserts with Andrea and Joe.

70

I'm relaxing in the back of the limousine, enjoying some music and just reminiscing on the last two days of my life, when my phone rings. I know it's my mother because I have a special ring set for when it's her number. I'm thinking it's important because she rarely calls my cell phone.

"Hi, Mom. How are you?" I try to make my voice sound as jovial as possible.

"Well, sweetheart, I'm just fine. I'm sitting at my dining room table drinking a cup of coffee and reading the newspaper. I decided to read the newspaper because I got a phone call from my friend Linda. You remember Linda Klapper, don't you, sweetheart? Anyway, Linda tells me that she can't believe I've been keeping your and J.B.'s relationship a secret. Imagine that. Me keeping secrets."

Oh, shit. Her calling me sweetheart is the equivalent of other mothers' using their children's full names, like Tina's becoming Christina or Chris's turning into Christopher. It's not good. How did I not see this coming? I should have called her this morning and warned her, but I was just so busy with the movers and all that I forgot completely.

"Listen, Mom, it's not what you think. He is a friend of one of my clients and he just asked me to show him the town because he's visiting here. I had no idea it would be in the papers and it was nothing more than a dinner... Mom?"

"No, no, no. Don't you worry about me. I'm sure you didn't intend to humiliate me to Linda who will tell Gail and Gail who will tell Jean who will tell— Well, you get the picture. I'm just going to have to quit the garden club, I suppose. I couldn't stand to hear them tell rumors about how I'm obviously not a good mother or my daughter wouldn't keep such secrets from me."

"Mom, it's really not like that. I promise. I'm not keeping secrets from you. There just wasn't anything to tell. You know that if something big was happening in my life that you would be the first person I would go to. You know that, don't you?" I'm saying this with my fingers crossed and hoping I don't end up burning in the fiery pits of hell. My mother would probably be about the fiftieth person I told, but she seems genuinely hurt, and if I wasn't completely positive that she was made of stone, I would say that it sounds like she's crying.

"Oh, you're just saying that to make me feel better."

"I'm not, Mom. I mean it, and how about this? I'm going to see him again this afternoon at my client's house where he is staying, so why don't I get some autographed pictures for you to pass out when you meet with your garden club next? I'll bring them on Sunday for you, okay?"

"Mia, that is just wonderful. I can't wait to call Linda and tell her that we're going to have genuine autographed pictures. I'll see you Sunday then, and please, don't forget my lasagna dish."

She's gone. She hung up. I hear that loud Hallelujah voice go off in my head. Can you imagine being a child and growing up with that? It took me a good 20 years to figure out that I wasn't completely crazy. I had this huge revelation after one of our particularly excruciating phone calls: She's the crazy one. I knew it then without a doubt. All these years of second-guessing myself and my thinking she said something when she would swear she didn't, it was all her craziness. And the guilt. She should have been a Catholic priest with the guilt trips she dealt out. I had always been so proud and enamored of my dad before he died, but when I finally figured my mom out, he became a fucking saint. Sorry about the *f* word, it's the Pappas Brothers coming out in me. I'll be fine in about 24 hours.

We make it to San Mateo, and I spend some time catching up with Romolo and his beautiful wife before buying six homemade cannoli. I get back in the limo and ask the driver to take me to the liquor store so I can pick up a bottle or two of wine. As we're driving down the streets I start to feel a little nostalgic. I grew up here, and every time I come back I'm overwhelmed with memories. Sometimes Frankie and I drive here just to go to a particular restaurant that we used to love when we were younger. There have been many trips made solo by each of us to Romolo's when the other has been depressed. It's just about the best surprise we can give one another.

After I'm done picking up the wine, I ask the limousine driver to make one more stop at the house where I grew up. It doesn't look much different even after all these years. Frankie's house was next door to mine, and our bedroom windows were right across from each other. Neither of us had any brothers or sisters so we used to call each other sisters from another mother. In fact, we still do. We still are. I let the driver know that I'm done looking, and he begins to drive back toward the freeway and San Francisco. I know that I've got a good 45 minutes before we get to Andrea's house so I decide to call Frankie. It would be nice to reminisce right now with my sister.

CHAPTER TEN

Before I get the chance to call Frankie, my phone rings. Frankie is calling me first.

"Hi, Frank. What's up?"

"Hi, Mia. What are you doing?"

"I was just about to call you. J.B. invited me to Andrea's for dinner and when I stopped off at the Pappas Brothers to pick up my first order of gems they got me a limo as a surprise. So, guess what?" I feel like I'm talking a mile a minute. I usually feel this way with Frankie. She hates talking on cell phones so I have to rush myself.

"What? Besides that being so cool of the Pappas Brothers."

"I had the limo driver take me to San Mateo so I could get some cannoli from Romolo's to bring to dinner, and afterward we drove by our old houses."

"Awww, I wish I could have gone, too. I love that. Maybe on our next "me" day we can go do that."

"I'm down. We'll make a day of visiting San Mateo."

"Okay, so I'm glad you're sitting down in the limo because I have some things I need to tell you and you're not going to like them." Frankie sounds serious and for that reason I'm glad I am sitting down in the limo, too.

"I'm ready. Tell me," I say.

"Okay, you know who that whiny, bitchy girl named Star Nutley is? She's the one that's the heir to the Nutley Candy Bar fortune?"

"Of course I know who she is, aren't you planning her twenty-first birthday party?"

"Party? It's a freak show I'm orchestrating over here. You'd think it was her twelfth birthday party, not her twenty-first. The guest list is a huge who's who of Hollywood and these people have no idea what they're in for. But I can complain about that later. I have to tell you what she said. I was talking to her on the phone this morning and she said that she saw on TMZ that J.B. was in town, and she wants to find out if he will still be here for her party so she can invite him. Then she told me she is really good friends with his girlfriend who called her today all pissed off about these rumors she is hearing of him with another girl. So I said, 'He has a girlfriend?' and she said, 'Of course, you know, Olivia Lucas from that soap opera "Hope's Chest." And then I asked her if she was sure and she started flipping out on me, so I dropped the subject. Did he tell you he was seeing somebody back in L.A.?"

This was a lot of information to take in all at once. Could he have a serious relationship back home? I just had no idea.

"He never said. Well, he didn't say he didn't and he didn't say he did, so I don't know."

"Are you okay about this? It doesn't seem right that he would give you the whole knee-buckling kiss if he was with somebody else." Frankie was right. I guess I just assumed he was single after he kissed me.

"I need to find out before another kiss happens, Frankie, because even though this sounds insane: I'm starting to fall for him. And if he does have a girlfriend, I don't care if my knees buckle to the ground. I can't be with somebody who does that."

"Amen to that, girl. If I were you I would try and find out some answers tonight before it goes any further. And Mia, I'm not done yet."

"I had a feeling you weren't," I say. "Go ahead, lay it on me."

"I had a client lunch meeting today that was a couple of blocks from my office, and I decided to walk it. I left a little early and gave myself some time to window-shop. I was browsing at the things outside all the shops as I was walking, and I came to an antique store. They had the greatest street sale going on and I see the cutest end table in front of the window, so I start to check it out. I'm right in the middle of opening the drawers when I look up and there, Mia, IS YOUR ARMOIRE! It's right in the window."

"Wha-wha-what?" I can't speak. I can't believe it. "What the hell did you do?"

"I stormed inside and demanded to see the owner. The man told me he was the owner and I told him he was selling stolen goods. I said that his armoire in the window belonged to my best friend who hand painted it herself and she recently had it stolen from her. So he said, 'Tell your friend to show me a police report that proves it's hers and maybe we'll talk about it.' So, you did file a police report, right?"

I'm just quiet. Partly because I can't believe this is happening and partly because I didn't file a police report.

"Mia?" Frankie probably thinks the call has dropped or maybe that I've passed out.

"No, I'm here. Sorry. I didn't file a police report, Frankie. I just didn't see any need to. I mean, I didn't think it would help. I'm sure it's too late now. Did you ask the guy where he got it? How much was he selling it for? Did you look around to see if he had any more of my stuff?"

"Okay, forget about the police report. You're probably right about that. The owner just said a man had come in saying he was moving out of state and needed to get rid of a few things. He's selling it for two grand and I only saw one more of your things."

"Oh my God, two grand? I painted that myself and he's going to profit two grand on it? That is ridiculous. What else did he have of mine?" I'm really pissed off now.

"He had your wooden chest with all your grandma's quilts still inside. Don't worry, sweetie, I bought it back for you. I'm so sorry all this is happening, I hope having the chest back helps a little bit." Frankie says this like she's about to cry, and I am, too.

"I love you, Frank. You got back the only thing that was important. Thank you so much. I will totally pay you back. I'm so sorry that you had to be the messenger." I said this and I meant it. I feel more badly for her having to call and tell me all these things than I do for myself.

"I love you, too. You try to have a good time tonight and remember that we have no idea whether or not that bitch Star is telling the truth."

"Okay, Frank. I'll call you tomorrow. Thanks again." We hang up, and I'm feeling so overwhelmed with information. I want to scream, but I'm afraid the limo driver will dump me off on the freeway for scaring the shit out of him. It was easier for me when I still had no idea what John had done with my things. Maybe I was holding out hope that he had just stored them somewhere because he was so angry and that eventually he would return them to me. Hell, he could have maneuvered a furniture hostage situation and I would have bought my stuff back if it came down to it. To actually know he sold everything, especially my chest with Grandma's blankets, that is almost too much to take. It makes you feel like you never really know somebody, even after sharing intimate secrets and living together. They can turn around and do something that you would have bet your life they would never do.

I'm still not sure what to think about the whole Joe situation and whether or not that girl Star has her story straight. I do know that I have no right to be upset after one date with him, but that doesn't explain why I feel a little pinch in my heart. He didn't actually come right out and say he was single, but at dinner he did say all the tabloid rumors weren't true. Isn't that the same? And if he has a girlfriend back in Los Angeles, why would he invite me out to begin with, then invite me out again and kiss me the way he kissed me? It doesn't make any sense.

As the limo pulls up in front of Andrea's house I decide that I'm not going to mention what Star said tonight or even bring up the subject of relationships. I'm also not going to talk about the whole furniture fiasco because I don't want to risk getting upset or worse off, teary eyed. I've still got a couple of hours to start work on Andrea's casket until it will be dinnertime. Maybe I can lose myself in my work and try and clear my head a little. There, I've made up my mind that I'm going to leave everything I have found out from Frankie behind in the limo. I'm just going to close the door on it when I get out and leave it sitting in there. I'm going to have a nice time tonight. Let the next passenger deal with my emotional baggage.

CHAPTER ELEVEN

Andrea opens the door and envelops me in a huge hug. It feels good, and I hold on for an extra long time. She's not looking well at all, but I tell her she looks wonderful. She's got a pink pashmina wrapped around her shoulders and a multicolored pastel scarf tied around her head. She's the picture of elegance and I tell her that, too. I show her the pattern I've completed, and she's so overwhelmed she starts to cry. Of course, I follow suit. Andrea tells me she's cooking a wonderful five-course meal and she'll leave me to my work. I want to ask her where J.B. is, but I don't want to look obvious.

I go about setting out all of my tools. My first job is the hardest, tracing the pattern onto the casket. It takes the better part of the afternoon, but it's done to perfection. I want to get started on applying the jewels this afternoon because I'm estimating this job is going to take about thirty hours. I'm starting to lay out the gems and trying to decide what I'm going to do first, the wording or the pictures, when I hear somebody open up the French doors. Andrea had the casket set up outside because she thought it was such a beautiful day that I would like working better out here. She was right: it's beautiful, really warm with just a hint of a breeze. I look up to see who's coming and it's Joe.

"Hey there! How are you?" He looks amazing. He looks way better than I remember him looking last night. How can that be, it hasn't even been twenty-four hours and he looks better?

"Hi Joe! I'm good, thanks. Just trying to get some work done and enjoying this weather. How are you?" I can't believe how calm my voice sounds when I'm freaking out inside. I'm just so not used to this; I've never fallen apart this much around a man before.

"I'm doing great now that you're here. It's really good to see you." And with that he walks up and gives me a hug. Oh God, he smells good. Maybe if I chant "Please don't have a girlfriend" under my breath the whole night, it will turn out that it's not true. Forget it, I'll either get caught or I'll look like a crazy person. He releases me from the hug but keeps his hands on my shoulders and stands back like he's sizing me up.

"You are so beautiful. Have I already told you that today?"

"No, you haven't and thank you. You're not so bad yourself." Did that sound dorky?

"Thank you back. I've been watching you work from the window. Andrea wouldn't let me come out here because she said I'd be disturbing you."

Oh fuck (Pappas Brothers; sorry), I can't believe he's been watching me this whole time. I'm trying to scan my mind quickly to reassure myself that I didn't do anything disgusting like pick my butt or sneeze and not cover my mouth. I'm pretty sure it's been a G-rated afternoon for me.

"Anyway," he says. "Andrea said for you to start wrapping it up because it's almost time for dinner. We're going to eat outside, is that okay with you?"

"That's perfect. I'll start packing up."

"Mind if I watch?" Joe askss this with a sweet little smile on his face.

Andrea starts walking toward us and says, "You've been watching her long enough. Go set the table, lover boy."

All three of us start laughing, and Andrea gives me a wink before she and Joe walk back into the house. I wonder if Joe told her anything or if she was just generalizing about Joe's normal behavior. From what Joe has told me about Andrea, they have been very good friends for a long time. Joe was a co-star in one of Andrea's movies, and they have stayed close ever since. Maybe if I get the chance to be alone with Andrea tonight, I will try to probe her and find out if Joe has a girlfriend. I finish packing up my stuff and go join Joe at the table, which he has just finished setting. The sun is starting to go down, and the sky looks amazing. Andrea has only turned some of the outside lights on, and Joe is starting to light the candles on the table. It's all so intimate and inviting.

I walk inside to see if I can help Andrea and she hands me some dishes to bring outside, which smell absolutely wonderful. I haven't eaten anything since the Chinese food this afternoon, and until I smelled this food I had no idea how hungry I am. As I'm walking out the doors, Joe is walking in to help bring some dishes outside, too.

"Why doesn't Andrea have help?" I ask Joe in passing.

"She does. She sent them home for the night."

I'm glad to hear that she has help. Even though I don't know her very well, she seems like the type of person that would want to do everything herself, and eventually she's going to have to rely on other people to take care of her.

All the dishes are in place and both Joe and I have taken our seats. We're just waiting for Andrea to come out. All of a sudden we hear soft, slow music and both of us start looking around for the speakers. They're everywhere, but they blend in so well outside that you don't even notice them. It's the perfect touch. Andrea comes out, and I'm happy to notice that Joe stands up and pulls her chair out for her. That's another one of my favorite things that men do. Everything looks and feels wonderful.

"Okay, dig in," Andrea says.

We all start to help ourselves to everything laid out on the table. There's so much of it and I'm so hungry that I have to pace myself so I can make sure I try it all. There are huge prawns as big as my palm with a cocktail sauce Andrea tells us she's made herself. There are three different kinds of bread to choose from and fried calamari with aioli sauce, which Andrea has also made herself. The main courses are ahi tuna, which she has seared and added cilantro to, and cappellini pasta with baby shrimp in a cream sauce. A true seafood feast. Every bite of it is more delicious than the last, and we're having the best time talking, eating and drinking wine.

"You are such an amazing cook, Andrea. Did you teach yourself to do all this?" I ask.

"My third husband would only eat seafood," she says. "So, after it was clear that he was going to stick around longer than my second husband, I decided to take some cooking lessons."

"How many times have you been married?" I ask.

"Four, but the last one was only for two days so we had it annulled. The first one was Billy and it lasted twenty years, and God rest his soul, he was the best one. The second one lasted less than a year and the third one lasted two years. I think I kept hoping that they would measure up somehow to Billy and they never did. It wasn't their fault. It was mine for always trying to compare and not just loving them for who they were, instead of trying to make them who they would never be. I believe in soul mates, as corny as that sounds, and Billy was mine."

"I don't think it's corny at all," Joe says. "I believe in soul mates, too. I think you can be happy with somebody even if you never find your soul mate, but I don't think you'll ever have the type of love that you and Billy had."

"How do you know he was your soul mate, Andrea?" I ask.

"I'll tell you something and you tell me what you think, because I've had so much time lately to soul search that I don't know if what I've come up with is crazy or just fate. I feel there's a reason for everything, even for my getting sick. When I found out I was going to die, and I'm okay saying that now; I am going to die. When I found that out my first impulse was to curse God and ask him why, but when he didn't answer, I thought I would find the answers myself. You don't know this, Mia, but I was an orphan. I spent the first eighteen years of my life living in and out of foster homes and never being happy. I met Billy when I was seventeen and we were married that same year. He was the only family I have ever had. I thought when we found out I couldn't have children that he would leave me, but he said I was enough for him. I thought he would be insecure when I got famous and started acting in movies, but he loved that all the limelight was on me. And when he died, I thought I would die, too. Instead, I just went from man to man looking to replace him and I couldn't. So now I think God wants to spare me from looking any further and he's just going to send me to be with Billy. I'm going to be with my family again, I'm going to go home."

Andrea starts to quietly cry when she has finished talking, so I grab her hand. I had been crying through most of her story, and I couldn't help myself and I let out a huge sob.

"Oh, honey. No need for you to cry. I'm the one that's dying over here." Andrea and I start laughing and I reach over to embrace her. The best feeling in the world is laughter through tears. We both look over at Joe, as it seems we've temporarily forgotten about him. To our amazement Joe is crying, too.

"You're still here?" Andrea says. This time all three of us are in hysterics.

"I'm off to bed, you two. I am exhausted right down to my bones. Please leave all of the dishes and everything else. I've already told my staff what to expect and they will take care of it in the morning. Thank you for a wonderful evening." And with that, Andrea is gone.

"She didn't even give me a chance to thank her," I say.

"She knows you enjoyed it, don't worry. That's all the thanks she needs. I hope she gets a good night's sleep because she has a lot of visitors coming tomorrow, and she insists they all stay with her and that she entertain them." Joe looks serious as he says this. I know he is really worried about her, and it's endearing.

The wind is starting to pick up outside, and two of the candles go out. Joe leans over and blows out the rest of them. I have such a funny feeling inside right now, it's hard to describe. Half my heart and mind are here with Joe and in this moment, but the other half is with Andrea. What a strong, remarkable woman she is. I knew that I liked her immediately when I first met her, but I had no idea how much I would admire her.

"How about we go inside? You're starting to shiver." Joe takes my hands and helps me up as he says this. We walk inside and go through the house until we reach the living room. Both of us gasp at the same time as we see what is set up. There are candles lit everywhere, soft music is filling the air, a bottle of champagne is chilling on ice, and there is a dessert plate with strawberries dipped in chocolate along with the cannolli I brought. It's so romantic.

"Did you do this?" I ask.

"Not me," Joe says.

"Andrea." We both say at the same time and smile.

CHAPTER TWELVE

Both of us take a seat on the couch and Joe begins to open up the champagne. I wasn't planning on this whole seduction scene, and now I don't know what I'm going to do. I don't want to bring up what Frankie told me Star said, but I also don't want to take this relationship to a more intimate level until I'm sure that Joe isn't seeing somebody else. Who knows if Joe even wants this to be romantic? He's not the one that set it up. Maybe he was just planning on walking me out. Oh shit! I have no way to get home. I decide this will be a good icebreaker because honestly, now that I know Joe didn't plan this, I'm starting to feel a little uncomfortable wondering if he is even into it.

"Joe, I just remembered I got dropped off here today, so I think I should try to find an Uber. If there are none in this area, calling a cab is going to take forever. That will give us some time to have a little dessert and champagne."

"Whoa! Wait a minute." Joe says. "Andrea went through all this trouble, there's no rush. I can drive you home later if you like."

"If you're sure it's no trouble." I can't refuse him, even if I want to. Because even though I'm trying my damnedest to protect myself and not get hurt, the truth is, I really want to be with him. In fact, if you had asked me earlier what the perfect end to this night would be: you're looking at it. But my phone call with Frankie changed all of that, and I'm just so confused.

"I'm absolutely sure it is no trouble at all." And with that, we are kissing. I didn't even know it was coming and it's incredible. I can feel his hands on the back of my head and he's playing with my hair. Now they're moving to touch my face and his mouth feels warm and soft. Did I mention that he smells incredible? His kisses are perfect, slow and passionate, but at times a little more aggressive and urgent. He moves his mouth and starts to kiss down my neck. Oh my God! This is heaven. I know I have to stop him, but I want to enjoy this for just a minute more. When I feel his hands start to unbutton my top, I pull back.

"I'm so sorry. I just got wrapped up in the moment. Are you okay?" He's looking up at me with those beautiful eyes and I'm so torn. I want to scream that I'm fine and put his hands right back where they were, but I can't do it to myself. I owe myself better and I have to keep remembering that. "No, I'm fine. I'm sorry, too I just thought it was moving a little too fast for me. Is that okay?" I sound like a little girl when I ask him this. As if I'm looking for his approval.

"It's more than okay. I want you to be comfortable. In fact, I wanted to ask you something anyway. I've been invited to a last minute party on Saturday night." Joe says this and then hesitates like he might be considering asking me. I hope he does, that would really answer any questions I might have had. "Anyway," he continues, "I'm open tomorrow night and I'd really like to see you as much as possible while I'm here. I know it's short notice, but do you have any plans?"

Wait. Is he asking me out for Saturday night or tomorrow? I'm just kind of staring at him trying to remember what he's just said, but as soon as he mentioned Saturday, I got wrapped up in my own thoughts.

"Mia, tomorrow night? Do you have any plans yet?" That solves it. He's not inviting me to Star's party and I know exactly why. I'm glad I didn't ask him yet because now I know my answer with out having to say a word. It was fine for him to invite me to a black tie event with him tonight, but not Saturday night because his stupid girlfriend is going to be there. All of a sudden I'm not feeling very well.

"I'm going to have to look and see, Joe. I've been so busy that I haven't even checked my calendar the last couple of days. Would you mind if you took me home now, I'm starting to get very tired?" And pissed off! I'm sure the annoyance came out in my voice, but I could really give a shit right now. I just want to go home, get into my new bed and call Frankie.

"Sure, I'll take you home. Are you alright?" Joe says this like he is very concerned and for a second I almost feel bad.

"I'll be fine. I've just had a long day." I hope I sound less annoyed than I am, but I really do want to go home. I need to talk to Frankie and tell her what has happened. I know sometimes after we talk to one another we make each other realize that we're blowing something out of proportion or that we just read too much into something. Unfortunately, I don't think that will be the case this time.

Joe and I walk to his car and once again, he's the gentleman and opens up my door for me. We ride part of the way to my house without talking until I can't take the silence anymore.

"Do you know who is coming to stay with Andrea tomorrow?" I ask.

"I know who every one is by name because the majority of them are pretty famous, but I only know a couple of them personally. There's Sophia Camp, Natalia Layne, Isabella Taylor and Tony Case. Most of them are bringing either their spouses or their significant others. I think Andrea said that Tony is bringing his Dad with him. Apparently he has been working non-stop and he's going to kill two birds with one stone and make this a trip to see Andrea and a catching up period for him and his Pop. Do you recognize any of those names?" Joe asks.

"I do recognize some. I know who Tony and Natalia are and I think Isabella is a soap star, right?" I ask.

"Yes, she's on the show "Hope's Chest." Have you ever seen it?" Joe asks.

Oh shit! This territory is one I don't want to go into right now. I can't believe he's asking me if I've ever seen his girlfriend's soap. And some one from that show, I'm sure Olivia's friend, is going to be staying at Andrea's. This is a nightmare.

"I don't really watch daytime television. Sometimes I TiVo Ellen, but that's about it." I say. I decide to take a chance. "Isn't Olivia Lucas on that show, too? Do you know her?" I ask.

I'm dying to see his reaction but it's so damn dark in the car that when I look over, I can't tell if his facial expression has changed or not. I think my tone sounded a bit accusatory, but I can't help it.

"Yeah, she's on that show, too. Although Andrea told me that she and Isabella aren't friends. I have no idea why." He answers.

That's it? Great. I got nothing from that. What do I do now? Say, 'But do you know her?' and sound like a psycho. I don't think so. Then he'll know that I know about Olivia. Do I care if he knows? I think I do. I think for some reason I'm holding out hope that he'll come clean or that it's all some kind of huge misunderstanding.

"Oh, so you don't know her?" I ask. I just rearrange the question so it doesn't look like I'm probing as much as curious.

"No, I know her. I just don't know why she and Isabella don't get along." He answers.

Now he's really trying to change the subject. Who gives a shit if Olivia and Isabella get along? What the hell is he even talking about? To me, that's a dead give away. He's guilty and now I know it for sure. God, I can't breathe. I roll down the window and half stick my head out so I can take some deep breaths of air. I notice that we're almost to my house and I'm so grateful I almost squeeze myself through the window and jump out.

Right as Joe comes to a stop in front of my apartment, cameras start flashing. It's crazy. There are at least five paparazzi there and they are literally on the windshield of the car taking pictures. Were they hiding in the bushes? They popped out of nowhere. I wonder how long they've been just waiting outside of my house.

"I have to go, Joe. Do you mind if I leave my tool bag in the back of your car? I really don't want to get out of the car and go grab it. It's just my tools; Andrea put the jewels in her safe for me." I ask.

"No, it's no problem. I'll bring it in Andrea's house for you. I'm so sorry about all of this. I feel so terrible but there's nothing I can do to stop it. Do you want me to try and park and walk you up?" Joe asks.

"No. No way," I say. "I'll be fine. I don't want to give them more then they've already got. But thank you for the offer and thank you for a really wonderful time tonight."

"You're welcome. I'll call you tomorrow, okay?" Joe asks.

"That would be great. Goodnight." I'm saying this as I'm opening up the door and I'm not sure he even catches my goodnight. I'm really prepared, though. I've got my door key in one hand and I'm holding my shoes in the other hand so I can make a run for it. Today will go down in the history books as the first time ever that I sprinted up the stairs to my apartment. I almost don't recognize the place when I walk in because of all the new furniture. My television is still sitting on the cardboard box, but I couldn't find an armoire that I liked when I went shopping with the girls. Speaking of the girls…

I set my things down and grab the phone. I hit one on the speed dial and wait for Frankie to answer. No luck. I go to speed dial two which is her cell phone and wait again for her to answer. As soon as she does I tell her that we need an Auntie EM and for her to call Dee. She says that she's on her way. An Auntie EM is an emergency meeting. If we just say an EM we know that we only have to plan the meeting for as soon as possible, but if we say an Auntie EM, it means right now. It doesn't matter where you are, who you're with or what time it is, it's right now. The Auntie EM is always at the person's house that called for it, because typically they are under the most stress and should just stay put and wait. The only duty the Auntie EM caller has to fulfill is making sure they don't kill themselves until the others arrive. When I call an Auntie EM, Dee is in charge of bringing the cocktails and Frankie is in charge of bringing some kind of snack food, preferably filled with sugar, salt or chocolate.

As I'm rummaging through my drawers trying to find something more comfortable to wear, somebody knocks on my door. How could the paparazzi have gotten in and how dare they knock on my door at this time. It's almost eleven at night. There is one other person that lives on the second floor and I'm hoping they didn't accidentally buzz them in.

"Who is it?" I ask.

"It's Frankie. Open up."

I open the door and Frankie is standing in the hallway outside my apartment wearing big, flannel pajama bottoms and a t-shirt that goes down to her knees. She's also carrying a bag of pork rinds.

"What are you wearing? And how the hell did you get here so quickly?" I ask.

"Shut up and let me in. Those idiots outside just took pictures of me through the glass door looking like this and running up the stairs. Oh, and I was at Charlie's. These pork rinds are all he had." She winks at me as she says this last part.

"Holy shit! You were? What about the bad breath thing? DID YOU SLEEP WITH HIM? YOU SLUT! YOU DID!" I scream.

"I didn't. Calm down. He made me dinner and I spilled something all over my shirt so he let me change into some of his clothes."

"And that's the best he could do?" I ask.

"Well, when I went to leave his house to go home, all those paparazzi were standing outside so he told me I could sleep over and he gave me some pajamas. It was innocent. He even told me that I could have the bed and he would take the couch. In fact, it's all too innocent; I practically had to feel myself up tonight. And you were right, that bad breath thing was just a fluke, he's fine."

"I'm so happy for you, Frankie! I really am. You've waited so long for this to happen and it's all finally working out. Come on; come help me set some munchies up before Dee gets here. If she finds out all we have is pork rinds, we're going to spend the night consoling her instead of solving my problems. She is coming, right?" I ask. We start to walk into the kitchen.

"She's on her way. She was out on a date with some new guy. Said she really likes this one but she says that a lot so we'll have to wait and see. I've been keeping her updated on everything with you and J.B. so you won't have to fill her in too much. I also told her about seeing your armoire and she completely freaked out about it. Said there was a reason and all that bullshit. So, give me a hint. What happened?" Frankie asks.

"Not a chance. Just start digging in my pantry." I say this to

Frankie because part of the EM is that we have to wait for all three of us to be here before we can start discussing the situation. One person always arrives before the other, and the first time it happened and things had already been discussed, the other person's feelings were very hurt. Luckily for Frankie, my buzzer goes off right then.

"Who is it?" I ask.

"Who the fuck do you think it is? Let me in, these people are on top of me with all their cameras." Dee screams. I buzz her up and open the front door and wait. She comes in looking like a movie star, literally. She's wearing a black cowboy hat and her blond curls are coming out from the bottom. She has on faded jeans with cowboy boots and a tight, white tank top that I made for her with the words "Spoiled Bitch" written on it. If I were going to switch teams, Dee would be my dream girl. The fantasy quickly ends when I notice that Dee is pissed off. The Dee of "everything has a reason" is really upset.

"Now that is just ridiculous. They have no clue who I am and they're snapping away like crazy. You think I'm mad now, you don't know what mad would have been if I had showed up here in my pajamas like usual on EM nights. They have no shame, screaming all these personal questions at me and coming about an inch from my face. The nerve. You know I complain about those stairs, Mia but I'm willing to hoof it up here to see you. The stairs and the paparazzi together, I just don't know." She's talking and swinging a paper bag with our cocktails inside of it like a mad woman.

"Well, Dee, it's good to see you, too. Come on in, have a drink, stuff your face and help me with my problems." I say this with a forced smile that Dee recognizes.

"Holy shit, Mia! The new furniture looks beautiful." Dee says.

"You're right. I didn't even notice until now. It all fits so nicely." Frankie adds.

"I know," I'm beaming. "I love it; thank you guys so much for helping me pick it out and encouraging me to buy it."

We all take turns jumping on the couch and getting comfortable. I make sure all the drinks are filled, the pitcher is close by and the snacks are spread out on the table before I begin to talk.

"Dinner went great. Everything was perfect, the food, the conversation and the company. I couldn't have planned it better. After dinner, Andrea goes to bed and it's just Joe and I. We're in the living room drinking champagne and kissing. He starts to unbutton my blouse so I stop him. I don't want to go any further until I know what's up with him and this Olivia girl. So, he asks me out for Friday night but it's how he asks me out." Dee and Frankie are just staring at me.

"He says that he's been invited on really short notice to a party for Saturday but he's free tomorrow night and he wants to spend as much time with me as possible before he goes back home." I finish and wait for a response.

"I don't get it." Frankie says.

"You idiot," Dee answers for me. "He doesn't want to invite Mia to the party even though he's just said he wants to spend as much time as possible with her."

"Oh, right."

"But wait," I add. "It gets worse. He's driving me home and I ask him who is coming to stay with Andrea tomorrow because she has all these guests arriving, and he starts listing names. One of them is Isabella Taylor who is in that soap opera with Olivia Lucas. So, I try to not be obvious and I ask, 'Isn't Isabella Taylor in "Hope's Chest" with Olivia Lucas?' And he says, 'Yes and Andrea told me that her and Isabella don't get along but I don't know why.' So I said, 'So, you know Olivia Lucas?' And he completely ignores my question until I have to ask him again, and when I finally do ask him again he says he knows her and starts talking about how she and Isabella don't like one another. And I'm thinking, who cares that they don't like each other, why don't you just answer the damn question instead of changing the subject." I'm talking really fast now and I hope Dee and Frankie have gotten most of what I've just said.

"He's trying to change the subject because he's guilty of something. It's avoidance." Dee says.

"That's exactly what I was thinking. It just turned out to be this big nightmare. The paparazzi were right outside my house when we pulled up, and they were all over the windshield. It was crazy. I don't know if I can deal with this. But when he was kissing me tonight it felt so good. I've never gotten a weak in the knees kiss before and he's so kind and sweet and attentive. He just makes me feel so good and I can't believe that he would hurt me. Does any of this make sense?" I ask.

"Of course it makes sense," answers Frankie. "He's an actor.

What does he care if he hurts you, he'll be leaving here soon and he'll never have to think about it again. Just one more conquest to add to his list. I don't like him and I don't trust him. And I tell you what, Mia, you're coming with me on Saturday. As the planner of this freak show I'm throwing, I get to bring a date and you're going to be it."

"No way. I can't. I don't want to look like a fool, like I'm stalking him."

"You won't," answers Dee. "He never told you where he was going; only that he had plans. For all he knows, you have no idea where he's going to be on Saturday. I think you have to go if you feel this strongly about him. It's the only way you're going to be able to find out for yourself if he's seeing this Olivia person."

Dee is right. I have to see it for myself if I'm going to believe it. I can't invest anymore of myself in Joe if he's not in it for the right reasons.

"There's one more thing," I add. "I've never even stopped to think about what will happen if this does work out. He's in Los Angeles, and he's this really famous person and I'm all the way in San Francisco. I'm already going nuts with the paparazzi after only two days, how would I be able to handle it all of the time?"

"I wouldn't think about that right now, Mia. You've got so much to deal with first and when that time comes, if it comes, you'll work it out. If this is meant to be, you will find a way to deal with the obstacles that come with it." Looks like the old Dee is back. We're all just quiet for a little while, munching on potato chips and drinking our cocktails. Dee breaks the silence.

"What are you going to wear?" We all just look at one another like the most important question of the entire night has just been asked. Well, it probably has.

"You have to look drop dead gorgeous. I mean, you really have to do this up. You can wear something of mine." Dee offers.

"Oh," I say. "Right, I can wear one of your dresses as a scarf around my neck. I don't think so. I'll look like a sausage trying to get out of a casing. No thanks."

"You've got a beautiful body, Mia. We'll find one that's a little big on me."

"I know you're trying to be sweet, Dee," says Frankie. "But it's not working. We have to shop. Mia, I'll be here first thing tomorrow morning. I only have a couple of hours to give you because planning this circus is taking up all of my time."

"I know you're trying to be sweet, Frankie," says Dee sarcastically. "But it's not working. We all know that if Mia needs to shop, I have to be the one she goes with. I'll be here first thing tomorrow morning, you plan your circus." Frankie and Dee glare at one another.

"Ladies, ladies. No arguing. But sorry, Frankie – Dee does have a point. Plus, she'll probably be able to get me a discount." I wink at Dee and she smiles back.

We spend the next hour or so finishing off the cocktails and talking about Dee's new boyfriend and Frankie's dilemma with Charlie apparently being a prude. I finally walk them to the door and right as I'm hugging Dee goodnight, she says, "Where's Bob?"

CHAPTER THIRTEEN

The next morning I am ready at ten am sharp. I'm checking my e-mails and doing some side jobs while I wait for Dee to arrive. I'm attacking this shopping experience as a job. I've got to get in, find something fantastic, and get over to Andrea's house to get some more work done on the casket. I was thinking that I could also go shopping tomorrow if I don't find anything today, but Dee told me that I have to spend all of Saturday afternoon getting a manicure, pedicure, my hair and make-up done. I don't know what I would do without my girls. I see an e-mail that I recognize is from my mother and right as I'm about to open it, I hear really loud voices from outside my door.

"Move it up! That's it boys, the slower you go, the longer it takes and the worse the pain will be. Move it up!" It sounds like Dee.

I get up and open my front door and try to look down the stairs. I can't see anything yet. I wait a moment and I see a man turning the corner backwards, and he's carrying something really large. What the hell is going on? As he starts to back up the stairs I'm seeing more and more of the object. IT'S MY ARMOIRE! Oh my God! I swing the door open all the way allowing the movers access inside my apartment. I'm so overwhelmed. This is amazing! As soon as the second mover rounds the corner my view is blocked, so I stand to the side and wait for them to move the piece of furniture inside.

"That's it, boys. You're almost home. Keep it moving!" Dee

sounds like a drill sergeant. She appears right after the last mover has come through the door.

"See that cardboard box, gentlemen? That's where the armoire goes. Now be careful, my friend hand painted that herself." Dee is looking over at me and smiling as she says this. I run over to her and give her a huge hug.

"How did you do this? Oh God, Dee – I hope you didn't buy it. I'll pay you for it if you did. I can't let you buy me a two thousand dollar present."

"Buy it? Are you kidding me? It was free."

"But how?" I ask.

"Remember Fernando, that really cute Puerto Rican cop I used to date until he finally admitted to me he was gay?" Dee asks.

"Of course I remember him; he was one of my favorites." I answer.

"Well, I went to the station this morning and paid him a visit. I told him what was going on, and he said he would go over there with me and see if he could scare the owner a little bit into giving you your armoire back. Turns out he was so scared that he even offered up his moving men to return it to you." I hug Dee again. I still can't believe I have my armoire back.

"See Mia," Dee says. "I knew there was a reason that you couldn't find an armoire you liked when we went shopping. You were meant to have this one back."

For once, I agree with Dee's reasoning and thank her about fifteen more times. As soon as the movers are done setting up the armoire, we leave to go shopping. Dee insists on driving because apparently she has "good parking karma." She claims it is because she has given up so many parking spaces in the past, and if you live in San Francisco, you never give up a parking space.

Our first stop is Neiman Marcus. One of Dee's ex-boyfriends has a sister that works in the "One of a Kind" department, where they have designer gowns and only one of every style they have exists. Dee assures me that the most terrible fate one can befall is showing up at an event where someone is wearing the same thing as you. And God forbid they look better in it. Although I could never imagine anybody looking better than Dee in anything. As I said before, I don't have a negative body image, I'm just aware of it when somebody has a drop dead figure and I'm not afraid to compliment them on it. While I'm your standard size six, Dee is a size two on a bad day. So, you see what I mean about the sausage casing now.

When we enter the "One of a Kind" department it's like going into another world. We're immediately offered a latte, champagne or spring water and there are large, plush sofas everywhere. In the center of it all is a mini circular runway, I'm assuming for modeling the clothes, but hoping that's not the plan for me. Dee asks for Christine, the sister, and the receptionist leaves to go find her. When Christine appears, Dee hugs her and introduces us. Christine looks very elegant and her body is tan and well toned. She's dressed impeccably with her long, brown hair up in a french twist and I can tell she means business. Dee starts to explain to her the type of dress I'm looking for. I think I overhear her using the term, "Make him crawl on his knees." Christine turns to me and looks me up and down.

"You're a size six, right?" She asks

"Yes, I am." I answer.

"Just give me a minute, I'll be right back." And she disappears from where she came from.

Dee and I sit waiting anxiously and I'm starting to get a little excited. I've never worn a one of a kind dress before and the idea of it makes me feel special. It must be similar to what movie stars and models feel like when a designer custom creates something just for them. I don't even realize I'm biting my cuticles until Dee yanks my hand out of my mouth.

"Can I pace in here?" I ask.

"Hell no you can't pace in here," Dee says. "Sit still and stop biting your cuticles. You know you should get manicures regularly. If your nails looked nicer you wouldn't want to mess them up by eating your skin."

Eating my skin? How gross is that.

"For your information, I don't eat my skin, Dee. I spit out the pieces of cuticle that I bite off."

Dee is looking over at the receptionist who helped us earlier. She has just stopped whatever she was doing at her desk to look up at us. Dee lowers her voice to a whisper.

"I am refusing to have this conversation with you right now."

Christine saves the day and comes back carrying three dresses. She holds them up one by one and tells me not to judge any of them until I've tried them on. She hands them all to me, asks me my shoe size and has the receptionist escort me to the dressing room. The first one I try on is an all white strapless number with blue and white piping on the very top around the bust area. It looks a little bit sailorish to me, or maybe for a more formal backyard barbeque. I come out of the dressing room and the receptionist points to the mini runway. Am I supposed to model for them on this thing? I look at Dee and she points to it, too. I step on the stage in my bare feet and notice that Christine is missing.

"Who designed this dress, Popeye?" I ask Dee. "I feel like my purse should be a can of spinach."

Dee gives me a very mean glare so I try to please her by doing a fake runway show until Christine comes back holding three boxes of shoes. She hands me a pair that are supposed to match the sailor dress and I put them on. Her and Dee start whispering to one another and tell me to walk the runway again. I do another model impersonation and wait for a verdict. They both shake their heads no so I grab the other two boxes of shoes and return to the dressing room.

I like the second dress much better. It's a pale blue color and it's made of a sheer, georgette fabric. It's very fun and flirty and it moves with you when you walk. It has spaghetti straps and a sash at the waist that I'm not very good at tying. I check the other two boxes of shoes and there is a silver pair of low sandals, and a pair of very high black, strappy sandals. The last dress that I haven't tried on yet is black so I'm going to guess the silver pair goes with this blue dress. I put the shoes on and look at myself in the mirror. Not bad. I make my way to show Christine and Dee and do my runway walk again. They both shrug but don't say no or yes. They just point to the dressing room and I leave them to their whispering.

The third dress is the black one. I immediately fall in love with it. It's strapless like the first one but it's got a very low back and a tulle skirt that hits right above my knees. It makes me feel like a sexy ballerina. I put on the strappy, black shoes and I'm in love. It fits the top part of my body like a glove and really accentuates my back. I leave the dressing room for hopefully the final time and take my last walk on the runway. Dee actually gasps when she sees me and Christine gives me an opera clap. Two thumbs up! Looks like I'm ready to go.

I go back to the dressing room to change and when I come out, Dee is hugging Christine good-bye and I thank her and shake her hand. I'm really happy with what we've picked out, and Dee can't stop talking about how great I look in the black dress. The receptionist asks me if I'll be taking the shoes, too and I tell her that I will. They're Louboutins so I know I'm in for some damage, but I just about pass out when she tells me the total is $4,789.32. Are you kidding me? That's over two months of mortgage payments for me. I think I look as if I'm going to put my wallet away because Dee takes it out of my hand and gives the receptionist my American Express. I quickly snatch it away and hand her my Visa. This outfit is going to have to go on the installment plan. I might be dating a movie star, but I certainly don't have the bank account of one.

When I first started making decent money, I began paying off my credit cards one by one. The largest check I wrote out was for about five grand, and that was the total of one card that I had been living off of for a year. It's hard for me to imagine paying that amount for one outfit no matter how much I make now. It just seems so frivolous to me. The down payment on my apartment was fifty thousand dollars and I just spent ten percent of that on an outfit? I've got to be out of my mind. I ask Dee in a whisper if she thinks I might be able to return it after I wear it and she gives me another mean look. I sign the credit card receipt with a shaky hand and Dee suggests we call Frankie to meet us for lunch.

We decide to go to The Garden Court restaurant in The Palace Hotel on New Montgomery Street. The restaurant is located where the hotel's former carriage entrance used to be and a stained glass dome covers it. It's very beautiful and close enough to Frankie's work so that she can walk there and meet us. She's waiting outside when we arrive and we all hug and make our way inside. Dee shows her my new dress and shoes and Frankie loves them both.

"Okay, I have some good news," says Frankie. "Star asked me to call and confirm her hair appointment for tomorrow afternoon, and at first I was going to completely tell her off and remind her that I wasn't her personal assistant, but I got an idea. So, I agreed and when I talked to him to confirm, I asked if he had any other openings for tomorrow and he said he did. So Mia, you're booked for two o'clock. Don't be late and I have no idea how much it costs, I just know if Star is using him he must be one of the best."

"You really need to grow some balls, Frankie," Dee says. "You would have never told that girl off. In fact, if she had asked you to come euthanize her dog you would have agreed."

Frankie looks really offended. "Just because I don't happen to tell people exactly what I'm thinking, whenever I'm thinking it, does not mean I need to grow some balls. At least I wouldn't have already dated and broken up with her brother."

"Whoa, Ladies," I interject. "Dee just doesn't want to see people shitting on you, Frankie. Isn't that right, Dee?" I look over at Dee for confirmation.

"That is right. You seem to have no problem telling me off. That was a very good insult, Frankie. I'm proud of you."

Frankie looks perplexed, but decides to take it as a compliment and smiles. Somehow Dee has managed to make Frankie think her affront was therapeutic.

I try to change the subject, "Thanks for making that appointment for me, Frankie. I will definitely go."

"You're welcome, now let's eat." Says Frankie.

The rest of lunch goes by with casual conversation about Star's party. Frankie asks Dee if she wants her to try and get her in, but of course, the guy Dee is dating is on the guest list so that is taken care of. I'm grateful they will both be there; I don't know how much support I'm going to need. When the plates have been cleared and we're about to divvy up the check, Frankie reaches into her bag and pulls out a magazine.

"I didn't want this to ruin our lunch so I waited. I saw it at the newsstand on my way over here. I'm sorry."

She hands me the magazine and it's the new *US* Weekly. The cover has a picture of a movie star with the words "Breaking News" over her head because she is off to a re-hab. Way in the bottom left corner there is a two-inch by two-inch picture of Joe and I coming out of the Italian restaurant. Right next to it in yellow writing it says, *"Is this another sister in law?"* Holy shit! I start frantically flipping through the pages looking for the article.

"Page 46." Frankie says as she reaches into her bag and pulls out two more copies. She hands one to Dee and keeps the other one for herself as we all start looking for page forty-six.

The first thing I notice when I find it is all of the pictures. They show pictures of the moving men bringing my new mattress into the apartment, there's a picture of me when I almost went down the stairs in my Giants hat, there is the same picture that is on the cover but a much larger version, and the final one is of Joe and I getting into the cab. This is unbelievable.

"Why do they have pictures of the moving men?" I ask out loud.

Dee starts to read the caption under the picture, *"Did J.B. purchase this bed for new gal pal Mia Roman? 'They went furniture shopping and jumped on all of the mattresses to try them out,' says a source."*

"What source?" I ask.

I read the caption under the cover picture to myself, *"After an intimate meal in San Francisco, Mia and J.B. take a stroll in Little Italy. 'They were very romantic and held hands the entire time,' says the restaurant owner."*

"I can't do this," I say. "One of you read me the article. I just can't believe this bullshit."

Dee starts to read; *"Since coming to San Francisco last week to visit a sick friend, Joe Barrick seems to be spending a lot of time with local Mia Roman. Mia is the owner of "Gem It Up," an elite jewel designing business to the stars. Sources say they met at a trendy downtown bar and have been inseparable ever since. "Romantic dinners out every night and dancing sometimes until dawn," says a friend of the local. The last woman we caught J.B. with turned out to be his sister-in-law, and outsiders are still wondering why someone like Joe Barrick would date someone like Mia Roman.*

The big screen hunk has been linked most recently to "Hope's Chest" star Olivia Lucas, but we've seen a string of models and beautiful actresses come before her. Reps for Olivia and J.B. declined to comment on the state of their relationship, but a friend of Olivia's tells Us Weekly 'Olivia is furious over the relationship and is going to San Francisco to confront J.B. in person.' I guess the only thing left to do is sit back and watch the sparks fly."

I bury my head into my arms when Dee is done reading. I can't believe this is happening to me. Why would people make all these things up? Dancing until dawn? I've never even danced with J.B. before.

"Dee, you haven't ever dated an attorney have you? Because I want to sue the shit out of this magazine."

"Oh Mia, you can't," says Dee. "It's all just assumptions and quotes from sources that mostly don't even exist. Nobody takes this shit seriously, it's purely entertainment. Please don't be upset."

"I have to go. I have a lot of work to do at Andrea's. I'm not even going to be there on Saturday because of the party tomorrow, and Sunday I have to go to my mom's. Oh God, my mom. I need to call her before one of her friends reads the article first and tells her about it."

"Come on, girl. I'll drive you to your car." Dee says.

We all kiss good-bye and Dee and I drive back to my apartment in silence. At one point she grabs my hand and gives it a kiss. We pull up in front of my car and I open the door to get out.

"Mia?" Dee asks.

"Yeah?" I answer.

"At least they mentioned your business. That's got to be a good thing. Whenever something bad like this happens, I look for the good in it and that's the good I could find."

"You're right, that is something. Thanks for taking me today, Dee. I'll call you later." I close her car door and walk over to my car. I hang up my dress in the back and put my shoe bag there, too. After I get buckled up I turn the ignition key, but before I can put my car in gear, I start to cry. I don't know how long I was sitting there for; all I know is the flashing of cameras right in my windshield took me out of the moment.

CHAPTER FOURTEEN

I arrive at Andrea's house to be let in by one of her staff. There are a lot of people socializing and laughing in her main living room and dining room. It's the last place I want to be right now. I'm trying to figure out how I can go around the house to sneak into the backyard when I remember that Andrea has all the gems in her safe. She spots me anyway and comes towards me. Her greetings are always warm and welcoming and today is no different. She gives me a hug and notices something is wrong.

"Are you okay, Sweetheart?" She asks.

"I've just had a tough day, but I'll be fine. Do you think you can get the gems for me?" I ask.

"No working today. I insist that you come and meet all of my friends. Have a cocktail and some hors d'oeuvres and just relax."

"I really can't, Andrea. I don't think I'm in the mood to socialize right now. I'm really sorry." Tears start to come to my eyes as I'm saying this.

"Oh, Honey. Come upstairs and you and I will have a talk."

"I couldn't do that. You have all these people here; you can't abandon your guests for me."

"I can so, now come on." Andrea takes my hand and starts to lead me up the stairs. On the way we pass an intercom on the wall and Andrea hits the kitchen button. She waits for a response and tells the woman to bring a pitcher of margaritas, two glasses and some chips and salsa to the master suite.

I've never been upstairs in Andrea's house before and as we're walking down the hallway I get glimpses of some of the rooms that have the doors open. There is one guest bedroom decorated in a familiar Ralph Lauren linen and it is beautiful. There is a large bed covered in throw pillows with a massive flat screen television set on the wall. We pass by what I think is Andrea's office and it's done up in mahogany and deep forest greens. When we finally reach the master bedroom, I can't believe my eyes. Her entire bedroom has windows for walls. It's amazing! The view is truly spectacular. Andrea motions upwards and I look at the ceiling, which is also all glass. The sky is a crystal clear blue today and the sun is just slightly shining through. I've never seen anything like it.

"I had this done because there are times when it's just too cold to sleep outside, so I like to feel like I am. When I was younger, Billy and I would sleep outside under the stars, rain or shine. It didn't matter; we had each other for warmth. Want a look?" Andrea asks.

I nod my head yes and she jumps on the bed and lies on her back. I follow her, and both of us just stare up at all the beautiful blue. Someone knocks on the door and Andrea tells them to come in. A woman walks in with a large tray that has the drinks with chips and salsa on it. Andrea thanks her and we both get up. It takes both of us to carry the tray over to her sitting room where we place it on the table and take our seats in large, over-stuffed chairs. Andrea pours us margaritas and grabs a chip for dipping.

"Okay, Honey – What's got you so down?" She asks.

I decide that I am going to tell Andrea everything. I start as far back as John moving out and stealing all of my furniture. I talk about Joe and my first date and our run-in with the paparazzi and the *US Weekly* article. I explain how I found out about Olivia and that I still can't confirm if it's true, and I end with the party tomorrow night and my apprehension at what I might find out if I go. Andrea listens intently to everything, nods in all the right places and seems genuinely interested in what I have to say.

"I'm sorry that your ex-boyfriend stole your things from you and left like he did. The only thing I can say about that experience is it's better you found out now what he is capable of. I couldn't imagine what he might have done later in life if you got married and had children and something didn't go his way."

I had never thought of that before and it was a very good point. It kind of reminded me of something that Dee would say.

"And the paparazzi, what a nightmare. The only way to avoid them is to live inside a bubble. Once they want you, it's very hard to avoid having your photo taken. I've found that even if you give them what they want, they will still persist and always want more. I just try to look my best when I'm going out of the house and hold my temper in check if I think they've gone too far. A lot of them actually pester you unrelentingly because they want you to get upset and they want to catch it on film. I say it's a small sacrifice to deal with paparazzi for what I have in return." Andrea hesitates after this and refills both of our margarita cups.

"Finally, I want you to know something about Hollywood. When you live there long enough, your life starts to emulate the movies. Joe has been raised in the limelight and he's been famous for so long that it's the only life he knows. You see, he dates all these women looking for something that he just can't seem to find. He has so much to offer the latest model trying to break into the acting business or the newest starlet that wants to be in a picture with him. He never knows who really likes him for him and to be honest, I don't think any of them ever do. I don't think any of them ever really take the time to get to know the real him – They're so wrapped up in the fact that they're with J.B."

"But what about Olivia?" I ask.

"I know that Joe went out with Olivia a couple of times but found out that she was trying to get a role in a picture he had already signed on for. He left town quickly after he heard that I was sick, and he didn't have a chance to end things with her properly. But, I want to do something I don't normally do, and that is tell you something Joe told me in confidence."

"No, don't do that Andrea. I would never want him to find out accidentally and be upset with you."

"No, don't worry. I think you need to know," she says. "He told me that the short time he has spent with you has been like no other experience he's ever had with a woman. That for the first time in his life, he knew that you were with him for no other reason but that you enjoyed each other's company. He was allowed to be himself around you. He liked that you ordered a full meal instead of eating one piece of lettuce from a salad, and he liked that you were up front and honest with him when the paparazzi arrived."

Andrea pours the last of the margarita pitcher into our glasses and we are both silent for a while eating the chips and dip.

"What do you think about me going to the party tomorrow night?" I ask.

"I can't tell you what to do about the party," Andrea says. "You're going to have to make that decision for yourself. But if you feel like you need to go, then go for you. And one more thing, he said he loved that you call him Joe and not J.B."

"Thank you, Andrea. I'll remember that. Thank you for everything. I've got a lot to think about. You've really helped me and I appreciate this so much."

"I enjoy spending time with you, there's no need to thank me for something I like to do already." Andrea smiles and grabs my hand.

We spend a little more time talking about her health and the people who have arrived today. She tells me that one of her friends has brought along his father and Andrea lights up a little bit when she talks about how sweet he appears to be. We finish what is in our glasses and stand up to go back downstairs.

"Come with me for a moment." Andrea says.

I follow her through her bedroom into a door that is a walk-in closet the size of my living room at home. There are rows upon rows of clothing on hangers and they are all sorted by color and style. There are shelves filled with hundreds of pairs of shoes and sweaters that are folded neatly in place. Andrea walks over to her safe and starts to put in the combination. I turn around respectfully and admire her perfume collection until I hear the click of the safe opening. She reaches in and pulls out my container of gems.

"Oh, thank you for holding these. I'd be a mess if I had to carry them around with me."

"You're welcome. Did you say your dress for tomorrow night was all black?" She asks.

"Yes, all black." I answer.

"Oh, good. Try these on."

Andrea hands me the most beautiful necklace I have ever seen. It is an inch or so wide choker made completely out of diamonds. There is also a pair of diamond studs that look like they're about five carats total.

"Oh no, I can't borrow these. God no. Could you imagine? I can't."

"You can and you are." Andrea says as she starts to put the choker around my neck.

"Now lift your hair up so I can do the clasp." I oblige and when she is done I take the earrings and put them in my ears. Andrea turns me around so I am facing the mirror, and I look beautiful. I can't believe that diamonds can make a person look beautiful, but they can. They completely frame my entire face and it looks so sparkly, I feel like a princess.

"Are you sure? I mean are you really, really sure?" I ask.

"Knock 'em dead." She says.

We head back downstairs and Andrea takes me around the back of the house and through the kitchen into the backyard. My bag that I left in Joe's car is sitting by the casket. I turn around and hug

Andrea.

"Is Joe here today?" I ask.

"He left before I woke up and I haven't seen him since."

Andrea walks with me over to the casket and we both look at the design that I traced onto the wood. I start to pull the gems out of their case while deciding where I'm going to start.

"How do you decide where to begin, Mia?" Andrea asks.

"Why don't you pick." I tell her.

She points to a heart pattern and says, "I think that would be a perfect place to start."

CHAPTER FIFTEEN

The rest of the afternoon goes by quickly while I sober up in the sun and start applying the jewels to the casket. It's coming along really nicely, and I'm happy with my progress so far. I'm also glad that Joe hasn't made an appearance today because I have no idea how I would deal with seeing him right now. When I'm done for the day, I give Andrea back the gems to put in her safe, and I drive home listening to some oldies that remind me of my dad. I make a special effort to try and find a spot as close to my apartment as possible. It takes me a couple of turns around the block, but I finally get one that's close enough for me to make a run for it. I don't spy any paparazzi this evening and it makes my mood lift a little.

When I check my machine there is a message from Joe:

"Hi Mia. I'm sorry I didn't get a chance to call you earlier and confirm our plans for tonight, but I had to pick up a friend from the airport. I wish I had your cell phone number because I'd really like to see you still, so call me when you get this. Bye."

What kind of an idiot does he think I am? Since when does it take all day to pick up a friend at the airport? And I know that "friend" happens to be Olivia, which upsets me even more. I check my caller ID and it turns out that Joe has tried to call several times but only left one message. It still doesn't change my mind, I'm not going to call him back or see him tonight.

I'm going to dedicate this evening to taking care of me. I start out with a long, hot bubble bath and when I've soaked for an extra long time, I shave my legs for tomorrow night. When I'm done with the bath I give myself a pedicure. I know most women out there like to have their toes done, but I prefer to do them myself. I paint them with a natural light pink color, and the yoga antics of giving myself a pedicure is worth it. They look both neutral and fantastic. I'm going to bring the polish tomorrow when I get my manicure so I can have matching fingernails. As my toes dry I turn the light on my magnifying mirror and grab the tweezers. This is a sticky situation because I definitely can't go too far with my eyebrows tonight. I force myself to do a little maintenance and then leave them alone. The final step is a hydrating facemask that feels cold and refreshing when I apply it.

My plan is to catch up on my reality television while the mask sets, so I turn on the TiVo and go straight to "The Bachelor." It's so hard for me to believe that these people come together under such strange circumstances and have the chance to find true love. I wonder how many of them really last? It's becoming more and more common to see the faces of reality show contestants turn up as television correspondents or in the tabloids with another famous person. It makes me start to think about what Andrea said today about Hollywood, so I get a pen and paper and make a list of all the Hollywood couples I'm familiar with that have been together a long time. The list is very, very short and after I've written down some of the names, I remember that they eventually broke up only to be seen a couple of weeks later with somebody new.

This leads me to another idea and I start to make a second list of famous people who are married to non-famous people. This list actually turns out to be pretty long. I'm surprised by how many there are. Sometimes they're photographed and seen together so much that you start to think the non-famous person is actually famous just by association. If I'm trying to prove to myself that J.B. and I can make this work, I don't know if I've succeeded. Is that what I was trying to do with this little time wasting project? I don't know but my mask is cracking all over.

I rinse my face and snuggle into my new bed. I need one more look at the *US* magazine so I pull it out of my bag and start rereading the article and analyzing the pictures. Joe looks so handsome and we both look really happy. The picture of me in the Giants hat is awful but it's so fuzzy it's hard to even see me.

Oh no! I forgot to call my mom. I glance at the clock and it's a little bit past ten, and it's a Friday night, so I decide to give it a try. After the fourth ring I'm expecting the machine but she finally picks up. Her voice sounds like I've woken her.

"Hi Mom. Were you sleeping?" I ask.

"Oh Mia, um, no. I wasn't sleeping. How are you?"

"Are you sure you weren't sleeping? You sound like you were." I ask again.

"I think I would know if I was sleeping. What reason would I have to lie to you about whether or not I was asleep for cripes sake."

Did she just say cripes? All of a sudden I hear the phone being muffled and talking in the background.

"Mom? Mom? Are you there?"

"Well of course I'm here. Where else would I be?"

"Who were you talking to Mom?"

"Oh that? That was nothing."

Man, is she being weird.

"What was nothing? Your conversation that I just overheard? Who were you talking to and why are you being so weird?" I ask again.

"Listen Honey, I have to go now but I will see you on Sunday, right?"

"No Mom, I'm kind of creeped out right now. Is someone there with you? Are you being held against your will? Should I call the police? Use some kind of code phrase if something is happening to you." I'm starting to get nervous now. I know the woman is crazy but this is even beyond her.

"For cripes sake, Mia."

There she goes with the cripes again.

"I'm fine," she says. "I just have a friend visiting, that's all. Your imagination really does run on over time. A code phrase? My word."

"Okay Mom, you're right. I ask you ten times if you've got someone there after I distinctly hear you having a conversation and you evade the question until I think something is wrong, but I have an overactive imagination? And why are you talking like Marcia Brady with the 'my words' and 'cripes?'"

"I really have to go, dear."

"See Mom, there you go again. You don't call me dear."

"Okay now, I'll see you Sunday. Right. Goodnight."

She hung up. What do you know about that? My phone rings and the caller ID says that it's Frankie.

"Hi Frank. What's up? Why aren't you going crazy with last minute details for the party?"

"Nothing for me to do until tomorrow morning. That's when I get down on my knees and pray that all the people who promised to show up, actually show up on time and do everything right. What are you doing?"

"Ignoring Joe's messages and phone calls, and I just had a *Twilight Zone* conversation with my Mother. Do you feel ready for tomorrow?" I ask.

"I'm ready. I made a checklist for you to make sure you don't forget anything. Say 'check' or give up an explanation. Number one: Facemask?"

"Check."

"Number two: Shoe scuff?"

"Totally forgot. I'll do it now on the balcony while I talk to you."

"Number three: Legs shaved?"

"Check."

"Number four: Eyebrow maintenance?"

"Check."

"Number five: Not going overboard with eyebrow maintenance?"

"Check."

"Number six and seven: Pedicure and manicure?"

"Check to the first, the second is scheduled for tomorrow."

"Number eight, nine and ten: Accessories, including purse, jewelry and nylons."

"Check, check and not wearing any. The Louboutin's are sandals."

"What purse?"

"My cute, little Chanel evening bag."

"What jewelry?"

"You're going to freak out but Andrea loaned me diamonds."

"Holy shit! How fantastic is that! I can't wait to see them. Don't lose them, Mia and what is that noise?"

"Nice vote of support and I'm scuffing my shoes. Keep going with your list."

"Number eleven: Perfume choice?"

"Check. Chanel to match the purse." We both giggle at that.

"Number twelve: Bob?"

"Bob? What does that mean? Do you want that stylist to cut my hair into a bob? No way, Frankie."

"Oh no, I just didn't want to forget this so I put it on the list. Do you have the issue of *US* that I gave you at lunch today?" She asks.

"Of course, let me go back to my room."

"Okay, go to the page with the fuzzy picture of you wearing the Giants hat."

"I'm there." I say.

"Alright, this is a long shot but do you see the glass front doors of your building?"

"Duh, Frank, the picture is taken through them."

"Okay smartass, I'm just confirming. Look in the bottom left hand corner of the picture, outside, to the left of the glass doors. It might even be on the steps. See the pink thing?"

"IT'S BOB! That's Bob's collar. Oh my God! What is he doing outside? Do you think he's been living outside this whole time?" I'm really freaking out now and I'm crying. I want Bob back.

"Listen Mia, don't cry or your eyes will puff up tomorrow. Go grab a can of cat food and run downstairs and call his name."

"Okay." I sniffle.

We hang up and I go to the kitchen to grab some cat food and my keys on the way out. I open up the front doors to the building and slowly start saying Bob's name along with lots of here kitty, kitties. Nothing. I decide to walk a little further to the side surrounded by very tall hedges and say his name again. This time I hear a little meow. At least it sounded like a meow. I start to follow the noise while saying Bob's name and I hear it again. I go for the clincher and snap back the tin lid of the cat food can, and within seconds Bob has jumped out of the bushes and is in my arms. I'm so excited that I sit down on the sidewalk with him and let him eat his cat food out of the can while sobbing almost uncontrollably. He must have been starving because he's really eating fast.

When Bob is done, he looks up at me and starts licking his face and his paws to clean himself. I can't help the tears of relief from falling down my face. I lean over to put my arms around Bob and pick him up to go inside when I hear a noise and look up. Paparazzi. This picture will probably be the best one yet. I can't wait to see myself in print wearing men's pajama bottoms rolled up to my knees, a tube top (yes, a tube top – I was wearing a facial mask and didn't want to get any stuff on me), a sweatband in my head (same reason as tube top) and of course, the four inch Louboutin's. I snatch Bob up and start walking back upstairs with as much confidence as I can muster with the glare of his camera flash behind me.

CHAPTER SIXTEEN

I open my eyes to the sun rising, and I'm feeling better than I've felt for the last couple of days. I can't explain why. I could definitely find out some information tonight that will most likely break my heart, but right at this moment I'm not bothered by it. I start smiling when I hear Bob purring, and I look over at him lying on the pillow next to mine waiting for his breakfast. I have to remember to make an appointment with the groomer, who knows where this cat has been. I called Frankie back last night to let her know I found Bob and we went through some ideas of where he might have been. I won't bore you with the details; I'll just tell you the one that I liked the best. Frankie said that John might have given him to a shelter and somebody adopted him or maybe he just left him at a friend's house. Either way, we think Bob found his way home to me. You read and hear amazing stories all of the time about animals finding their way back home from hundreds of miles away, so it might be true. I have a new found respect for Bob if it is. Frankie toyed around with the idea that maybe he found his way home from Africa. And my mom thinks I have the over active imagination?

Bob follows at my heels all the way to the kitchen and waits there until I feed him his breakfast. I've got a lot of last minute side jobs to finish up this morning. Every Saturday at noon my friend Eleni from Federal Express comes to my apartment to pick up all of my outgoing packages for the week and drop off my new ones. About ninety percent of my business is generated from my web site and I've found that Fed Ex is the best way to go. I've never had a problem with them and I've also never had a complaint about my work, which is something I'm very proud of. I list my turn around time as four to six weeks on my website, but I usually like to complete small jobs in about two weeks or less. My goal has always been to give everything back to Eleni that she brought the week before, but I haven't met it yet. I still have hope.

My plan for the day is to finish up some work until Eleni gets here, take a quick shower and make it to my manicure appointment by one. I've got my hair scheduled for two and my make-up isn't until five so hopefully I can get a decent meal in between the last two. I take a seat on the couch and go to my TiVo to see what else I have to watch. I'm going to finish off "The Bachelor" because I've taped the whole season and it's actually getting really good. When they whittle down the women towards the end and there is only three or four left, the dynamic between them gets very interesting. Well, dynamic might be too nice a word – The catfights are entertaining. Time flies while you're working and watching reality television because the next thing I know, it's noon and my buzzer is going off.

I hit the button to talk to Eleni and let her know that I'll be right down. Eleni is the only one I'll go down the stairs for unless I have too many packages, and then she comes up and helps. But when I hit the buzzer, she intercoms me back.

"Oh no girl, don't think I didn't see the US Magazine article. I'm coming up."

Great! Not only do I not have the time for this, but I definitely don't want to go over this story again when I don't know the end of it yet. Eleni appears out of breath and with a bag that is loaded with new boxes.

"Oh my God, girl, my friend and I saw that magazine article and I said, 'That's my customer Mia. She did not snag the most eligible bachelor in Hollywood?'"

"It's not what you think, Eleni." I say.

"Well, you need to tell me what to think because you sure did look like a couple coming out of that restaurant."

"That was just me being nice to a friend of a friend. I took him around San Francisco because he's visiting here as a favor, it was no big deal."

"No big deal? Did you hold hands with the man as a favor, too? And by the way, nice furniture."

"Oh Eleni, don't believe that. I bought all this furniture myself."

"And the hand holding?" She asks.

I smile at the memory, remembering how that moment felt.

"Oooooh girl, I just knew it."

At that moment my phone rings and I don't make a move to answer it. Eleni and I are just staring at the machine together waiting for the beep.

"Hi Mia. It's Joe. I still haven't heard from you and I'm hoping everything is okay. I have this thing I'm committed to going to tonight but I really want to see you soon. Please call me when you get a chance."

Eleni and I both just stare at each other.

"I have to go, Eleni. I'm not trying to avoid your questions, I promise. I just have this huge thing I have to go to tonight and I've still got to take a shower and be at my manicure by one."

"You promise you'll update me next Saturday? All the details?" She asks.

"I promise you, I won't spare a one."

She helps me box up the rest of my things and we fill her bag so she can leave. I jump in the shower and I'm ready by 12:45. The place where I go on the rare occasions that I have my nails done is close to my house, so I walk there. It's a beautiful day and there are no paparazzi in sight. The salon is pretty upscale and there is only one manicurist because they mostly do hair, so I take a seat in the waiting area and pick up a magazine. There are several other women waiting with their smocks on and every one is pretending to read when we're really just checking each other out. The woman across from me has the *US* magazine open with my picture on the cover. I try to slouch down a little in my chair and now I wish I had worn my Giants cap. I see it happening in slow motion, her looking up from the magazine and looking at me, her mouth forming a big "O" and then her reaching into her bag for a pen.

"Can I have your autograph?" She asks.

"Oh, you don't want my autograph. I'm nobody." I answer.

I'm nobody? That didn't sound good.

"Oh please, I know my daughter would really love to have it? Her name is Analise."

She hands me the magazine and pen as she is saying this. I don't want to refuse her; I could just imagine the tabloids finding her so she can tell her story about how rude I was. I agree to sign the magazine and I feel like a fraud as I'm doing it. My name finally gets called for my manicure and I'm so grateful that her station is behind a partition.

When my nails are done I check for an Uber and it's ten minutes out, so I sit and dry under the machine while I wait until 1:30. The manicurist nail shamed me for my terrible cuticles and because my nails are so short. After the woman told me off for about twenty minutes, I finally agreed to buy some oil that would help them heal. I went with the same color as my toes and even though they don't look great, they look way better than before. When the Uber arrives I assume this guy has been here before because he gets out and opens the door for me while motioning to my nails.

"Don't want you to mess up your manicure." He says.

More like he doesn't want to miss out on a five star rating. We ride to the next salon in silence and I have to admit, I'm pretty excited to have Star's stylist doing my hair for tonight. It's located in Union Square and I love this area of the city. Tiffany's is here and Louis Vuitton, all the places the girls and I love to window shop at on the weekends. When we arrive, the Uber driver gets out again and opens the door for me. I decide to really give him the five stars because opening the door for me both times is unprecedented for a San Francisco driver.

I enter the salon and tell the receptionist that I'm here to see Dante. She leads me to a back room to change into a smock and I make my way back to the waiting area to read some more magazines. I'm happy to find there is no *US* Weekly in their stacks. It's two thirty and I'm still waiting. I hate being in these predicaments because normally I would say something after a half an hour but this is not normal, this is Star's stylist. I'm sure he's sitting in the back eating a sandwich and laughing because I certainly don't see any men at all doing hair right now. I change my tactic a little bit and ask the receptionist if she thinks I have time to go grab a quick bite to eat, she just shakes her head no.

I start to do the things that I hate to see other people who are waiting do. Like sighing really loudly and throwing my magazines back down on the table with a thud. Whenever I see somebody acting that way I always feel uncomfortable and now I'm doing it and I can't stop myself. When it hits three o'clock, I've had enough. I approach the receptionist again and she's talking on the phone. I can tell by what she's saying that it's a personal call.

"Um, excuse me?" I say.

She looks up at me and continues talking.

"Excuse me." I say even louder this time. She puts her call on hold and just stares up at me exasperated.

"You told me a half an hour ago after I had already been waiting a half hour that I didn't have time to get something to eat and I could have sat down at a restaurant it's been so long." I'm really pissed off. Not so much at the waiting but at her flippant attitude. She's about to say something when really loud, laughing voices emerge from the back of the salon. I look up and Star Nutley and Olivia Lucas are walking towards me. I can tell they both just had their hair done. I'm breaking out in a cold sweat and my cheeks are so red that I can feel them burning. I do my best to turn towards the wall with out looking awkward when the receptionist's intercom beeps and a voice comes through saying,

"Christina, you can send my next client back now."

She glares at me and gives me the fakest smile I have ever seen.

"Dante will see you now." She says.

I stay turned toward the wall as I hear Star and Olivia approaching. I can see out of the corner of my eye that the receptionist is looking at me wondering what the hell I'm doing. She says good-bye to Star and Olivia and I hear the noise of the front doors opening and closing letting me know they've left.

"Excuse me; I said that Dante can see you now."

I give her my fakest smile back and head towards the back of the salon.

"Hi, you must be Dante?" I say as I stick out my hand for him to shake.

"I am." He says and shakes my hand back. He doesn't even bother to look up at me and I'm a little disturbed that he doesn't even ask my name.

"Have a seat and let's take a look. This is your first time here, yes?" He asks.

"It is." I answer and pull the ponytail out of my hair to let it down.

"It's long, very brown, almost mousy brown. Is this your natural curl?"

Mousy? What does that mean? Whatever it means, it doesn't sound like a compliment.

"Yes, this is my natural curl." I'm gritting my teeth. I feel like punching him. So much for the good mood I woke up in this morning.

"It's too long. We cut, no?" Dante says this and looks in the mirror straight at my face. I look back at him in the mirror and I'm sure my face looks horrified at the thought of him thinking my hair is too long because he drops the strands that are in his hands and steps back like I just morphed into an alien.

"What's wrong?" I ask. He looks absolutely frightened.

"I can't do your hair, no way honey. You've got to go."

"What are you talking about? It's not that long. I mean, it's pretty long but it's not like I'm Rapunzel or anything."

"You're Mia Roman." He shrieks.

"I know." I say.

"Oh, honey. If Star and Olivia find out you were even here I'm done for. You've got to go."

"You're kidding me, right? I have nothing to do with those women. I'm just another paying client."

"No way, no way, no way. You've really got to go, I'm sorry. There will be no charge." He says and starts to walk away.

"No charge? I should charge you for making me wait an hour for nothing." He's already gone, though. I can't believe this. What the hell am I going to do now? Well, I can run home and do my hair

135

myself before my make-up or I can try and find another salon that has some one available to do my hair now. I go change out of my smock and walk outside the salon. The fresh air feels good so I take some deep breaths and look around me. I start walking a little bit down the street looking for another salon close by. I'm not worried about whether they'll do good work, because all the places in this area are very nice, I'm just worried that they won't have an opening.

I find a salon that is brand new a couple of blocks down and it looks inviting. I walk in and ask the receptionist if someone is available to style my hair immediately and she says she'll check for me. I've got three thirty on my watch now so I need to be done here by four forty-five the latest to make it to make-up by five. The receptionist comes back and tells me if it's just a style, there is someone who can fit me in. I'm so happy I could cry. She takes me in the back and I change into my second smock of the day and pray this person doesn't know who the hell I am. I take a seat and wait for a short while until a man approaches me and shakes my hand.

"Hi, I'm Luca. How are you?"

"Hi, I'm Mia. I'm doing great. Thanks so much for taking me at such short notice."

"No problem, Sweetheart. Do you want to go ahead and take down your hair for me?" He asks.

I take the ponytail out and reluctantly wait for his assessment. He starts running his fingers through my hair and tossing it this way and that.

"Look at this beautiful mane. It's so healthy and it has so much natural body. I love the deep, brown color, too. Are you thinking of wearing it up or down?"

"Down," I say meekly. I'm afraid he's going to say, 'Just kidding! Your hair is mousy brown and your split ends are so bad I have to take five inches off.'

"Oh, good. Because even though I like doing up-do's, your hair is just too beautiful to hide. So, what's the special occasion?"

Luca and I talk non-stop for the rest of the time that he's doing my hair. He has the chair turned around so I'm not facing the mirror because he wants to surprise me when he's done. I find out all these fantastic things about him and he's so open and honest and kind. I even find myself telling him about Joe and what happened at the last salon. Luca agrees that it was unprofessional, especially after he made me wait for an hour. When he's done, Luca asks if I'm ready to see and I nod my head yes. He spins the mirror around and I can't move. Who is that person?

"I look like a movie star." It's all I can say. I have no make-up on and I'm not even dressed, but I look like a movie star. I start to cry again and I figure I might as well get it all out now before my make-up appointment. Luca has added to the curls in my hair by using several different roller sizes and making my whole head this curly, crazy mess of beauty. It looks so exotic and sexy. I hug Luca and go in the back to change. When I re-emerge he tells me there's no charge.

"What?" I ask.

"No charge, just make me a promise?"

"Anything," I say. "I'm in love with you right now."

"Promise me when you're at this event tonight and anybody asks you about your hair, you'll tell them my name?"

"They won't have to ask, I'm going to volunteer that information to anybody who will listen." I say. He wouldn't even take a tip from me.

There is a small gourmet deli next to the salon, so I request an Uber and grab a quick sandwich. I practically inhale it I am so hungry, this is what happens when you don't eat all day. The Uber pulls up at four fifty and I'm going to just make it for make-up. Frankie has a limo through her work and she is going to pick me up at eight thirty, the event starts around nine. We'll probably be the first one's there but Frankie has to be, and I have no choice because she's my date. She promised me she was going to call Dee and find out if she could be on time so I won't be solo while Frankie is running around.

The make-up goes well and I'm home a little after six. I feed Bob dinner and take some more me time before doing the finishing details on my look. I'm finding it hard to relax with my hair and make-up completely done. I don't want to lie down because I'll mess up my hair and I don't want to drink or eat anything because I'll have to brush my teeth and I'll mess up my make-up. I end up watching the rest of "The Bachelor." He picks the wrong girl in the end. They always pick the wrong girl.

CHAPTER SEVENTEEN

Frankie is right on time. I take my shoes off before I go down the stairs; I've learned my lesson about that the hard way. Charlie is coming out of his door when I reach the bottom landing.

"You look hot, Mia."

"Thanks, Charlie."

"I told Frankie I would come out to see what she looks like." He says.

I never even thought Frankie might want to invite Charlie to be her date to this event. How selfish of me. I go outside the front doors but stay in the background while the limo driver opens the door for Frankie. Charlie lets out a long whistle and gives her a hug. They talk for a little while before I approach them.

"Holy shit, Mia! Look at your fine ass! If I don't come back to your apartment tonight, Charlie, it means I've switched teams and you can find me upstairs at Mia's."

I give Frankie a hug because she always says exactly what I need to hear.

"Um, Frankie, may I please admire you?" I ask.

She does a slow spin for me and she really looks gorgeous. I would consider Frankie to be almost plain looking on most days. She hardly ever wears make-up and dresses in black almost every day. She's only five feet, two inches but you'll never find her without a pair of heels on. Even her sneakers have heels. Frankie is a natural redhead and her short hair is straight as a board. Tonight she is wearing an emerald green dress that makes her green eyes and red hair stand out beautifully. She lost one of her contacts this morning and her glasses give her this smart, sexy look. I tell her so and she winks at me. We both laugh and say good-bye to Charlie.

The event is being held at a place called "Ruby Skye" on Mason Street. Frankie gives me the lay out while we're driving there. She says it was originally built in the 1890's and used to be a Victorian playhouse. It has two stories and four rooms with their own executive chef and in-house catering. I can't wait to see it. She also tells me it was recently voted one of the top five hot spots in San Francisco and that the third season opener for "Sex and the City" was held there. It makes me feel really old. A couple of years ago I would have been living at a place called "Ruby Skye" every weekend, but we just don't go clubbing anymore. The only way I find out about cool, new places or old places that are now cool again is because of Frankie's event planning or because Dee is so connected. Apparently it can hold nine hundred people, which is the amount Frankie forced Star to stop her guest list at. Only four hundred or so responded yes. Frankie chose this place because of the separate rooms. A lot of the people attending will be Star's parent's friends and business associates, so she wanted to be able to have a separate section for them to hang out away from the younger crowd. It was a really smart idea and I'm both nervous and excited for the exposure this will give Frankie.

"Do you think it's possible I might not even see Joe if there will be that many people attending?" I ask Frankie.

140

"No way. They don't all come at once. Besides, I'll tell my people checking invitations at the door that I want to be notified when he arrives."

"Do you have to wear that headset thing all night?"

"I do, but they're so small now you can hardly see it. It's just an ear bud, I don't mind. Do you want to wear one in case we get separated so I can let you know when he gets here?"

"Um, no. I mean, I don't think so. Do you think I should? Won't I hear all the other stuff going on all night, too if I wear it?" I ask.

"You will, yeah. Maybe not such a good idea. Dee would say you'll feel it when he arrives if it's meant to be."

Frankie and I both start laughing at that. It is exactly what she would say. I keep touching Andrea's necklace and earrings. Even though the earrings are screw backs and the clasp on the necklace has about ten safeties, I can't help it.

"By the way, did you tell her she needs to be here on time so I'm not a loner loser?"

"I told her and she said she would do her best. I'm excited to meet her new guy."

"Me, too." I say.

"Hey Mia?"

"Yeah?"

"What are you going to do? When you see him, have you decided what your plan of action is going to be?"

"No clue. I'm winging it."

Frankie grabs my hand and we pull up in front of Ruby Skye. The limo driver opens the door for us.

"Stop messing with your jewelry, Mia." Frankie says as we start to walk towards the entrance.

There are four very large men guarding the front door and they all say hello to Frankie by name. She introduces me and they put a plastic band around my wrist. We walk in and I'm completely floored both at the place and what Frankie has done to it. It's incredibly ornate and has a mixture of modern furniture and older style leather couches that look almost regal. There are huge swags of organza draped on the high ceiling and a large movie screen in the center of the front room. A majestic looking fountain sits near the bar and Frankie tells me it's Cristal champagne flowing from it. There are tables everywhere and most of them are already set up with cold hors d'oeuvres.

"Do you want to eat something before the guests arrive?" Frankie asks.

"I don't think so. In fact, I think I feel a little nauseous. Should I be doing this Frankie?"

"Yes, you should. Do you really like him, Mia?"

"I do, I really do. These last two days of not talking to him have been so hard for me that it's made me realize I like him even more than I thought I did. And I didn't tell you this before, but Andrea told me he was seeing Olivia for a little bit and he didn't have a chance to end it with her properly before he came out here."

"Good, that means no matter what you see that you shouldn't

freak out right away."

"But Frankie, he picked her up from the airport yesterday and if he really wanted to end it, he could have done it by now."

"Okay, don't over react and don't jump to any conclusions. I have to go for a little bit and check things out in the other rooms and the kitchen. Will you be okay?"

"I'll be okay," I say and Frankie gives me a kiss on the cheek. There are no other guests here yet so I sit at the bar and order a martini. The bartender asks me what flavor I would like and begins listing all of what sound like delicious options. I decide on the green apple flavored one and the bartender tells me it's called an Appletini. I figure at least I'll look hip drinking it even if I'm not hip and I have no idea what the hell it is. It turns out to be amazing.

"Is there alcohol in here?" I ask the bartender.

"Plenty of it, don't let the taste fool ya."

Hard to believe they can make vodka taste this good. By the time Frankie has made her rounds and finds me at the bar, I've finished one of the Appletini's and I'm working on my second. Frankie joins me for one and we start checking out the people who are starting to come through the door. I ask Frankie if Star is here yet and she tells me the guest of honor usually arrives a little bit late. I recognize some of the people from movies and television, and Frankie and I comment on how strange it is to see them in real life. You can see how much thinner, prettier or just plain different they all look. It's hard not to stare, and we're both so caught up in our gossip and laughter that we don't even see Dee coming in.

Dee walks up to us and she looks unbelievable.

"I would so fuck you tonight." She says to me.

"I told Charlie I was switching teams." Adds Frankie.

We all laugh and comment on how great each other looks, and Dee introduces us to her new boyfriend. His name is Drake and he looks like a Roman god. He is well over six feet tall and has brown, long curly hair with these piercing hazel eyes. I feel like I should drop down and bow before him. He takes turns kissing Frankie's hand and then mine and we both look at each other and then at Dee. Dee just smiles and winks.

"We're going to go mingle, we'll be back soon." She says.

They walk away and disappear into the crowd.

"I'll never wash this hand again." Frankie jokes.

"Jesus. He's like Thor, God of Thunder! I've never seen anybody that massive and beautiful in my life. He's out of a book."

"Leave it to Dee," Frankie says. "I've got to do some spot checks; the place is really starting to fill up. Will you be okay by yourself?"

"Me and my Appletini will be just fine."

After Frankie leaves, I start scanning the crowd looking for any familiar faces. I don't expect to see anyone I know, just a lot of celebrities and I'm ready to people watch. I notice one of the girls from "The Bachelor" that didn't get picked and she is with an actor from a new sitcom that I recognize. I also notice one of Joe's co-stars from his most recent film. She just had a baby and you would never know. It seems that movie stars take off baby pounds in weeks. Hopefully she'll ask me to do her stroller. Should I give her my card? I decide against it because there is no open seats left at the bar and the thing that's even worse than being alone at a party is standing alone at a party.

All of a sudden a silence falls among the crowd and I hear people start to whisper. I'm trying to catch what they're saying when the person sitting next to me leans over and tells somebody else "She's coming." I'm assuming they mean Star Nutley. She enters through the front doors and the whole crowd starts screaming and singing "Happy Birthday." I'm trying to see if Olivia and Joe are with her but by this point she's lost in a crowd of people circling around her.

"Mia Roman?" I hear somebody say.

I look up and it's Dante from the hair salon. Since when do people invite their hairdressers to their birthday parties? This is just great. I smile at him and go back to my drink hoping he'll just forget he saw me.

"What are you doing here?" He asks.

How rude is that?

"Same thing you are. Enjoying a drink and a nice party." I answer.

"Were you even invited?"

"Um, Dante, right? That's your name, Dante?" I ask.

He just nods his head.

"Since you're insistent on asking stupid questions, let me throw one at you. You did see the four huge men in front of the door checking invitations, right?" I ask.

He just stares at me. Finally he nods his head again.

"Good, Dante. Do you think I could take them? I mean if I really wanted to get into this party and I didn't have an invitation?"

He just keeps on staring at me; his mouth is partly open like he wants to say something.

"Okay Dante, I'm guessing by the look on your face that you don't think I could do it. With that said, let's just assume that I was invited. Okay? Okay."

I turn back around and finish off my third Appletini. I'm about to get up and see if I can find something to eat when I hear a whispered "Bitch" coming from behind me. I turn around and see Dante walking away. Thankfully I see Dee and Drake and get up to join them. Drake is looking at Dee adoringly as she talks to a group of people. It turns out that Drake is in the show "Beach Blanket Babylon" and these are some of the cast members. We end up all finding a table together and I'm having a really good time. I'm working on my fourth Martini, this time I switched it up and I'm drinking a chocolate flavored one. I haven't seen Frankie since she last left me at the bar and I'm hoping everything is going okay for her.

The party is really picking up and people are starting to dance. One of the men at our table asks me if I would like to dance with him and I agree. We dance to two fast songs in a row and then the music slows and we decide to stay on the dance floor. I get to know a little bit about him and he is very sweet and funny. It turns out he is also a cast member in the show and so is his boyfriend who is sitting at the table with us. He tells me that every one has fallen in love with Dee and they all hope her and Drake make this relationship work. It turns out that Drake's love life has had as much turmoil as Dee's. They might be a match made in heaven.

By the time we leave the dance floor I'm starting to feel a little tipsy, so I make my way over to one of the tables piled with food. There is fresh sushi but I decide against it to avoid fish breath and go for some fruit from a beautiful platter that is made of an ice sculpture in the shape of a candy bar. What? Oh yeah, Star is the candy bar heiress. Frankie is good. I pop a melon ball in my mouth and just as I turn around I see Star, Olivia and Dante coming towards me, and they look like they mean business. Just the image of it reminds me of my high school years.

"Mia Roman, I don't think you were invited to my birthday party." Star says.

I'm trying to finish chewing my melon ball and they're all just glaring at me. If I weren't so mortified, I would probably think this whole thing was comical.

"Oh, hello Star. Happy Birthday."

"Do you have an invitation to my party, Mia?" She asks.

"Well, no. Not exactly. I mean, I came with a friend who was invited and told they could bring a guest."

"Who is your friend?"

I start to say Frankie's name and stop myself. This could really damage her career. Star had told Frankie point blank that Olivia was

147

her best friend, and that she was upset about the photos in the magazine. If she knew Frankie had invited me, Star would trash her and the company to anyone that would listen.

"Well, I think I'd rather not say. It appears you're upset with me for being here so surely you would be upset with whoever it is that brought me. By the way, what is the reason you don't want me at your party?" I ask. I'm hoping I confuse her a little bit. It works, because they're all just glaring at me again. It seems like minutes have gone by and suddenly I spot Joe, and he's walking towards me. He has a huge smile on his face like he's happy to see me. Then he notices Star, Olivia and Dante, and by all of our faces, he can tell something is up.

"Hello Mia. It's nice to see you here." He says, while leaning down and giving me a kiss on the cheek.

That was actually kind of reassuring. He even stays standing next to me so now it seems like we're having a face off, the two of us against the three of them.

"It would probably be even nicer to see her here if she had an invitation." Star says.

"J.B., she has no invitation and she won't tell us who brought her as a guest." Adds Olivia.

"Mia, what's going on?" Joe asks.

"Nothing is going on. Star here is upset for some reason that I am at her birthday party and she's demanding to know who brought me. I just would rather not say. In fact, I have no idea why she doesn't want me here. I've never even met her."

"You know damn well why I don't want you here. Everyone knows that J.B. is with Olivia and you show up hanging all over him in the paper." Star yells.

"Slut." Olivia adds while starting to walk closer to me.

Joe steps in the middle and says, "Now just hold on a minute."

I'm ready to go. I'm too old for this shit. Dee is walking towards us now and I feel like we're becoming a spectacle.

"Dee, I want to go. Please leave with me. Right now."

"Did that girl just call you a slut?" She asks.

"Yes, I did call her a slut. Do you have a problem with that?" Olivia has quite a big mouth for such a little girl. I'd never expect so much attitude from her; if I was a bystander I would probably be impressed.

Dee's eyes open really wide at this. I probably don't have to tell you that Dee is a take no prisoners type of girl. Whatever Frankie is, Dee is the exact opposite. She's the one you want on your side no matter what. I've seen a lot of people say something to Dee and as soon as they see her reaction, they quickly retract what they've just said. However beautiful she is, she can be twice as scary if you piss her off.

"I-happen-to-have-a-huge-problem-with-that," Dee says. Every word is being annunciated by Dee poking Olivia in the chest with her finger.

"Please don't do this, it's my birthday party!" Star whines, and she looks like she's about to cry. Man, did she wimp out quick.

"I don't give a fuck whose birthday it is." Dee turns around and says this within an inch of Star's face. Then she turns again and faces Olivia who also looks like she's going to cry. "It seems like you don't have a problem with my friend, you have a problem controlling your man. If he even is *your* man."

Two of the big bouncers that were standing outside when I came in are now walking towards us. I turn to look at Joe and his mouth is open in shock. I don't know which part he is shocked at, there's so much going on here it's hard to figure out. The guards tell us that we have to go and Dee grabs Drake by one hand and me by the other as they escort us outside.

CHAPTER EIGHTEEN

As soon as we get out the front doors, Dee and I start freaking out.

"I can't believe you just did that, you are so awesome!" I scream to Dee.

"I know, it was such a rush. What a bunch of bitches they are. I can't believe how tough they were acting and then they almost started to cry."

We both look at Drake.

"Oh God, are you mad at me Drake?" Dee asks.

"Hell no, I'm completely turned on." He says.

We all start laughing hysterically.

"You guys! What the hell happened?" Frankie is screaming and running out the front door of the club.

"Dee was amazing, Frankie. Star and Olivia tried to kick me out and Dee totally told them off, it was so great. Don't worry; I didn't mention your name at all."

"Oh my God, are you kidding me? I can't believe I missed it. Star is in there crying and saying that her party is ruined."

"I hope you don't get in trouble for this, Frankie." Dee says.

"No, I won't. She'll get over it in a minute; I think she's just kind of milking it for attention right now. Mia, what happened with Joe?"

"Nothing. He was just standing there, he didn't say a word. He looked really confused and shocked."

"I was confused and shocked!" I gasp and we all turn around to see Joe standing there. "I had no idea you would be at this party, and I didn't know why Star and Olivia and that hair dresser person were attacking you."

"Of course you know why they were attacking me. Olivia is your girlfriend and she saw all those photos of us, photos that would never have happened had you told me you had a girlfriend!" I was yelling at this point.

"Mia, please don't scream at me. I already feel like I was completely put on the spot in there and just because you were attacked, don't attack me."

I start looking around for Frankie, Dee and Drake for support, but they have backed off a little ways, far enough to not look like they're eavesdropping but still close enough so they can hear us. I lower my voice because I'm really not into another scene myself and I'm vaguely aware of paparazzi presence.

"You put yourself on the spot because you weren't honest, to me or to Olivia. You should have told me you had a girlfriend."

"Why did you come to this party, Mia? Did you come here to try and catch me? Did you even have an invitation?" He asks.

"Oh man, Joe, that is so low. Don't try and change the subject. I came to this party with my friends who all had invitations and the option to bring a guest. Now you answer my question."

"Okay, this is the deal. Olivia and I dated a couple of times before I came out here to visit Andrea. I found out she was going out for the same movie I had already been signed for and I wanted to end things with her, I felt like she was with me for the wrong reasons. I never had a chance to talk to her before I left and doing it over the phone just isn't my style."

"Did you pick her up from the airport yesterday?" I ask.

"Yes, I did Mia."

"And you didn't have a chance then?"

"I already committed to go to this party with her, I didn't think it was appropriate to pick her up from the airport and then break up with her."

"Appropriate? You seem to have a very distorted view of appropriate if you think dating two women at one time is better than breaking up with one of them because it doesn't fit into your schedule."

"That's not what I mean. I just felt an obligation to attend this party with her. I didn't know you were going to be here. I wanted to tell you all of this yesterday, but you wouldn't call me back or answer your phone."

"You shouldn't have waited until the last minute to tell me the truth. You've had plenty of opportunities to deal with this and you just chose not to. I have to leave, Joe. I don't want to be here anymore, this is too uncomfortable for me, all of it." I'm starting to tear up a little bit and I don't want him to see me cry. I don't know whether or not I should believe him. Was he really going to tell me the truth yesterday? I feel that if I stay here and talk to him any longer that I will believe anything he says because I want to be with him so badly.

"Please don't leave like this, Mia. Let me go with you. Please."

He's really pleading with his eyes and he's holding his hands together like he's practically begging me, but I can't. I can't do this right now, I'm so hurt by him and I do the worst thing possible – I try to hurt him back.

"Go back to your party, J.B." I immediately feel terrible after the words come out of my mouth. I should have called him Joe. He looks at me with such sadness and disappointment in his eyes and turns and walks back into the club.

I'm really crying when Dee and Frankie walk back over to where I am. I'm trying to tell them I shouldn't have called him J.B., but I'm sobbing so hard they can't understand me. We go over to the side of the curb and I sit down in between them and finally get out what I was trying to say. I tell them about how Andrea said he really loved the fact that I called him Joe instead of his Hollywood nickname of J.B.

Frankie gets paged through her ear bud, so she flags her limo and tells the driver to take me and Dee wherever we need to go.

"Where's Drake?" I ask Dee.

"I sent him home. I can see him later, don't worry."

We hug Frankie good-bye and she promises to come back to my place as soon as she's done with the party. Dee and I get inside the limo; I put my head on her lap and just cry the entire way back to my apartment. Dee asks the limo driver to make a stop, and she leaves me in the limo alone so she can run into a convenience store. When she comes back, she's holding a big, brown bag.

It seems like it takes us an hour to climb the stairs to my

apartment. I'm so depressed, and I know that what started out as a night of me looking like a princess, has now turned into me looking like pure shit. I open the front door and throw myself on the couch and start crying again. Dee brings the bag into the kitchen and comes and sits next to me a couple of minutes later. I look at what she has set on the table and I can't help but laugh. There is a cheap bottle of red wine, about ten Nutley candy bars and several bags of potato chips.

"Is this supposed to make me feel better?" I ask through my tears and laughter.

"Hell yes! This is what people on death row request as their last meal."

We start drinking the wine and I put my head on Dee's shoulder and continue crying.

"This was worst case scenario, Dee. I never even thought about Star and Olivia approaching me at the party. And Joe is wrong any way you look at it. He should have told me about her. If he was really planning to end it with her and it was only a couple of dates, there's no reason why he couldn't be honest with me."

"I agree with you, Mia but he also came outside to talk to you. If he really had any feelings for Olivia, he wouldn't have risked upsetting her more by coming to find you. I'm not sticking up for him; I'm just trying to point out something you might not have noticed."

"Oh, how noble of him. Lying to me, getting caught and then chasing me down to defend himself." I'm not buying Dee's apple pie take on him.

"I saw him, Mia. He wanted to come with you, he was practically pleading with you. That was not the look of a man who wants to be with somebody else."

"I know, it was the look of somebody desperately trying to cover their ass." I sit up and open a bag of chips.

"Okay, so what are you left with? It seems you have two choices: You can forgive his lie and this whole misunderstanding and decide you like him enough to give him another chance, or you can decide this is all too much for you and there aren't enough feelings there to pursue it any further. But you do have a choice, and he seemed genuine to me, Mia. The way he was looking at you and wanting to be with you seemed real to me."

"He's a fucking actor, Dee. That's his job." I yell.

"He wasn't acting when he came outside, he wasn't acting when he said he wanted to leave with you, he was making his choice. Now it's your turn to make one."

"Not tonight, okay? Tonight I just want to get drunk, eat and cry, okay?" I ask.

Dee nods at me and we end up browsing through Netflix and watching some romantic comedy favorites. Every once in a while, one of us will pause it when we come up with a new thought or idea about the events that happened tonight. At one point, Frankie calls to check in and she lets us know that Star is fine and the party is back to normal. Both Dee and I eventually fall asleep on the couch, drunk off cheap, red wine and disgustingly full from all the junk food.

My door buzzer rings, waking me up, and I turn and look at the clock. It's nearly two in the morning. I teeter over to the intercom and ask who it is.

"It's Joe, Mia. Or J.B., whatever you want to call me. Can I come in?" He asks.

He sounds drunk; his words are kind of slurred. That makes two of us.

"No, Joe. Not tonight. I can't do this again tonight. You have to go."

Dee starts waking up and she's rubbing her eyes trying to figure out what is going on. I point to the intercom and whisper that Joe is here.

"Let him in. Why are you whispering?" She asks.

"I don't know." I start to laugh and then Dee starts to laugh. Joe buzzes again and I don't want to answer because we're both in hysterics now. Joe keeps on buzzing and every time he does it, Dee and I laugh even harder. She's trying to say something, but I can't understand what it is through her fit of giggles.

She points to the mirror by the front door and says, "Look."

I walk the short distance to the mirror and look at myself. That does it, I'm on the floor laughing so hard and both Dee and I have mascara-streaked tears running down our faces. I look like a crazy, bush woman. My hair, which was so pretty and full, has turned into a mass of kinks and knots giving me a giant sized Afro from me sleeping on it. My perfect make-up is now running down my face and I look like a raccoon. After a couple of minutes we finally regain control and I start to get up off the floor. Joe rings the buzzer again and Dee and I look at each other and the laughter starts all over.

I finally stand up, straighten my dress and walk over to the intercom. I'm doing my best not to look at Dee because I don't want to start laughing again. I hit the button and say, "Yes?"

"It's Frankie, let me in."

Frankie? I look over at Dee and she shrugs.

"Is Joe out there with you, Frankie?" I ask.

"No," she says. "But there is a black limo double parked in front of your house. Is that Joe in there? Wait, wait, wait – He's getting out." She lets go of the button and Dee and I can't hear anything anymore.

"Should I go out there?" I ask Dee.

"Not looking like that." She says and we both start laughing again.

I sit down on the couch and Dee and I both just wait, staring at the intercom. It finally buzzes.

"Yes?" I ask.

"Mia, it's me. Let me in." It's Frankie's voice.

"Are you alone?" I ask.

"No, I'm with Joe. Let us in."

"No, Frankie. I can't see Joe right now."

"Look, Mia, he's really upset and he wants to talk to you. Just buzz us up."

"I can't tonight, Frankie. Tell him I will talk to him tomorrow."

I hear the intercom go dead for a minute and then it buzzes

again.

"Frankie?" I ask.

"Yes, let me in now."

"Is he gone?"

"YES!" She yells. "Now let me in."

I look over at Dee and she shakes her head no. I hit the button.

"We don't believe you." I say.

"For fuck's sake, he's gone. Now let me in."

Dee shakes her head no again.

"We still don't believe you." I say. Dee starts to laugh and I can't help laughing, too.

"Did she just say, 'For fuck's sake'?" Dee asks and we're back with the hysterics. It's quiet now, so we know Frankie has let go of the button. I don't know whether to stand there or go sit back down, all I know is that I'm exhausted. I'm starting to get a headache and I just want to go to bed. I'm back on the couch with Dee and she's digging in her bag for some aspirin, we're both going to need it tomorrow. Somebody knocks on the door.

"You get it." I say to Dee.

"Hell no! It's not my door."

"But how did they get in, I didn't buzz them up?" We both look at each other.

"Charlie?" Dee asks.

I'm so mad Frankie did that.

"Please go answer the door so I can wash my face and change. Please, please, please?" I beg Dee.

"Fine. Go."

"Oh shit, Dee, hide all the candy bars and stuff, okay?"

Dee starts throwing all of the junk food and the empty wine bottle back into the bag that it came in. The knocks on the door come again.

"I'm coming." I hear her scream. "For fuck's sake." She starts laughing and even though she can't hear me anymore, I'm laughing, too.

I run in the bathroom and clean up my face with some eye make-up remover, and then I reapply more powder so I don't look like the walking dead. I go to my bedroom next, where I change out of my dress and into jeans and a t-shirt. My hair? Oh no, I don't know what to do. There's no way that I can brush it out unless I can find a weed whacker. I gather it all up and twist it on top of my head. I look in the mirror and it's worse then before, I'm about five inches taller it's so high. Okay, calm down. I start digging for a scarf and the only one I can find is a pastel thing that I forgot about years ago. What the hell, I have no choice. I wrap it around my head and it actually looks kind of chic. I'm off to the living room.

I walk slowly around the corner and I'm trying to spy to see who's here and what's going on. It's almost impossible to peek around without being seen so I stand behind the wall and just listen for a minute. I hear both Dee and Joe's voices, but not Frankie's. I can't hear either of them clearly enough to make out what they're saying. I hear laughter now and it makes me smile because I know Dee is the cause of it. She can charm anybody within five minutes when she turns it on.

Eavesdropping isn't all it's cracked up to be when you can't hear well enough, so I start to walk into the living room. Dee is sitting on the couch facing the hallway so she sees me first. Joe is sitting on the other end of the couch and his back is to me. As soon as Dee spots me she starts to laugh. I have no idea why she is laughing but I'm assuming it has something to do with my pastel scarf. I smile at her and make a cutting movement with my hand across my neck so she'll stop. Turns out she can't stop, which just makes her laugh harder. Joe finally turns around and I drop my hand quickly and say hello to him. He says hello back and he looks so sad.

The buzzer goes off on my intercom and Dee stands up.

"That's my Uber, Mia." She walks over and gives me a kiss and a hug then she shakes Joe's hand and tells him how nice it was to meet him. I walk her to the door and she whispers to me that she likes him before she goes down the stairs. I guess that makes one of us.

"I like your friend Dee, she seems very sweet." He says.

"Joe, what are you doing here?" I ask.

"Don't you mean, J.B.?"

"I'm sorry about that, I really am. I was hurting and I wanted you to hurt, too. I didn't mean it. There's just no way anything can be solved tonight, so I don't know why you came here. I told you at Ruby Skye I didn't want to do this tonight."

"I can't not do this tonight. I need to tell you how I feel because I'm afraid if I wait until tomorrow, if I give you time to sleep on it, then you won't give me a chance to explain."

"You already tried that and I don't accept your explanation. You might have been doing what you thought was right, but you didn't consider me." I catch myself starting to yell again so I make an effort to lower my voice.

"Did you know I would be at that party tonight, Mia?"

I'm surprised by his question. I don't know whether or not I should tell the truth. I decide if I'm not honest, I'll be just as bad as him.

"I knew, yes. The girl you just met outside, Frankie, she is my best friend and the person who planned the whole event for Star. I was her guest tonight and I went because I wanted to see you with Olivia for myself."

"If I can forgive that, can't you forgive me?" He asks.

"I didn't lie to you, Joe. Now let me ask you something. After everything that happened tonight, did you break it off with Olivia?"

Joe just sits there silently. I'm too tired to stand any longer, so I go and sit next to him on the couch. He reaches for my hand but I pull it away.

"I didn't, Mia. But it wasn't because I didn't want to. I feel nothing for her. All I do is think about you and wonder when we can be together. I called you about ten times yesterday because I wanted to see you so badly last night. Don't you understand how I feel about you?"

"No, I don't understand. Because if you feel so strongly about me, you would have done whatever it took to end it with Olivia. You just keep giving me all these excuses and it makes me doubt you even more, it makes me doubt your intentions. You're always so worried about other people's intentions with you, well, now I'm worried about yours with me."

"But there is nothing material I need from you. You can't get me a part in a movie or help my career in any way. What could I possibly want from you besides your company that I love so much?" He asks.

"You could want the same thing that you wanted from every other girl I've seen you photographed with in the tabloids."

"Are you calling me a womanizer?"

"I'm not calling you anything, but if the shoe fits…"

I immediately feel bad. I can't believe I just said that. I don't even talk like that. Joe starts to get up from the couch and I want to apologize, but the words won't come out of my mouth. He leans down and gives me a kiss on the cheek.

"Goodnight, Mia." He says and walks out the front door.

It was like it happened in slow motion. If anyone happens to be keeping score, I'm now two for two with the insults.

CHAPTER NINETEEN

When I wake up the next morning my mouth feels as dry and scratchy as sandpaper, my head is throbbing badly, and there is something wrapped around my neck so tightly I feel like I'm choking. It's that stupid pastel scarf. I try to rip it off my head, but the minute I sit up I get the spins and I have to lie back down. The clock says it is ten and Bob confirms this by putting his face in mine and letting out a huge meow because I'm late feeding him breakfast. I hear the phone ring and fumble for it on my nightstand, of course I can't find it. I end up knocking something over but it hurts too much to lift my head and see what it is. The machine goes off and my mom leaves a message telling me not to be late. I'm having lunch at her house at one, which gives me three hours to recover. Impossible!

There's a noise coming from the living room and my memory of last night starts to come back in bits and pieces. There is no part where somebody spent the night and I'm starting to get creeped out.

"Mia, it's Frankie." Thank God. Frankie has my spare key.

She walks in my room with a cup of hot coffee that has steam coming off the lid. She's also holding a bottle of aspirin and a blueberry muffin. She is my savior.

"Okay, one caramel macchiato, your favorite, two aspirins and something to put in your empty stomach. How are you, Sweetie?" She asks.

"I want to die." I say, and throw the covers over my head.

"You do that for a minute and I'll go feed Bob."

164

Bob is tormenting Frankie. He's one smart cat. I guess he figures, she's standing, why can't she do it. I wish I could stay under the covers all day. I want to lie on the couch with my big, down comforter and watch my shows and eat the rest of the junk food Dee bought yesterday. Joe hates me, now Andrea is going to hate me and if I don't get my ass out of bed soon, my mom will hate me, too. I lift myself up as slowly as I can and take a drink of the coffee while swallowing the two aspirin. When Frankie comes back I am sitting up.

"You're going to need a Roto Tiller to get through that hair. Want to talk about what happened?" She asks.

"Want to tell me why you let him in and where you went?" I ask.

"I went to Charlie's to seduce him and I let Joe in because he was practically crying in his limo about you."

"Did your seduction work?"

"No. I had the whole garter belt thing working for me under my dress and everything and he just wanted to kiss and cuddle. Do you think he's gay?"

"No, he's not gay. He's just a gentleman and you don't know what the hell to do with him. Give him some time. You should appreciate that he's not trying to get into your pants so quickly."

"But I want him in my pants. I'm this crazy, slutty girl when I'm around him and I can't help it. Maybe it's because I've been so attracted to him for so long, maybe it's because I just need to have sex."

"The party ended okay?" I ask.

"It was perfect. The only other hitch was that Dante guy tripping on the dance floor. Someone had to drive him to the emergency room because he thought he might have sprained his ankle."

I start to laugh. It really hurts my head to laugh.

"I thought you might like that one. You want to know what I saw Joe doing after you left?"

"No, I don't care." I yell. This also hurts my head.

"Okay, then I won't tell you that he just spent the rest of the night brooding and drinking whiskey. I also won't tell you that I didn't see him with Olivia once after you left and when I saw him getting into the limousine to leave, Olivia came running after him and he just closed the door."

"Unless her head got caught in the door, I don't care."

"When I was with him downstairs, he kept going on and on about how real you were and you probably don't want to hear this, but I think he's sincere about you."

The moan I let out hurts my head. Great, now both of my best friends are siding up with him.

"HE'S AN ACTOR!" I yell. "He can make you believe anything, that's why he gets paid millions of dollars to do movies. He can even cry on cue. It was only two dates, Frankie, that's not enough for this to be worth fighting for."

"Are you sure? My parents got married after one date and they've been together thirty years." Frankie says.

My phone starts to ring and Frankie asks if she should answer it. I shake my head no and tell her I can't find it. I watch her start to look around for it and she finds the picture frame I knocked over earlier. She disappears by the side of my bed for a minute and reappears with the telephone.

"Your Caller ID says that it's your mom."

I shake my head no more violently than last time and Frankie just smiles. She knows my mom well from living next door to me for so long. The machine beeps and my mom's voice booms through the apartment. I have to remember to turn that thing down.

"Mia, pick up the phone. Fine, I don't mind being ignored as long as you're still here by one. I have two surprises for you when you get here. I'm not going to give you any hints, but you need to make a list of three questions you want answers to before you come. Okay, see you soon."

I roll my eyes and it hurts my head. When are these aspirin supposed to kick in? I need to take a shower. I hope I have a full bottle of conditioner because that's what it's going to take to get these knots out of my hair.

"What do you think your surprises are?" Frankie asks.

"Who gives a shit?" I answer.

"Okay grumpy Grace, I'm going to go now. Charlie and I are going to go get a bite to eat. Maybe I can get him drunk at lunch and make him have sex with me."

"Maybe you should buy a vibrator and give the guy a break." I say.

"No, Michelle would probably use it while I wasn't home."

"Gross. Thank you for the coffee and stuff. I'll call you when I get back."

Frankie blows me a kiss good-bye and I put my head back under the covers. Every once in a while I grope for my coffee and bring it under the blankets with me to take a sip. Eventually I bring the muffin under, and when I feel Bob jump on the bed, I drag him under, too. When the coffee, the muffin, and Bob are all gone, I decide to drag myself out of bed. The aspirins are finally starting to take effect, so I get in the shower. I hear my phone ring when I'm in there, but since I haven't answered it all morning, I'm certainly not going to get out of the shower for it now. It's probably my mom again. She does this every time I'm supposed to come to her house. She will call and call until I pick up. So, you ask, why not just answer it and get it over with? It's my secret way of torturing her, although I'm usually the one that feels tortured.

I've conditioned my hair twice, and I feel like I've lost half of it by the time I'm done with the shower. It's made my headache, which was down to a dull throb, come roaring back. I take two more aspirin and call my mom back. I promise to be there on time and to write down the three questions. She sounds like an excited little kid and it's actually kind of nice. She lives in Marin, which isn't very far from me. I usually leave my house for our Sunday lunches around twelve thirty to get there on time. It's only eleven thirty now, so I make my own pot of coffee and start opening the boxes Eleni dropped off yesterday. I recognize most of the names and items from Internet orders until I come across a box with no return address. It has no FedEx markings on it, and then I remember the other day I got this package in my regular mail and just threw it with my other work orders. I'm about to open it when the phone rings again.

My Caller ID says that it's Andrea, and even though I want to talk to her so badly, I just can't deal with it right now. I end up letting it go to my machine.

"Hi Mia. I was going to call you to ask how the party went last night, but Joe filled me in this morning. I'm not going to put my two cents in because it's probably not even worth half a penny. I just want you to know that if you need to talk, I am here for you. Hope to see you tomorrow."

Even though my curiosity is killing me, I don't want to call Andrea back now. I don't have the time and I'm trying to clear my head before I go to my mom's. Who knows what's in store for me there. I go back to opening the unmarked box and there's a t-shirt inside with a note. I open it up and it reads: *Dear Ms. Roman, I've heard through the grapevine that you do very good work and I would like for you to decorate my t-shirt. Please write the words, 'J.B. is my boyfriend' across the chest area. Send back C.O.D. when complete. Thanks, Olivia Lucas.*

There is no return address and it makes me come to the realization that she sent this t-shirt as a cruel joke after she saw the photographs of Joe and I. I should find out her address, write something a little different on the t-shirt and send it back to her. Or, I could write something on it and wear it myself. I don't normally advertise by wearing the clothing I make, but perhaps this would be an exception. I would just have to make sure that I got photographed in it. This would be one time I would gladly pose for the paparazzi. Now I just have to figure out what I should write.

I'm going to deal with it later because I have to get ready to go to my mom's. I pull out a pen and paper and I'm trying to figure out what my three questions should be. I'd like to know what it's for; it would help in the kind of questions I ask. Maybe it's part of some game she wants to play. I know if I don't do it, she'll be upset for weeks. Okay, here's my list:

1. What are the winning numbers for the next SuperLotto?
2. Where did Bob go when he disappeared for so long?
3. Did someone really see Tupac at 7-11?

I'm really happy with my questions. I doubt my mom will be, but I fold up the piece of paper, put it in my purse and head out the front door. It's a really nice day outside and whatever the weather is like here, it's usually a little warmer in Marin. My favorite bridge is the Golden Gate and I have to ride over it to visit my mom. The speed limit might be a little slow and the toll might be a little high, but it's a wonderful drive and it's worth it. I once walked across it when I was in the eighth grade for a class field trip. I remember being so young and feeling so cool that I was in San Francisco. They told us on that field trip that they're constantly repainting the bridge, and as soon as they've finished, they have to start all over again. I know there's symbolism in that, but the hell if I know what it is.

CHAPTER TWENTY

"Come on in, Sweetheart." Either my mom is mad at me or she's got company over. Those are the only two times she calls me Sweetheart.

I walk into her house, the one she bought after my father died. I've never lived here and I was against her selling our old house, the one I grew up in. She said the old house held too many memories for her and I understood, but I was still heart broken. You see, the memories it held for me were all good ones, and I loved coming to visit and feeling my father around me. The memories my Mother held were all good ones, too, but having them around her day and night proved to be too much.

I walk inside and there is a very nice looking, older gentleman sitting on the sofa. My mom introduces him as Daniel and he shakes my hand and does that thing I love by putting his other hand over mine. He has very gray, thinning hair; pretty hazel eyes and a smile that makes you smile back. I love contagious smiles. My mom is acting so nice I almost want to puke. Don't get me wrong, I'm happy to see her being nice, but I haven't seen her act like this in about twenty years. And when she did act like this twenty years ago, it was never towards me.

Daniel and I drink iced tea and share small talk while my mom finishes making lunch. I find out that he is a retired doctor, a general practitioner. His wife died of cancer several years ago and he has one grown daughter who is married with two children of her own. He lives in Marin, right down the street actually, and he and my Mother met online. I just about pass out when I hear this.

I bought my mom a computer last Christmas and she wouldn't even turn it on for the first two months. She was afraid of it because she had never used one before. She has yet to get a cell phone, doesn't even know what an iPhone or iPad is and usually refuses to call anything but my home number. So for her birthday in February, I hired somebody to come to her house and give her private lessons on how to use it. Ever since then, you can't get her off of it. She's the type of person that sends you about fifteen of the stupidest jokes every day and then wants to talk to you about them when she sees you next. I always delete them. I knew that she went to online support groups to chat and talk to other widows whose spouses died of cancer, but I never thought she'd make a love connection there.

My mom calls out to us and says that lunch is ready, so we make our way into the kitchen. Daniel seems very soft spoken and kind, I like him already. During lunch they talk about their first date and I find out they've been seeing each other for over a month, on a daily basis. The more I watch my mom, the more I see that her acting nice is because she's truly happy right now. I might make her out to be more of a monster than she is, it's just that she and I never clicked when I was growing up. I was always a Daddy's girl and I think she resented that because she only had one child. She tried very hard to have more children but after several miscarriages, she gave up. Both my parents had to work and we were always struggling to have a middle class lifestyle. It wasn't until my father died and my mom sold the house and got life insurance money that she was able to retire and relax.

We finish our lunch and go back to the living room. Daniel offers to clean up the kitchen while my mom and I talk. Unbelievable! I really like this guy. After he leaves the room, my mom moves closer to me on the couch and grabs my hand.

"Isn't he wonderful?" She asks. She's beaming like a teenager.

"He really is, Mom. He seems very patient and kind. I guess that comes with being a doctor. Why didn't you tell me about him sooner?"

"I've meant to, but I didn't want to jump the gun. I thought I would wait until he and I had spent some more time together before you two met." She looks at her watch after saying this.

"Well, the surprise is almost a half an hour late. Did you bring the questions you wrote down with you?"

"I did. What is the surprise?" I ask.

"I hired a psychic to come and do readings for us today. Isn't that exciting?"

"Um, no. It's not exciting. It's creepy. I don't want a reading. How did you find this person?" I don't believe in psychics, I never have. There's a medium on television that Frankie and I watch and make fun of while we try to figure out how he staged everything and got their information beforehand.

"She came to my garden club and did a reading for the other ladies, but I wasn't there that day. So, I called her and asked her to do a private one for each of us. You're first."

"No, I'm not first. I'm not going to have a reading, Mom. I'm sorry, I don't believe in it."

"Oh, you'll be fine. I heard from Linda that she was very accurate. I'm going to call her and see why she's late."

I hate when she just disregards what I've said like I'm a child. She gets up and grabs her purse and digs through it until she finds the phone number on a piece of paper. I hear her dial the number and she's sitting in front of me holding the phone. I look up at her and she winks at me. What does that mean?

"She's not answering. Maybe that's a sign." She says.

"Yeah, a sign that she is ignoring you."

"Come on, Honey, this will be fun! Please? Do this for me?"

"Fine, I will do it." I say.

"Oh, goodie. Now let me see your questions."

She just said goodie. I dig through my purse and pull out the piece of paper that has my questions written on it. I hesitate for a moment and she holds out her hand so I hand them over. I watch her open the paper and read until her smile starts to fade. She doesn't look mad, just really serious.

"Mia, Honey, these can't be your questions. You have to ask real questions about yourself. You don't want to waste the reading having her answer these."

I can't believe she is saying this with a serious face. Like this lady could answer any of those questions anyway. She really believes all this psychic stuff. The doorbell rings and saves me from having to respond to her. I wait on the couch until my mom comes back with

Daniel and a woman she introduces as Sandy. Even though I don't believe in the psychic stuff, I do get an initial feeling when I first meet somebody or go into a new place, and I like her energy. My mom tells Sandy that I'm going first and her and Daniel go into the kitchen and leave me and Sandy alone in the living room. I ask her to take a seat and she opens her bag and starts pulling out some candles and incense. I wait while she sets everything up and then takes a seat across from me.

"Do you have any specific questions for me?" She asks.

I kind of wanted to stick with my list, so I go for the easiest one.

"Do you know where Bob went when he was gone?"

"Is Bob human?"

Well, now shouldn't she know this?

"No." I answer.

"I think Bob got out when your door was left open too long. I think he was right outside the entire time he was missing."

That makes me seem like an asshole! How could I not know that my cat was living in front of my house? I like Frankie's story better.

"Do I have to ask you questions? Can't you just tell me what you see or feel?" I ask.

"Sure, we can do that." She says, and sits back a little bit on the couch so she can look at me.

"I see that something is troubling you but it's kind of hazy. I see a person around you who has initials for a name. For some reason I'm seeing a lot of stairs, like an endless stair case going up and up and up."

Whatever. She probably saw the article in *US* Weekly.

"I also see a star, the shape of a star. Is that a person's name?" She asks.

I nod my head yes. I'm starting to get into this now.

"Do you see love in my future?" I ask.

She's quiet for quite a long time. This isn't looking good.

"I do," she finally says. "I see you struggling before you come to terms with the love that's already there. I see trust issues that need to be overcome. Who is sick?"

"My friend Andrea. What do you see for her?"

"I can't tell because she doesn't know what she sees for herself right now. Your friend Andrea came to the conclusion that it was her time, and now she might be changing her mind."

Wow! This is really interesting. She's right about the first part, but I had no idea that Andrea might be changing her mind. Oh no, I'm buying into this.

"Did somebody really see Tupac at 7-11?" I ask. I need to get back to my original list of question, she's really freaking me out. But instead of becoming angry or upset, she just laughs.

"You started to get into this for a second and you got freaked out, right?" She asks.

Jesus, she's really good!

"Right." I say.

"Don't worry; it happens all of the time." She reassures me.

"Okay, then how do I resolve the trust issues that you say I need to overcome?"

Oh, Honey, that's for a psychiatrist to answer, not a psychic."
She laughs.

I laugh, too. She's right. I forgot for a second that I wasn't
sitting here having a conversation with a friend.

"Can you tell me anything else? Anything else you see that I
might want to know?" I ask.

She's quiet again for longer than before. I hope this ends on a
good note.

"I see that you have a good heart and that your heart has been
hurt before, so now you're wary. If you're going to make a decision
not to be with someone that you really have feelings for, don't make
that decision based on past hurt. You might think the reason you are
choosing not to be with him is something else, but in most cases, it
has to do with pain you haven't let go of. I guess what I'm saying is,
don't let your past dictate your future."

I start to tear up a little bit thinking about what she's said. Is
that what I've been doing? I never even gave myself time to mourn
John leaving me or to forgive him for what he did, even though I
would only be forgiving him for me. I stand up to thank Sandy and
give her a hug. If she's not psychic, she certainly is astute. I go in the
kitchen to get my mom and tell her that she's next, but she stops me
and says that Daniel is going to go now. I'm happy because I want to
spend a little time with my mom alone. I don't know why, but I feel
like telling her the truth about Joe.

We spend the next half hour having one of the best

conversations we've ever had. She listens to everything I have to say without being judgmental or jumping to any conclusions. She also doesn't blame me for driving him away last night. When I'm done telling her absolutely everything, she offers up no advice.

"Aren't you going to tell me what to do?" I ask.

"No, Mia. That's not my place. I stopped trying to tell you what to do a long time ago. I will tell you that I love you, and that I want the best for you, like every parent does. I'm sorry you're hurting and that you have to make a decision that could prove to be pretty big. No matter how many times you tell this story to somebody, or someone gives you advice on how to handle it, you're still going to ultimately do what is right for you. You always have, and look at how special you've turned out."

Oh no, I never thought my mom would make me cry tears of sweetness. I have to remind myself to send Daniel some flowers or something, I'm positive he is responsible for this change in her. Speaking of Daniel, he is done with his reading and his timing is perfect. I hug my mom good-bye and whisper to her that I really like Daniel, and then I shake his hand and tell him how lovely it was to meet him.

My ride home is quiet and instead of thinking about things, I listen to some oldies instead. Sometimes when I'm driving at night and listening to my Dad's favorite music, I feel like I can smell him. It's such a comforting thing, and I know it is my mind remembering his smell, not the smell itself, but I don't care. I appreciate it when it happens. Maybe I'll ask my mom if she knows any mediums.

I spend the rest of Sunday night doing side jobs in front of the television, eating junk food, drinking wine and screening my telephone calls. All in all, a very unhealthy night. My hangover is making me tired earlier than usual, so I grab Bob and we get into bed. I ask him if he was living in front of the building, but he doesn't answer me. I remember that I haven't seen my iPhone in quite some time or checked my e-mail for that matter, so I begin my search. I have to call my cell from my home phone, but I finally find it and bring it back into bed with me. When I open up my account, I think there must be some kind of a mistake. There are over a hundred orders here, this can't be possible. I start opening them up one by one and they are all legitimate orders.

My first thought is, I can't do this. It's all too much. I know that it must be a result of the *US* Weekly article. I've always been very business minded aside from being creative, and I try to force myself to think about this logically. The first thing I do is e-mail Dee and ask her if she's interested in a job working for me. Even though Dee's life is very glamorous, she's never had a decent job. She goes from one thing to another, never finding anything that suits her. I've always told her that if my business did well enough, I would hire her.

The second thing I do is make a To-Do list for tomorrow:

1. Place order for more gems and adhesive.
2. Figure out how much more supplies I will need.
3. Make space inside office to handle workload.
4. Call FedEx to make two drop-offs/pick-ups a week.
5. Call Paulie (my website designer) and ask him to change the turn-around time on the website to eight to twelve weeks.

Okay, that should cover it for now. I try to fall asleep, but my mind is racing with everything that has happened in just the last two weeks. It takes me a long time before I finally fade off into a very restless night's sleep.

CHAPTER TWENTY-ONE

First thing the next morning, my front door buzzer goes off. I feel like I just closed my eyes but when I turn and look at the clock, it's already almost nine. I stumble out of bed with Bob meowing at my heels for breakfast and press the talk button.

"Who is it?" I ask in a very grumpy voice.

"Dee. Buzz me in."

I buzz her up, unlock my front door and go into the kitchen to feed Bob. I see Dee coming in and she's holding two cups of coffee in her hands, which immediately makes me less grumpy.

"One Caramel Macchiato for you." She says with a big smile and gives me a kiss on the cheek.

I take the cup and give her a big hug to thank her.

"What are you doing here so early?" I ask.

"Dee Mooring, reporting for duty."

"But what about your job?" I ask.

"I quit this morning. I'm ready to work for you; I have been since you started this company. Let's go. What's first?"

The rest of the morning and early afternoon fly by with Dee and I cleaning up my office to make work spaces for the both of us and getting all of my materials organized. I show her how to place orders with the vendors and how to estimate how much of the materials we're going to need. I show her how to check the website for e-mails and how to process the orders and make sure payment has been made. Then, we go through the boxes that arrived on Saturday and I show her how to match those against the paid orders on the website. And finally, how to start applying the patterns and the gems. Thankfully all of my patterns are organized, I don't get very many custom orders through the website because they can be quite costly.

I show Dee the order from Olivia and she makes that her first test project. She ends up creating a custom pattern from scratch while I go and get us some lunch. When I come back, she has written the words:

Jealous

B*itch*

across the chest of the t-shirt.

"What is that for?" I ask.

"Well, I'm sure she'll recognize this t-shirt if you wear it because of the color and style. It has two meanings, one is that she's obviously a jealous bitch, and the other is the big, bold first letters that spell J.B.'s name. Now, you just have to wear it when you know you'll be photographed."

"Well, I don't think I have the guts to wear the t-shirt, but besides that, you get an A+ for creativity and workmanship. The application you did is great! I can't believe you finished this in the time I was gone. I'm really impressed, Dee."

"But you have to wear it to get back at her for sending this to you, that was so fucked up and nobody will know what it means except us and her, if she sees it."

"I'll think about it. Let's eat lunch."

I drive over to Andrea's and leave Dee at my house to finish working for the day. I'm really happy with my decision to hire her, and she seems equally as happy. I let her know that the crazy amount of orders coming through right now might not last, and her job is based on that. She didn't care considering she changes jobs as often as she changes boyfriends. We started to talk about salary and I could tell she was uncomfortable asking. So I took the initiative and asked her what she was making at her last job. When she told me, I told her I would double it and that was that. After I got over the shock of how much she's been living off of, I asked her how she managed to dress like she did and have her own apartment with that kind of salary. She told me with a wink that she's always managed to just make it work and that people like to buy her things.

When I arrive at Andrea's she immediately wants to take me upstairs to talk, but I ask her if she will come outside with me and talk to me while I work. I feel like I should already be done with her casket because of the amount that she is paying me. Not to be morbid, but we have no idea how much time she has left and I really feel it's important for her to see the finished product. She doesn't seem too concerned, and she actually looks fabulous today. By the looks of it, she might not need this casket any time soon.

As I'm working Andrea tells me about the state Joe was in when she saw him yesterday morning. He told her everything that happened, including all the things that were said when he came back to my house. He said he felt terrible about not doing more when Star, Olivia and Dante were ganging up on me.

"It seems your friend Dee handled that situation just fine. She sounds like a girl I'd like to meet." Andrea says this with a smile on her face that looks like she's reminiscing of the way she might have been when she was younger.

"You would fall in love with her, just like everybody else does," I say. "I actually hired her today to come work for me. It seems that *US* article really did a lot for my business, if nothing else good came out of it, at least that did."

"Good for her. I hope she does well with you and I hope your good fortune lasts long after that silly article is forgotten. By the way, you should know that after Joe left your house on Saturday night, he went to go see Olivia."

I stop my work and look up at Andrea.

"He told me that he didn't do it because of what you said, he did it because you made him realize it was something he should have done a long time ago, no matter what the circumstances were. He was just making excuses to himself when he didn't want to do it over the telephone or do it right when she arrived from the airport. He just didn't want to face having to do it at all."

"Is he here, Andrea? I'd like to talk to him. I'd like to apologize for the way I treated him. And it's not what you think. It's not because of what you just told me, it's because I've just realized what a fool I've been."

Andrea is quiet and it makes me nervous. Perhaps he told her he didn't want to see me if I came here today. I don't know what to think.

"Andrea, is he here?" I ask again.

"He left this morning, Sweetheart. He went back home, to Los Angeles."

I tell Andrea I'm fine, that it's no big deal, but I'm only saying this because I want her to go back inside. I want to be by myself so I can let out these tears I am trying so hard to hold back. I blew it! I can't believe how awful I was to him, and Dee and Frankie kept trying to tell me in the nicest way that I blew it. I just blew it! He went back home to get away from me, from the harshness of my words and actions. I should have never gone to that stupid party and caused a scene that ended up putting him in a terrible predicament. What can I do now? I can't call him and beg him for forgiveness, I'll look pathetic. It's too late for me to say I'm sorry because the damage is already done.

Andrea finally goes back inside of the house and I take a seat outside and cry and cry and cry until I feel I have no tears left inside of me. I spend the rest of the afternoon getting lost in my work and making great progress on the casket. I'm figuring only two more days and it should be complete. When I'm done packing up for the day, I bring the gems to Andrea to put inside her safe. She introduces me to a man named Don Case and tells me that he's Tony Case's father. I vaguely remember Joe telling me that Tony Case was coming to visit Andrea and bringing his Father. I guess this must be the guy. Tony Case is an actor and he's about the same age as Joe but he does a lot of Indie films. Joe told me that he does one big motion picture every year or so, that way he can afford to do the

Independent movies he loves. I think that's fantastic. I also really like his Father and the way Andrea looked when she was introducing us.

When I get home, Dee is still plugging away. She updates me on everything that has happened while I was gone. Both of the orders we placed for materials were confirmed via e-mail, Paulie changed the turn around time on the website already and FedEx called and said they would be making drop-offs/pick-ups on Wednesday and Saturday now. Dee has finished a lot of orders already, and I check them all to find out that she is doing wonderfully. The last thing I need to teach her is how to wrap the finished product up in the packaging and fill out the form so it's ready to ship off. I do the first one while she watches and she finishes the rest.

Dee tells me I had some messages while I was gone, but she let the machine pick them up because they were on my personal line. She has a funny look on her face while she's telling me this, and I'm assuming it's because the volume is so loud on my machine that she heard everything already. I walk over to listen to the messages. The first one is from my mom.

"Hi Honey. I just wanted you to know I had such a nice time visiting with you yesterday. Daniel thinks you're a doll. Call me back because I want to tell you about our readings. Bye!"

There was no, "Where are you, Mia?" or "Pick up the phone." It was all "Honey" and her being very sweet. I'm thinking I could get used to this. I press erase and go on to the next one. It's Frankie.

"Hey! I tried to call you on your cell but it's turned off. I heard you hired Dee and I'm so excited! I want to invite you guys to Charlie's house for dinner tonight. He's going to cook for all of us if you can make it. Let me know."

I hit erase and move on to the next one. Dee comes into the room and stands next to me. I'm glad because I just about pass out when I hear John's voice.

"Hi Mia. It's John. I know you probably didn't expect to hear from me any time soon but I'm back in town. They pulled our funding. It's a long story but I'd like to see you. I'm staying at my sister's house and the number here is 415-555-8261."

I hit the save button and before I have a chance to freak out, the last message plays.

"Um, hi. It's Joe. I meant to call you earlier but I haven't had the chance." He hesitates a moment. "Well, that's not true. I did have the chance but I didn't know what to say to you. I'm back home now, in Los Angeles. I wanted to be the one to tell you that before you found out some other way. I also wanted to tell you there are no hard feelings. I'm glad I met you, Mia. I'm glad I had the chance to be your friend."

I lean against the wall for support, and then slowly slide down until I'm sitting on the floor. Dee slides down with me and we both sit together.

"Had the chance to be my friend? Had? Does that mean we're not friends anymore? He didn't even ask me to call him back. I blew it! I really did, and you guys tried to tell me but I wouldn't listen." Dee tries to say something but I'm not done yet. "And who the hell does John think he is calling me. I don't give a shit if a lion ate one of his legs off in Africa; he has no reason to ever call me again. He'd like to see me? Are you fucking kidding me? I'll see him in hell."

I feel a little bit better now. I really needed to vent uninterrupted.

"You'll see him in hell? Dee asks.

I look at her and we both crack up.

"No sitting around and sulking, let's call Frankie and tell her to have Charlie whip us up some dinner. He's never been with all three of us together; he has no idea what he's in for."

CHAPTER TWENTY-TWO

The next week goes by really quickly. On Wednesday, FedEx dropped off about fifty boxes and Dee and I have been working around the clock. I finished Andrea's casket and she was beyond thrilled with it. She told me it exceeded any expectations she could have had. In the end, it doesn't seem like it was a time sensitive job at all, considering Andrea looks as healthy as ever. Dinner at Charlie's went really well and Frankie was proud to announce they've progressed to third base. On Thursday night, we all went and saw Drake in "Beach Blanket Babylon" and then to an after party that was a lot of fun.

It would seem like I'm living my normal life again, but after Dee leaves for the night or I come home alone from being out, I'm always sad and depressed. I think about Joe constantly and it takes every ounce of my emotional strength to not call him. John left another message sometime during the week and I ignored it again. I deleted his first message because Dee said I might come home drunk one night and call him at his sisters if I still had the number. I didn't think that would ever happen, but I took her advice just in case. I kept Joe's message and I listen to it about fifty times a day. I'm obsessed with it. After dinner at Charlie's the other night, Frankie came upstairs and we all listened to it together so we could analyze it.

I've been invited to a dinner party at Andrea's house on Saturday and I'm really looking forward to it. I wish I wasn't dateless, but the only person I want to be with right now is Joe, and that's impossible.

On Friday I've been invited as a guest to a morning talk show called "Mornings on 2." It is on a local channel two station, and they want to talk about my work and for me to bring a couple of samples. They're going to say my website address on the air and I never thought I'd say this, but I don't know if we can handle more orders. Dee suggested hiring somebody from a temporary agency, and if this morning show appearance makes our order count any higher, I think I will do that.

After Dee and I are done working all day on Thursday, we meet Frankie for dinner at Puccini and Penetti. We ended up eating here one night because an ex-boyfriend of Dee's was bartending and we fell in love with the food. We try to come at least once a month and I'm pretty sure I've tried everything on the menu. One time when we came here for dinner, I had stopped right before to pick up some pictures I had blown up of my father. They were for a photo collage I was making of him for my mom. One of them was a beautiful eight by ten in black and white of just his face when he was in his late thirties or early forties. There are framed pictures hanging up all over the restaurant and in Dee's drunkenness, she took one of the photos off the wall and exchanged it for the one of my Dad. It's still there, almost two years later. So, if you're ever in San Francisco, don't forget to eat at Puccini & Penetii and take your best guess at which picture is my father.

Our plan is to have dinner and do a little shopping for my television appearance tomorrow. I've already called Andrea to make sure she watches, and my mom and Daniel are going to watch, too.

After dinner we head over to Neiman's to look for a summer suit. I want to wear something in a pastel that looks semi-professional with a tee underneath that Dee made especially for me. It is white with baby doll sleeves and it says, "Mornings on 2" but the number two is actually the networks logo. It is all done up with sparkling cubic zirconia's and it looks too cute. We end up picking a light blue pantsuit with a short jacket that looks better when it's open, so you can see the tee. I already have the perfect shoes to match, so I get out of there without breaking the bank.

The morning show goes extremely well. I'm surprised by how calm I feel on camera. I think a lot of it has to do with the hosts making me feel so comfortable. They really talk up my work and they have photographs of famous people pushing strollers I've created for them and the one Rolls-Royce I decorated. They also show the things I brought in as examples and they say the name of my website several times. We made an agreement beforehand not to talk about Joe and I'm grateful they did not bring him up. I'm very satisfied with the experience, it was more than I could have hoped for. As soon as I walk out of the building and look at my iPhone, I can see I have tons of texts and missed calls already. People I haven't talked to in the longest time are calling and messaging to congratulate me, and of course my mom, Dee and Frankie all called to tell me how great I looked, etc. I'm feeling really good about everything until my phone rings with a number that I don't recognize. I answer it and it's John.

"Hey Mia. So you're famous now and you decide to ignore

me?" There is laughter in his voice that I recognize as nervousness.

"I'm not famous, John and I'm not ignoring you – I'm trying to avoid you."

"Don't be that way, Mia. I've missed you a lot. I thought about you every day in Africa and I wanted to call you so many times and tell you about all my experiences. I wish you could have been there with me."

"John, have you lost your mind? I mean, really, have you? You rob me blind, sell the things that are most important to me, steal my cat and now you want to talk about your African adventures?"

"I didn't steal Bob." He says.

"Okay, John. You know what?" I ask.

"What, Mia? Because I didn't steal your cat."

"Fuck off, that's what!" And I hang up.

God that felt good! Aside from being therapeutic, he really deserved it. I never thought the best way to get over a guy would be him stealing my things and selling them, but it worked like a charm. I'd rather chew razor blades than see him right now. I'd rather drink a glass of somebody else's spit. Okay, I'm sure you get the point. My phone rings again and I'm assuming it's John calling back before I even look at the caller ID. I'm wrong, though, it's another number I don't recognize.

"Hello?" I say.

"Hi. Mia?"

"Yes, this is Mia. Who is this?" I ask.

"It's Joe, Mia. How are you?"

I halt in mid-step and start looking for a place to sit down because I feel faint.

"Mia? Are you there?" He asks.

Oh God, I need to talk. I need to say something back.

"I'm here. I'm sorry. I was just looking for a place to sit."

Like he gives a shit. The truth is, I don't know what else to say.

"I just wanted to tell you that I'm on my way. I'm going to fly down; I'm at the airport now so I should be there in about an hour or so. Are you going to go to the hospital and keep Don company?"

"Joe, what are you talking about?" I ask.

"Didn't you hear? Oh God, I'm so sorry Mia. Andrea is in the hospital. Don had to take her this morning. She's not doing well at all, Mia. I feel so guilty that I ever left. Can you go right now to St. Francis and be with her and Don?"

"Oh God, Joe. Oh my God! What happened, Joe?"

"I don't know all the details, Angel. Don just left me a message saying she was in the hospital and to come right away."

Did he just call me Angel? I can't believe this is happening; it's not her time yet. I'm not ready for her to go. She looked so good the last time I saw her and she sounded so happy when I called her to tell her about the show yesterday.

"I'm on my way right now. I'll see you as soon as you get here."

I hang up and try to hail a cab. As soon as one stops, I jump in and tell him St. Francis hospital. I open my wallet, hand him a hundred dollar bill and tell him to drive as fast as he can.

CHAPTER TWENTY-THREE

When I get to the hospital, the information desk tells me where I can find Andrea. I look for Don first in the waiting room, but I can't find him. When I ask the Intensive Care Nurse what room Andrea is in, she tells me that unless I'm family, I can't go in. I tell her that I am family and she reluctantly gives me the room number. I figure if I didn't know Andrea had no family before I met her, this woman probably doesn't know either. She tells me that I can't go in until her current guest comes out; only one at a time.

The waiting room is very simple and sterile. The chairs are uncomfortable and all the magazines outdated. There is a big sign telling me to turn off my cell phone, so I call Frankie, Dee and my mom to tell them what is going on. Fortunately for me I get voice mails for all, so I just leave messages telling them where I am and that my cell phone will be turned off. There is a television in the corner hanging from the ceiling and there is so much static it's hard to watch. There isn't a remote in sight and I would have to stand on Lebron James' shoulders to reach the dials, so I start digging in my purse for something to keep me occupied. I promised myself in the cab on the way here that I wasn't going to get weirded out like I usually do in stressful situations and overwhelm people with stupid questions.

Before I can start pacing and biting my cuticles, I hear footsteps hitting the tile and I look up to see Don in the doorway. He looks so tired and sad. I know I've only met him once, but I stand up and give him a long hug and I wait for him to let go.

"How is she?" I ask.

"Not good. Not good at all. They're running some tests now." He starts to cry and I lead him over to the uncomfortable chairs.

"We made a decision just yesterday, you know. She and I decided that we wanted to have the chance to make a relationship, to be together. She called her doctor this morning and left him a message saying she wants to try chemo again, that she doesn't want to give up. She changed her mind, she was so happy, and now this." He breaks down in tears again, so I just sit with him and hold his hand.

"Please go in and be with her now, Mia. I know she would want to see you."

"Are you sure it's okay?" I ask.

He nods his head yes and I get up to find Andrea's room. The door is slightly open, so I peek in and see a room that looks more sterile than the waiting room. Everything is white, including her hospital gown and the sheet she is under. She has tubes running from her arms and nose and her eyes are closed. I crack the door a little and it makes a squeaking noise, Andrea opens her eyes, sees me and smiles. Joe was wrong, Andrea is the angel. She looks so peaceful even though everything surrounding her screams the opposite. I walk into the room and slowly close the distance from the door to her bed. She reaches out her hand; I grab it and take a seat that I'm assuming Don moved to be next to her.

"You were great this morning." She whispers.

"Thank you." I say. "I kept trying to act like you. Your quiet confidence and your eternal elegance. I know I failed miserably, but I tried. What happened, Andrea?"

"I knew that if I didn't get more treatment, this is where I would eventually end up. I just didn't think it would happen so soon. I'm going to be okay, though, Mia. Do you want to know why?" She asks.

"If it has anything to do with Don, I already know. He told me you changed your mind yesterday."

"I thought I got sick to be with Billy, but I was wrong. I got sick so that I could appreciate somebody besides Billy. When, not if, I pull through this, my doctor said that I could start treatment again. Will you stand by me, Mia? I'm going to need all the support I can get. I know that we haven't known each other long, but I feel so close to you because of the circumstances that have thrown us together. If it's too much for you, I'll understand."

"I will stand by you no matter what, Andrea. No matter what."

She squeezes my hand and closes her eyes. I sit there for a while wondering if she's just resting or if she's fallen asleep. The door opens and a nurse comes into the room. She tells me that I have to leave for a little while and when I look back over at Andrea, her eyes are open again.

"I'll be in the waiting room, Andrea. Also, Joe called me and he is on his way."

"He needed an excuse to see you again; lucky for him I got sick." She winks at me and I leave her with the nurse.

196

Back in the waiting room I find Don sitting around a whole assortment of foods from the cafeteria.

"It's important that you eat in times like this. Most people forget to eat and they get weak. Andrea needs us to be strong, so come have a seat."

I eat until I'm full and Don persuades me to eat some more. He's even gotten different desserts and I'm really stuffed, but the more I eat the happier Don seems, so I eat some more. I finally tell him that I just can't eat another bite or I'll throw up and he stops persisting. I'm being serious; I do feel full and nauseous. Don and I pass the time by getting to know about one another. Don used to be a film producer and he tells me that he's very proud of what his son has accomplished as an actor. He also tells me that he was married for a very long time and his wife left him for someone else. He's never been with anybody since and that was almost ten years ago. Love was never something he thought he'd find again until he met Andrea. He only came here as a favor to his son, who wanted to spend some time catching up with him while visiting a sick friend. I heard him whisper to himself that love works in mysterious ways.

We both took turns visiting Andrea again and sitting by her side. She slept through my second visit but I was happy to be able to be there, even if she didn't know it. Eventually Don and I both fall asleep inside the waiting room. I must have been emotionally exhausted because that's what it takes to fall asleep on those chairs. I wake up with a jump when I feel something touch my face. I look up and it's Joe. He's stroking my cheek and I've never seen a more welcoming sight. He mouths out the word "hi" and I start to stand up, but he stops me and drops to his knees in front of me. We fall into a tight embrace and I don't ever want to let go. He's nuzzling and kissing my neck while he continuously tells me that he's sorry.

"No, no, no. I'm sorry, Joe. I really am. I should have given you the benefit of the doubt. I should have believed your intentions were good and that you would eventually break up with Olivia."

"I did. Break up with her, I mean. It's over."

"I know, Andrea told me."

We hug again for the longest time.

"Have you been in to see her?" He asks.

"I've been in twice. She was awake the first time and although she didn't look very well, her attitude is really positive. The second time she was asleep, so Don and I just sat with her."

"Will you come with me to see her?" He asks.

"I can't, Joe. They only allow one person at a time because she's in Intensive Care."

"We'll sneak, come on." He says this with a sly smile on his face so I take the challenge. After we're sure Don is still asleep, we leave to go see Andrea.

We start walking down the corridor like we're on some kind of secret spy mission. Joe makes me take the lead because I know where the room is. He pulls a ski cap and some sunglasses out of his pocket. He hands me the hat and puts the glasses on himself.

"What is this?" I ask.

"We don't want to call attention to ourselves, this is our

disguise."

"Joe, I think a ski hat and sunglasses in a hospital will call plenty of attention to us. What the hell are you doing with these anyway?"

"I always carry them in case I don't want people to recognize me or if I want to avoid the paparazzi. Put the damn hat on, where's your sense of adventure?" He asks.

I reluctantly put the ski hat on, and once it's on my head I realize it's the kind that goes completely over your face with eye, nose and mouth holes.

"Oh, hell no. I am not wearing this."

Joe gives me a pouty look, so I put the mask over my face and continue walking down the hallway. We see a nurse coming and Joe opens the first door we come to and we run inside to hide. It's really dark inside and I think it's a storage room of some sort. Joe and I are face to face in the dark; we're both breathing heavy and trying to stifle our laughter. He leans in to kiss me and it feels so good. How could I have ever turned this away? His hands start trying to remove my ski mask while we keep on kissing and we get tangled and laugh. When he finally peels off the mask, I feel his hands go to the back of my head while he starts playing with my hair.

"I missed you, Angel." He whispers.

He did it again. He called me Angel. Maybe he calls everybody Angel. Maybe he called Olivia Angel. I'm not going to read too much into it even though every time he says it my stomach feels like I'm on a roller coaster. Is that love? Maybe I'm just sick from all the food Don made me eat.

"I missed you, too." I whisper back.

Joe ends the moment by opening the door a crack and letting some light in.

"The coast is clear." He says.

We start walking down the hall again, but this time we keep our hat and glasses off. When we reach Andrea's door it is open and we can see her sitting up in bed wide awake. As soon as I move out of the way so Joe can enter, a huge smile spreads across her face. I stand in the background while they embrace and Joe takes the seat by her bed. I take the seat by the window and look around Andrea's private room. Don was told that he would be allowed to sleep here with her if he'd like, and I know that will take away some feelings of his helplessness.

While I'm sitting watching Joe and Andrea talk, it brings back a lot of memories for me that I've stored neatly away for a long time now. When my father was dying of cancer, we had several similar visits to the hospital. The thing that stands out the most was how he always put on a brave face in front of me. I remember once walking to his room and before I got to the door, I heard him crying. I mean really, really crying. I walked in to try and comfort him, but as soon as he saw me, he sat up straight and put on a smile for me. I knew then that he was trying to hide his fears from me because he wanted to protect me. At that moment, I couldn't have loved him more. I made him scoot over in his bed and I got in with him. We lay like that for hours, talking, laughing and even falling asleep together. It is the single best memory of my father that I have.

I sit there quietly and catch little bits and pieces of what Andrea and Joe are saying to one another. They're whispering and I don't know why. It seems everybody whispers in hospitals when somebody is sick. I catch her telling him something about how him and I look positively glowing. Do I look glowing? I hope I do. I excuse myself from the room and find the exit to make some phone calls. The first person I call is my mom and thankfully she answers. I fill her in about Andrea and Joe and she tells me that she and Daniel watched the morning show and she is proud of me. This is too much. I think I'm starting to like her. Next I call Dee to find out how everything is going at the home office. She sounds really concerned about me and then it turns into excitement when I tell her about Joe. I ask her opinion about the whole "Angel" thing and she thinks Hollywood-types call everybody by those kind of names, so I shouldn't read too much into it yet. Even though this bums me out, I'm going to take her advice. I also ask her to call Frankie and fill her in because I want to get back inside the hospital.

When I get back to the waiting room, Don is awake. I tell him that Joe is in with Andrea and he says, "Good" and winks at me. I wonder if the winking is a Hollywood thing because I've been winked at more times in the last couple of weeks than I can count. We start talking about all the new friends we've made in the past couple of weeks and how they've changed our lives. I share with him the news about my mom's new boyfriend Daniel and how much her disposition has changed since he came around. I also tell him that I liked Andrea from the second I met her and that I never had any hesitation about doing the casket for her.

Don asks me if I have ever read Kurt Vonnegut's *Cat's Cradle*. I tell him that I haven't and ask him why.

"Because in his book he talks about a 'carass.' It's when people, very mismatched, different people are brought together and they feel an affinity towards one another. They don't even know why, they just do. I think Andrea, Joe, you and I – We're all part of a carass."

It was the most perfect way to describe us and I wanted to tell him that. To thank him for clarifying what I've been trying to articulate for a while now. Before I have a chance to respond to him, Joe appears in the waiting room and he and Don shake hands.

"Why don't you two go ahead and go for the night," Don says. "I'm going to stay here with Andrea and if anything happens, I'll call you. It should be fine, though. You go on home and get some sleep."

We all hug good-bye and Joe and I get on the elevator to leave the hospital.

"How did you get here from the airport? And is that all you brought with you?" I ask him this because he's holding a small duffle bag. If I were going on a trip it would probably be the equivalent of my make-up case.

"I took an Uber from the airport and yes, this is all I brought with me. I don't need much. If I run out of clothes, I'll buy some more."

"Where are you staying? Do you have Andrea's house keys?"

"No. I'll just check into a hotel. Can you recommend one

close?" He asks.

"Yeah, I can. How about a cute, little, three story walk up in Little Italy?"

"Are you sure?" Joe doesn't know if I'm joking or not.

"I'm positive." I say and he grabs my hand as we try to hail a cab.

Once we get in the cab, Joe starts talking on his phone to his agent so I grab mine and call Dee praying she is still at my house. As soon as she picks up I try to whisper as loud as I can because I don't want Joe to hear me.

"Is my house clean?" I ask.

"What? Mia? I can't hear you."

"Issss myyyy house cleeeeeean?" I ask.

"You're with a queen? Who is this queen, Mia?"

Oh brother! This isn't going as planned. I look over at Joe and he's deep in conversation so I change tactics. This time I blurt it out loud enough for her to hear but very quickly so maybe Joe won't catch it.

"I still don't know what you're saying about some queen. Just bring her here, Mia. I'll straighten up for you."

I hang up. I just don't know what to say to that. Where would I ever meet a queen and why would I bring her to my house? Joe looks over at me and I smile.

CHAPTER TWENTY-FOUR

As soon as we pull up in front of my apartment, the paparazzi come out.

"Did you ever stop to think that your agent or your publicist is telling these people we're here so you get in the tabloids?" I ask.

"They wouldn't do that to me."

"I just think it's too much of a coincidence to have happened twice already, Joe."

We start walking up the stairs and Joe asks me when my birthday is.

"May ninth. Why?"

"Because I'm going to buy an elevator for your building as your birthday present." He says completely out of breath. "Do you think the other tenants would mind?"

"Why don't you just buy the whole building and then they won't have a choice."

"Would they sell to me?" He asks.

I roll my eyes at him and keep walking up the stairs. I suppose if I'm going to be dating him I'll have to get used to how much money he has. When we finally make it to my apartment I am amazed at how it looks. It's only been about twenty minutes since I called Dee, but the place is immaculate. There is a huge vase of fresh flowers on the dining room table, one on the coffee table and another in the kitchen. Dee has pulled open all the shades, so the last of the setting sun is coming through. She's sitting on the couch with her hands folded in her lap looking like a proper schoolgirl.

"Hi Dee. You remember Joe."

"Of course. Hello Joe. Nice to see you again. All these flowers came for you today, Mia."

"Who are they from?" I ask.

"The cards are next to them, I didn't open the envelopes. Where is this queen, Mia?"

Oh God. That's why she was sitting that way.

"Joe, why don't you take a seat and make yourself comfortable. I'm going to go with Dee in the office so we can wrap up for the day." I move my head in exaggerated motions towards the office and Dee looks confused, but starts to follow me. As soon as we're inside I shut the door.

"There is no queen, Dee. I was asking if MY HOUSE WAS CLEAN because I was bringing home Joe. He was in the car with me and I was trying to whisper."

Her face turns red and then we both start laughing. After Dee and I are done in the office, she takes a seat on the couch with Joe and I look at the cards that came with my flowers. The first card is from my mom and Daniel congratulating me on my talk show appearance. The second one is from Dee thanking me for her new job and also congratulating me. The third one is from Andrea, and the card makes me cry. It reads: *There are people that cross your path in life and you know immediately that they will be your friend. I am proud to call you my friend. Congratulations on your much deserved success!* I show the card to Joe and Dee and it makes Dee cry, too.

"I can't wait to meet her; she seems like such a wonderful person."

"She is, Dee. She wants to meet you, too. I told her all about you and she said you sound like her kind of girl. How about I make dinner for all of us? Is everybody hungry?" I ask.

"I'm starving." Says Joe.

"I've got a date with Drake tonight. It's one of his only two nights off work this week so I'm excited to see him. Do you need me tomorrow, Mia?" Asks Dee.

"No way! It's Saturday. Thanks so much for this week, Dee. I can't tell you how grateful I am that you're here helping me now. And thank you for the flowers, I love them."

"You're welcome, Sweetie. I'll call you later. Bye, Joe. Nice to see you again."

Joe waves good-bye and I walk Dee to the door.

"Well, do you want some wine while I cook? Do you like music? Jesus, I don't know anything about your likes and dislikes."

"I would love a glass of wine if you have it. I love any kind of music, my taste is really eclectic, and we have forever to figure out each other's likes and dislikes. I know, how about for every question we ask one another, the other has to answer it, too?"

"Okay. I love wine; I don't care if it's red or white. My favorite drink is champagne and once a year on my birthday I splurge on a bottle of Cristal. I love every type of music as well, and you should know right now that I have a cat named Bob walking around here somewhere."

"I hate cats." Joe says.

"Me, too!" I say very excitedly. "I really do. I was bullied into taking this one. I love that you hate cats. Want to meet him?" I ask.

Joe looks at me like I'm crazy and nods his head yes. I start calling for Bob but he won't come so I pull out his cat food, it's time to feed him dinner anyway. I snap the lid and he appears quick as a flash from absolutely nowhere.

"Bob, this is Joe. Joe, meet Bob."

"Bobcat. Very clever. Did you think of that?" Joe asks.

"I did. All by myself." I answer proudly.

I feed Bob his dinner and get the wine out for Joe and I. I hand him the bottle so he can open the cork while I try to find an appropriate play list for the night. Joe pours the wine and hands me a glass.

"I want to make a toast," he says. "To forgiveness."

"To forgiveness." I answer back.

We clink glasses and he kisses me again. I'm not sure I'll even be able to cook dinner if he keeps kissing me like this.

"Cute t-shirt." He says, while taking off my suit jacket.

"Thanks. Dee made it especially for my morning show appearance today."

"Has Dee always worked for you?" He asks.

"No, she just started this week. I think that *US* Magazine article took my business over the top and it's the first time I've needed help. Did you see that article?"

"I don't read that shit." He says, while now trying to lift my t-shirt over my head.

I slowly move his hands away. "How about dinner first?"

He smiles and kisses the tip of my nose. He smells and feels so good I almost say fuck dinner and drag him into my bedroom so he can do the same to me. I don't know why I want to wait a little longer, but I do. I'm sure it will happen tonight at some point, but I'm not ready for it to happen right now. I want to share a little more with him before I share my bed. I was going to make a shrimp dish to bring with me to Andrea's tomorrow night, but since that's not going to happen, I use the shrimp for scampi instead. I put a bottle of Pinot Grigio in ice to chill while I cook, and then I go back in the living room to join Joe. He's turned the television on and he's browsing through my TiVo. When he sees me, he looks up and smiles.

"Do you have something to tell me?" He asks.

I look guilty because he's found my recorded reality show stash. Both Frankie and Dee know about my addiction, but nobody else does.

"I have a problem." I say and smile.

"I would say so," he says jokingly. "I'm afraid I have a confession to make as long as we're exposing secrets."

"I think that's only fair. Considering you exposed mine for me." I say.

"Okay, in the past ten years, I've never missed an episode of 'Hope for Tomorrow.' And before the ridiculing begins, I need to tell you why. When I was younger and still living at home, my grandmother got sick and came to live with us. It was her favorite soap opera and every day after school I would sit with her and watch it."

"That's so sweet," I say. "Is that really true?"

"No. No." Joe starts to smile. "It was the best I could do for an excuse. My Grandma is 82 and fit as a fiddle."

We both start laughing and I swat his leg with my palm. I leave the living room to go check the pasta and scampi. I'm having such a good time. I feel like Joe belongs here right now. My worries for Andrea are on the back burner until I can go see her again tomorrow. Like Don said, there's nothing that we can do and he'll call us if anything should happen. I set the table with candles and leave the flowers on it because they look so beautiful. I'm grateful John didn't steal my dishes and silverware. When everything is ready, I call Joe in for dinner.

He's impressed both with my cooking skills and how romantic everything is. I don't even feel a hint of nervousness, in fact, I'm very relaxed and I'm sure the wine is helping. After dinner, Joe helps me do the dishes and we laugh and talk the whole time. He tells me about the new movie he has already signed on for that he's going to start shooting in Los Angeles. He also tells me what a relief it is that he won't be working on location in some other state or country; he likes to be close to home. It gets me thinking about what our future is going to hold when Joe has to leave and go back to Los Angeles. I try to put it in the back of my mind so I can enjoy the time we have together now.

When the dishes are washed and dried, we grab the second bottle of wine and go to my bedroom. Joe compliments my new headboard and I gloat. I excuse myself to the bathroom to freshen up and stop at my dresser to slide my La Perla panties and bra under my shirt. These panties and bra cost what a woman's yearly lingerie tab should be, but I couldn't resist. Especially since Dee was with me telling me that La Perla is all she wears. I'm glad I bought them now, and that I finally have an opportunity as special as tonight to wear them. I'm also glad that I had that morning show interview today because I shaved my legs last night even though I wore pants. I change quickly and put my clothes back over the La Perla items. I'm looking around for a place to hide my other bra and panties, but there is no hamper in my bathroom. I open up the cupboard and stuff them in between one of the guest towels that nobody uses, not even my guests. Next, I brush my teeth, floss, smell my underarms just to make sure and freshen my face powder. I'm afraid he's going to have fallen asleep waiting so I go back to the bedroom.

Joe is sitting on my bed and he's lit all the candles in my room and turned off the lights. He's found some soft, slow music on the iPad he has playing in the background. The seduction scene before me is too much, and you know how when men are very excited, they can't hold it? I'm afraid that will be my downfall tonight. It's been a while since I've had sex and I don't think I've ever been attracted to someone as much as I am to Joe. I walk towards him and he stands up and hands me a glass of wine.

"I'd like to make a toast now." I say.

Joe raises his eyebrows and says, "Go for it, Angel."

"I want to toast to make-up sex."

"Don't you think you need to have regular sex before you can have make-up sex?" He asks.

"Is this your toast?" I ask sarcastically.

"Um, no. It's not. Continue, please."

"Well, would you like to have sex, get into an argument, make-up and then have sex again?" I ask him.

"I would. Should we choose the argument now?"

"No, because then I'll be thinking of how I'm going to support my position the whole time we're having the first sex." I say starting to giggle now.

"Okay, I've got it," he says. "A toast. To new sex, a good, unspecified brawl and make-up sex to follow."

We clink glasses, take a drink and fall all over one another. It's all very soft and sensual, yet there's still an urgency to it that I love. I know I've said this before, but he smells so damn good. I lift up my arms so he can pull my t-shirt over my head and he returns the favor by helping me unbutton his. When he finally takes off his shirt, I have to use all of my strength not to moan out loud. He has the most beautiful body I have ever seen. It's exactly like it looks in the movies. I always thought that was special effects and make-up, but it's his real body. Holy shit! We both start to unbutton each other's pants at the same time we're trying to kiss and it causes confusion making both of us laugh out loud.

We're down to only our underwear and we're lying on top of the comforter kissing. I'm trying to clear my mind and just enjoy this moment. There's been so much that has happened today that it's hard for me not to mix parts of it into my thinking process. I feel Joe's mouth moving from my neck down to my chest, and suddenly all the other things that were on my mind go straight out the window. He starts licking around my nipples and gently pinching them at the same time. My hands are gripping his head so tight that I think I might make his ears bleed. When he finally puts his tongue on my nipples, I really let go and moan out loud. By the way, this is through material – My bra is still on. I'm afraid of what's going to happen when his mouth is on actual skin.

He starts to slowly take my bra straps down and I'm thinking about screaming, but I hold it in. Thank God, because as he's removing my bra straps, his mouth starts working downward and the next thing I know, he's kissing my belly button. Now I should scream. Now I need to scream. He slides my panties down and oh-my-God. Forget about me making his ears bleed; I think I just squeezed his brains out of his head. He stays down there long enough for me to throw all caution aside and say, "Inside me. Now!"

When he finally enters me, it's amazing. I feel complete and satisfied before we even move. We sit there for a moment, just feeling each other's warmth and our bodies so connected.

"I missed you." He says again.

"I missed you, too."

We start kissing as he slowly moves inside of me. I have to push his mouth away because my moaning is superseding the kissing. I'm loud in bed, I can't help it. It lasts just long enough. Right between the time when you say, 'just come already' and the time when you're thinking, 'is that it?' The wine intensified my orgasm and my whole body is tingling as he slides out of me. We both lie on our backs out of breath, and he takes my hand and entwines it with his. After we rest up for a while we take a shower together and Joe wants to have sex again. Obviously he forgot our agreement, so I start it.

"You're an asshole!" I scream.

"What are you talking about? What did I do?"

I whisper to him that this is our fight.

"Oh, okay. You selfish, um, you selfish Susan."

"What are you? Two years old? You can do better." I encourage him.

"Okay. Okay. You selfish, ignorant, cheat! How's that?" He asks.

"Are you sure you're an actor?"

"Now that's low. But I forgive you. Are we made up now?"

I nod my head yes and we have make-up sex in the shower. After drying off we share some Ben & Jerry's ice cream and fall asleep. We wake up once more during the night to have sex again and I feel like it's a dream. I'm afraid when I wake up in the morning, my bed will be empty and I will have imagined this whole thing happened. I'm happier then I've been in months and I really, really want it to last. I want it to be real.

When I wake-up, Joe is still here, lying in my bed with me. I smile at him and shoo Bob away before he wakes him up looking for

213

an early breakfast. I hear a noise in the living room and before I'm able to get out of bed, Frankie appears in my bedroom doorway. She practically skids on the hardwood floor when she sees Joe in my bed and she starts jumping up and down doing a silent dance, spilling the coffees in her hands. I motion her out of the room and get up and put a robe on. When I walk into the living room, her mouth is wide open and she's quietly trying to scream.

"How did that happen?" She asks.

"He came to the hospital to see Andrea and we made up." I'm smiling from ear to ear as I say this. "Didn't Dee call and tell you he was here?" I ask.

"Um, no she didn't. I'm so happy for you! How was it?"

"It was so romantic and perfect, exactly what I would have wished for if you asked me my fantasy come true."

"Oh God, Mia. That's so great!"

Frankie reaches over and hugs me. I'm so glad that I have friends like Frankie and Dee that I can share this with.

"Did you sleep at Charlie's?" I ask.

"We didn't sleep." She whispers.

"Frankie!" I take a deep intake of breath and ask, "How was it?"

"Almost exactly what you just described, but not quite as many times."

Now it's my turn to hug Frankie.

"So, now do you believe me that he's not gay?" I ask.

"Oh, honey, he is so NOT gay."

Frankie and I talk for a couple more minutes and make a

tentative plan to share all the juicy details later tonight. I walk her to the door, feed Bob and go back to join Joe in the bedroom. He's sitting up and he smiles when I walk in. I just stand in the doorway staring at him. I put my hands behind my back and pinch my arm. Good, it's real. He moves back the covers so I can get back under and we cuddle and kiss the rest of the morning.

CHAPTER TWENTY-FIVE

I call FedEx and reschedule the pick up/drop off for tomorrow because Joe and I want to get back to the hospital as early as possible. We grab a quick lunch and head over to see Andrea with the paparazzi on our tail. I showed Joe the shirt and the note Olivia had sent to me. He was really upset about it, but he loved what Dee had written so I wore it for the day. It was fun thinking about dishing out a little bit of well-deserved revenge. When we reach the hospital, the security won't let the cameras inside and both Joe and I are grateful. Joe tells me on our way up in the elevator that the good thing about the paparazzi is they don't usually ask any questions; they just want to take your picture.

Don is in the waiting room when we arrive and he looks really happy to see us.

"They're letting her go," he says with a smile. "She's going to start treatment on Monday. The doctor says it will probably get worse before it gets better, but he also said she has a wonderful attitude which is a huge part of it. Why don't you go on in and help her get ready to go, Mia. Joe and I will wait here."

I kiss him on the cheek and make my way to Andrea's room. I peek through the door and she is still lying in bed with a nurse leaning over her.

"Knock, knock?"

Andrea peeks her head around the nurse and smiles at me.

"Hi Mia. I'm so glad you're here."

I walk over to her bed and the nurse finishes up taking her vitals and leaves.

"I hear you're leaving today?" I ask.

"I am. I'm going to start getting ready now. Can you help me?"

"Of course."

I help Andrea out of bed and grab her clothes that are hanging up so she can change. She seems a little bit weak, but in very good spirits.

"The paparazzi followed Joe and I here today, Andrea, so do you want me to make you up a little bit in case they're still waiting outside?"

"That would be great, but I have nothing with me. Do you have any make-up or anything in your bag?" She asks.

"I happen to have make-up and a scarf for you. I always carry a scarf because my hair is so long and my friend Dee drives a convertible. You never know when you're going to need it."

After Andrea is done changing, I help her with her hair and make-up. She actually looks pretty good, but she's worried about people viewing her as helpless because hospital policy calls for her to leave in a wheel chair.

"I have an idea," I say. "Why don't Joe and I go first and they'll follow us. The paparazzi have no idea who Joe is here visiting and they certainly don't know that you're getting released today even if they have a hunch it's you. After we leave, they'll come chase us and you and Don will be free to go in peace."

"Oh, Mia. I love it. Thank you so much. I would really

appreciate that. Will you both come back to my house? Don and I will meet you there in about an hour?"

"Sure." I give her a kiss and start to leave.

"Mia?" She asks.

I turn back around.

"I wanted to know if I could talk to you about something important to me when we get to my house. Is that okay?"

"Sure. Anything you need, Andrea. I'll see you there."

Now she has my curiosity peaked about what she could possibly need to talk to me about. Maybe she didn't like the way the casket turned out. Maybe she's changed her mind about the treatment. I have no idea and I try to put it out of my head before I see Joe and Don in the waiting room. I tell them my plan and Joe and I leave Don to take care of Andrea. As soon as we walk out the hospital door, the paparazzi are all over us. It's the first time ever that Joe and I are actually pleased to see them and have them follow us.

We walk a couple of blocks down the street looking for a place to have a coffee and relax. We find a café and make sure all the paparazzi are in tow before taking a seat outside. Joe goes in and gets us our drinks while I enjoy the sunshine and try to ignore the crowd of people surrounding me. It doesn't take long for them to start asking questions after they realize they have me alone. 'What does your t-shirt mean?' 'Are you and J.B. an item now?' 'Who were you visiting in the hospital today?' I'm so relieved when Joe comes back that I almost kiss him in front of everyone. Wasn't he just telling me that they didn't ask questions?

We drink our coffee slowly, and sometimes we just look at each other and laugh. We know that even though the paparazzi think they're getting the photo opportunity of a lifetime, we're actually getting one over on them. The longer the paparazzi stay, the more annoyed I become, and I really have to respect Joe for dealing with this every time he leaves the house.

After we feel like we've been there long enough for Andrea and Don to make their escape, we start walking back to the hospital. We're whispering to one another about what our plan is going to be so they don't follow us back to Andrea's once we get in the car.

"I can lose them." I offer.

"Okay Dale Earnhardt, Jr., I don't think so." Joe says with a smirk.

"Listen. I've lived here for a long time and I know my way around San Francisco very well. I got this."

"You got this?" He asks.

"Yeah, don't you trust me?"

"I trust you, Mia. I just don't want to play Fast and Furious today."

"Good. You trust me. It's decided. Let's go."

We get into my car and immediately all the paparazzi start running towards their vehicles. We already have a head start because the hospital parking lot is fairly large and they've got to find their cars, get inside, and then find us again. I pay for parking and drive onto the street. So far, so good. We get about a block away from the hospital and out of nowhere comes a lone paparazzi in his car, he's driving like a crazy man.

"Alright, Earnhardt. You're up." Joe says.

I start to speed up and take a sharp right, but he stays on my tail. I slow back down to a normal speed and eventually, when the time is right, I will sharp turn it again. I come to a stop sign and look in my rear view mirror to find that he's waving at me. Now I'm pissed off.

"Do you see that, Joe? He's waving at us. What an asshole!"

Joe just laughs. After the stop sign I check to see if the streets are all clear, there are only two or three other cars on the road. There is a double yellow line, so making a u-turn at this point would be highly illegal. Fuck it. I'm going for it.

"Joe, hold on." I say as I crank the wheel and do a u-turn in the middle of the street. I start barreling down the road at about twice the speed limit and make another sharp right turn, and then a sharp left turn. I'm not even paying attention to see if he's still behind me, I'm too focused on the road and on not getting into an accident.

The place where we've ended up happens to be a dead end. I look around and we're alone. Joe and I start laughing and high five one another. I make him admit that he was wrong to doubt me and then I gloat the entire way to Andrea's house.

"You could have gotten us killed." Joe says when he can't stand my gloating any longer.

"I wasn't thinking about that. I was thinking about protecting Andrea's privacy. I'm going to talk to her about getting a security gate."

"That's a good idea. I live in a gated community and I have my own security gate as well. I don't take any chances. They might be able to finagle their way past the security guard, but they won't be able to get onto my property."

I never even thought about the fact that Joe owns a house. I start to imagine what it might look like. He's got a whole other life back in Los Angeles that I know nothing about. It actually makes me feel nauseous. I want to ask him about it, but I don't know if that will make me more upset or not. What am I getting into?

"Hey," Joe says. "Are you okay? You look sort of pale all of a sudden."

"I'm fine." I lie. "I guess I'm just a little shaken up by my own driving, that's all."

We arrive at Andrea's house before Andrea and Don do, so we spend some time talking in the car and listening to music.

"Joe?" I ask. "What is your house like? What city do you live in?"

"I live in Beverley Hills and my house is really beautiful. I only just recently purchased it and it's almost completely empty. I have a nice bedroom set and I had a smaller room turned into a closet. I'm not big on buying a lot of clothes, but I like what I have to be organized. I have no living room furniture and there is nothing in my kitchen. It's kind of sad, actually. Want to come decorate it for me?" He asks.

"How do you know I have any decorating sense?"

"I've seen your apartment, it's gorgeous. Do you own your place?"

"I do." I say. "Kind of. I put a down payment on it and I have a mortgage."

For some reason I feel a bit inferior for a moment.

"What did you pay?" He asks.

Wow! Now I feel really weird. I don't want to answer that question. What a strange question to ask me. How do I get out of this? I guess my hesitation throws up a red flag for him because he looks over at me and raises his eyebrows.

"Was that too personal a question?" He asks.

"Not if you're my accountant." I answer, and hope for a laugh. He does laugh and I'm very grateful. I'm even more grateful when Andrea and Don pull up and put an abrupt end to our conversation.

We all go into the house and Don starts to make margaritas. I've learned by now that margaritas are Andrea's favorite drink. When I tell her that mine is champagne, she has Don pull out a bottle of chilled Cristal for me. At first I want to refuse because I don't know how I feel about drinking a bottle of five hundred dollar champagne. But, if she happens to have a bottle chilling, I'm game.

"Don and I have all this food and drink from the dinner party that was supposed to happen tonight. So, please, have dinner with us. We called and cancelled with the catering company but I had already fixed most of the hors d'oeuvres myself and stocked up on beverages."

"We'd love to." I say and look at Joe for confirmation. He nods his head yes.

We spend the rest of the afternoon outside in the sun talking, drinking and eating various hors d'oeuvres. When it grows dark and the backyard lights come on, Andrea takes my hand and asks if I will come inside with her. I get up and follow her into the living room. I'm starting to get that nervous, nauseous feeling back wondering what is going to happen.

"First, I want to say thank you so much for coming here today, for everything that you've done for me, and for everything that you've become to me in such a short period of time."

"You don't have to thank me, Andrea. I love being here and spending time with you."

"I'm glad you love spending time with me, because that leads me to the second thing I wanted to say. You know that I have no family. The family that I do have are my friends, and I'm proud to say that you're now part of my family. With that said, here is what I need to ask you. Don came here to spend a day or two catching up with his son and to take a little vacation. He had no idea that he would end up developing an attraction to me and staying as long as he has. He needs to go back home for a couple of days and get things sorted out before he can come stay here indefinitely. I don't want to be alone, especially since I will be starting treatments again on Monday. I know this is a huge favor to ask of you, but would you come and stay with me?"

"That's it? That's what you wanted to ask me?" I ask. "Of course I will, don't say another word about it. I thought it was going to be something terrible. I'm so relieved. Don't even think about it for another second. It's done," I answer.

"I need to tell you that it won't be easy, Mia. I'm going to be sick most of the time because of the treatments. I've hired a whole slew of nurses who will be here around the clock for my health needs, but I need somebody here for me emotionally right now. I'm so sorry to put you in this position." Andrea is crying now.

"Andrea, don't cry. You are not putting me in any position except for one that I am happy to be in. Please don't think you're putting me out in any way. I have Dee at home doing some work for me now and I can bring my things and do some work here. But I think that Joe was going to be staying with me while he was here, do you mind if he stays, too?" I ask.

"Of course. That was going to be my next question, if you wanted him to come and stay, too. I haven't told you yet how happy I am to see you two together. I'm happy that you worked out your differences."

"Me, too. It's all so much for me right now that I'm just trying to take it one day at a time. I don't have any expectations, but I also have every expectation. Does that make any sense?" I ask.

"Yes, it does. You want to protect yourself and not get hurt, but you still want to be able to enjoy what's happening. I know exactly how you feel. You've got to decide if you want to jump in head first and go all out taking a big risk, or if you want to just dip your toes in and test the waters first."

"What do you suggest?"

"I've always been a jump in head first type of girl myself." She says, and we both start laughing. "I know myself and I know that if I decide to dip my toes in first, I might decide that it's too cold and never try something that might turn out to be the best risk I've ever taken."

I sit on what she's said a while. It's so insightful and brave of her. I would love to be able to live my life that way. Even though Andrea has had a lot of ups and downs, she's really lived. I see that now and I'm even more enamored of her than I was before. We get up and join Joe and Don back outside to tell them what we were talking about. Don hugs and kisses me and won't stop thanking me for being his stand-in for a couple of days. Joe is the one who looks a little bit apprehensive and I can't figure out why. Don and Andrea start clearing the table and argue with us until we give in not to help them do the dishes. As soon as they are both inside, I try to find out why Joe is acting strange now.

"Are you okay, Joe? Is it okay if we stay here for the next couple of days?" I ask.

"Yes, I'm okay with that, but I need to tell you something Mia." He hesitates and I just stare at him, willing him to finish.

"What's up, Joe?"

"I'm actually leaving the day after tomorrow. I start filming next week and I need to be back in Los Angeles."

I don't know what to say to that. I'm just wondering why he didn't tell me this sooner. I'm trying to distinguish between whether or not having sex is dipping your toes in, or if I've already dived in head first. I want to ask him how we're going to make this work, but I also don't want to jump to any conclusions about this relationship and scare him away. I think I've already made the dive, because I feel like I'm in way over my head. The only thing I can think to do is play it cool.

"Okay, that's fine. I just didn't know when you were leaving again."

Joe doesn't respond to that and Andrea and Don come back outside. Andrea looks tired so I tell her that I'm tired myself and thank her and Don for everything. I'm in such a strange position because I'm not sure if Joe is coming back to my house with me tonight. I don't even know how to ask him. Shouldn't he just be getting up with me to go? I start kissing and hugging Andrea and Don good-bye and Joe still hasn't made any movement to come with me.

"Your things are at my house, Joe." I say, trying to get him to do something. To say something.

He looks up at me with those big, beautiful eyes and I feel like crying. What is happening right now? One minute we're a happy couple and the next minute he's completely unreadable. He keeps looking at me like he's waiting for me to say something more, and I keep looking at him like I'm waiting for him to get his ass up and come with me.

"I'll be fine without my bag for the night." He finally says, and it's the last thing I wanted to hear. I quickly walk over to him, give him a kiss on the cheek and say goodnight. I tell Andrea and Don that I will walk myself out and thank them again. I practically run to my car to avoid anyone seeing my tears. As soon as I'm in my car I pull out my phone and call Dee. When she answers there is music in the background and it's so loud I can barely hear her.

"Dee, I need to talk. Can you talk now?"

"Mia, I can't hear you. Talk louder." She screams.

"AUNTIE EM! NOW! MY HOUSE! CALL FRANKIE!" I hang up and start my car. I drive home crying the entire way. When I get to my apartment, a miracle happens. There's an actual parking spot right out in front. I'm about to get out of the car when I remember the paparazzi. I start looking around and I don't see anyone, so I get out. The second I close my door; somebody pops out of the bushes and starts taking photographs. The flashes are really blinding when they are that close to your face and I'm fumbling to find my front door key. I'm positive that my face is tear stained and I do the only thing I can think of, which is to guard it with my purse. God bless Louis Vuitton's big ass Neverfull. I find the key and as soon as I'm through the door, I run up the steps. What do these people want? Joe and I gave them carte blanche this afternoon but they still come back for more. How many pictures do they need?

I feel like a three year old as I throw myself on my bed face down. It just makes me cry harder because the bed smells like Joe. What the hell happened tonight? I just don't get it. Did I do something today to change his mind about me? Maybe this was it. Maybe he just wanted to have sex with me and I was right about him. I so didn't want to be right about him and I can't help feeling that I deserve this. I should have known better than to sleep with him last night. If I keep going from extremely elated to depressingly sad I'm going to need an anti-depressant soon.

I hear a noise and look up to see Frankie standing in the door of my bedroom. She's wearing one of Charlie's t-shirts and I can tell that Dee's phone call probably disturbed something.

"What the hell happened?" She asks.

I can't follow the rules tonight; I have to get this off my chest even though Dee isn't here yet.

"I don't know, Frankie. I don't understand it. It was so strange."

"Why don't you start from the beginning?" Frankie urges.

"Why don't you fucking wait for me?" Dee says, appearing behind Frankie.

They both get on my bed and I tell them everything. When I'm done spilling my guts, they both have nothing different to offer in terms of an explanation. They ask the same questions that I've been asking myself. Nobody wants to jump to the conclusion that he's just an asshole and maybe it just is what it is, maybe he just used me. Well, if Frankie and Dee are thinking that, at least they don't share it with me. I feel all cried out and very tired. My eyes hurt and I have a killer headache. There were no munchies or drinks tonight, just my best friends trying to make me feel better. It's late now and Frankie and Dee eventually get into bed with me. I'm not sure when exactly we all fell asleep, but having my girls here makes this the best night's sleep I've had in months.

CHAPTER TWENTY-SIX

When we all wake up the next morning, each one of us takes turns complaining about my one bathroom. I'm crazy enough trying to get ready in that small space alone, it's a disaster with three women at once. I'm still feeling depressed and confused after the girls' leave, so I go into my office to see how Dee has been doing and to get the packages ready for Eleni at noon. I check my e-mail first and go through my new orders. One of them is blank in the order section, but it has a lot of writing in the notes section. It's an e-mail from an agent of a huge rap group called *VIP*, apparently they want all three of their Bentleys blinged out with gems spelling their group name. They want it done for a video that is being made of their single that will be releasing soon. I'm very excited about the prospect of this job, because the agent is so detailed I can envision what he wants already. They're going to need all diamond solitaires for the writing and luckily for them, their group name is only three letters. He's left a phone number for me to contact him so I call right away.

My mood is considerably better when I hang up with Dave G., who is the group's agent. He was very personable and went into even more detail on the telephone. He did ask that I come to Los Angeles to do the work instead of having the cars driven out here. I agree after he offered to pay for all my traveling expenses. I told him that I would get back to him with an estimate by Monday evening after I went to go visit the Pappas Brother's. In the back of my mind I'm still hopeful that things between Joe and I will work out and I can combine business and a little vacation.

Eleni arrives, and as promised, I fill her in on all the details between Joe and I, all the way up until last night. Except unlike Frankie and Dee, Eleni finds something in the conversation that I missed.

"So, he tells you he's leaving the day after tomorrow, after you've finally apologized to one another and gotten your relationship back in check... And what do you say to him?" She asks.

"I told you, I decided to play it cool. I just said 'okay.'"

"Okay? Okay? You're telling me you just said, 'okay?' Oh girl, you're crazy. Now he thinks you don't give a shit that he's leaving for a couple of months. You didn't act sad? You didn't say that you would miss him and ask him when you would see him again?"

Oh God, I really blew it. I blew it again. This relationship is becoming a series of me just completely blowing it. I should have been myself and just said what I was feeling. He told Andrea the reason he likes me so much is because I'm so real and then I say something that was so far from what I was really feeling.

"I blew it again." I say to Eleni. Tears start to well up in my eyes even though I thought I was all cried out last night.

"No, you only temporarily knocked it out of whack. Tell me then, Mia, why did you act like you didn't care?" She asks.

"Because I didn't want him to see my weakness. To see how much I care about him and how much I would really miss him." I answer truthfully.

"Then the first thing you need to do is figure out if you're in this

230

for real or not. Because if you are, there should be no reason to hold back anything from him. In other words, shit or get off the potty. That's what my momma always says. Do this thing or don't, but don't do it half-ass. The second thing you need to do after you make your decision, is both tell him the truth and try to work it out. Or tell him good-bye, stop wasting his time, and walk away."

Eleni left me with a lot to think about. I did need to make a decision and her words reminded me of Andrea's last night when she talked about diving in or dipping your toes. I keep thinking of Andrea and how she wants to live again because of love. I decide that I'm not going to dip my toes and test the water, I'm going headfirst and I'm going to give this all I've got. No more being afraid of getting hurt, I'm doing this and I'm doing it right. As soon as I've made up my mind, I start running around my apartment trying to pack as quickly as possible. I can't wait to see Joe, tell him everything, and pray that he forgives me. Again.

As soon as I'm out the door of my apartment, the paparazzi start taking photographs. I'm too focused to care and luckily my car is parked right in front from last night. It also doesn't hurt that even though I got dressed quickly, I look cute. I don't know if any of them are trying to follow me to Andrea's house, but I'm driving so fast I probably lost them if they were. I'm on a mission and I feel so liberated that I've made up my mind.

I screech into Andrea's driveway, grab my bag and make a run for her house. I don't even realize that I'm sweating until I ring the bell and have to wait for an answer. I'm actually dripping in sweat and all of a sudden, I don't want Joe to be the one to answer the door. He'll think I'm insane. Thankfully Don answers and I'm glad because he does look at me a bit strangely.

"Is it hot outside, Mia?" He asks.

"Don," I whisper. "Can I sneak in and use the bathroom?"

"You can, but whispering won't help you. We all heard the doorbell." He whispers back with a smile and motions me inside the house.

I pass by and on my way I give him a kiss on the cheek. When I get in the bathroom I freshen myself up and take a seat to catch my breath before I go out and join them. When I feel like I'm back to normal, I go out to the backyard and Don, Andrea and Joe are all sitting in the shade, having margaritas and enjoying the beautiful day we're having. As soon as I get to the table and lean down to give Andrea a kiss, she looks at Don and he nods at her.

"Come on, Big Guy," she says. "Let's go get your things packed."

I take a seat and Joe and I just sit there in silence staring at one another. I know that I have to start talking but I don't know where to begin. I can't believe I busted my ass to get here so fast and now Joe's right in front of me and I have no idea how to tell him what I want and need to say. I finally blurt something out, but Joe doesn't hear it because he began talking at the exact same time.

"What? What did you just say?" I ask. Because I'm almost positive I heard him, but I can't believe it. I need to hear it again.

"I said that I think I'm falling in love with you. But you run so hot and cold that I don't know how you feel about me. You need to tell me, to be honest with me, so that I can back away now if you're not feeling the same. You didn't even care when I told you that I had to leave soon. You seemed so distant, like it didn't even matter to you that we were going to be separated."

"Okay. I want to say this right, so bear with me." I take a deep breath. "I acted the way I did last night because I was afraid of showing you how much I care about you. I purposely acted like it didn't matter to me that you were leaving, even though my heart was breaking. Since the moment you first grabbed my hand when we were leaving that restaurant, I've always felt like you were going to end up hurting me. I've put up this guard with you to avoid getting close, and I don't want to be afraid anymore. I want to be with you and take my chances." I hesitate for a moment trying to gather up the courage to finish what I'm trying to say. "Because I think I'm falling in love with you, too."

Joe gets up and drags his chair next to mine so we can sit closer. He grabs my hand and kisses my fingers.

"I think we have to think of ways together how we're going to make this relationship work with the distance that's going to be between us. I'm only an hour away by plane, which means that even visiting one another for the day is possible. I just think that eventually we're going to want more, that's what I see as our biggest obstacle. Do you agree?" Joe asks.

"I do agree. Do you have any suggestions?"

"I could buy a private plane." Joe offers.

"Oh, um, no. That doesn't seem very practical or economical. Could you really afford to buy a private plane? I ask

"I think so. I don't know how much they cost. Why? Do you need money?" He asks.

I'm so taken back I don't know what to say. I know he's trying to be nice, but I've just never met anybody who was so open about money and who asked me so many financial questions.

"I need a million," I joke. "Can you do that?"

Joe kind of raises his eyebrows like he's considering it.

"Joe, I was kidding. Dear Lord, are you insane?" I laugh. "I'm just fine, thank you for offering. Listen, I don't have any long-term answers right now about how we're going to make the distance between us work out. But I wanted to tell you that *VIP's* agent and I talked today, he's going to fly me to Los Angeles to do some work for them as soon as Don gets back. So, we've already got our first visit taken care of."

"I'll be filming," Joe says contemplating the visit. "But I'll have the evenings off if it doesn't turn out to be fourteen hour days. That could work. Something is better than nothing. Will you stay with me when you come?" He asks.

"*VIP's* agent said they would pay for a suite for me, but I'll figure out what the distance is between the job and your house as soon as I know the details. What time does your plane leave tomorrow?"

"I take off at three. Why?"

"Do you want to come with me to order the gems for *VIP's* job?

I want you to meet these two brothers that I get all my genuine stones from. Then I'll drive you to the airport."

"Yeah, I'd like that." Joe says with a smile.

Andrea and Don reappear so we can say our good-byes. I offer to drive Don to the airport, but he's already requested an Uber. Joe and I stay outside while Andrea walks Don out and we're prepared for her to be a little sad when she comes back outside. She surprises us by her huge smile and great disposition.

"I'm excited for tomorrow. I'm not looking forward to my treatments, but I want to be well again. I know you both think I'm crazy with all the talking I do about Billy, but I think this is his work. The same way I thought God wanted me to finally be with Billy, I think Billy asked God to send me Don. Billy was never the selfish kind. And I don't think it was Don that changed my mind; I just think it was Don that made me see I wasn't ready to go."

I normally don't talk about God that often, and it's not that I don't believe God exists, because I do. I just normally get annoyed when people are overly religious and try to push their beliefs on you. With Andrea, I know it's different. She told me when you get really sick and you think you're going to die; you start to reassess not only your life, but also all of the things you thought you believed in. She said you have to try and figure out how God is playing a part in all of this. If her reasoning is what is keeping her motivated to get treatment right now, that is all I need to know.

We spend the rest of the afternoon lounging by the pool and taking turns trying out Andrea's canopy bed that is outside. It's wonderful, and because the weather is so nice, Andrea offers it to Joe and me for the night if we want to sleep outside. We accept, and both of us are looking forward to spending the night under the stars. I cook dinner for everyone and I'm overwhelmed by the response I get from Greek lemon chicken and rice. It's a dish that my Mother taught me to make, and even though I think it's one of my best, I've never had anyone that I cooked it for react like Andrea and Joe.

They insist on doing the dishes because I cooked, so I take my time alone to call Dee and update her on the situation with Joe and the new *VIP* deal. She's extremely excited about both and tells me that she will relay our conversation to Frankie. At the last minute I decide to ask Dee if she wants to come with me to Los Angeles and help with the *VIP* job. Since Joe will be working a lot it would be nice to have company, and for the first time ever, an assistant on a big job. Dee screams so loud that I have to hold the phone away from my ear. I'll take that as a yes.

The rest of the evening is lost in conversation, laughter and of course, margaritas. When Andrea retires for the evening, Joe and I stay outside enjoying our buzz and the warm evening air. I love Andrea's house. It's like a quiet, little oasis in the center of a very busy city. The neighborhood where I live is so crazy and loud all the time. It's one of the reasons I bought there, because of the noise. Growing up as an only child can be lonely and quiet. Sometimes the silence was so much that I wanted to scream just to hear another noise aside from my breathing. Frankie moving next door was my saving grace. Sometimes when we're alone, I'll reach out and just hug her. She always asks why I just did that and I always say the same thing, for moving next door and saving my existence.

When it's time for Joe and I to get in bed, I'm so excited I can hardly contain myself. The idea of sleeping with him again is enough to take me over the edge, but it seems so exotic that we're in a bed outside. I'm out of La Perla and wasn't expecting tonight to happen, so I'm thankful to be wearing Victoria's Secret bra and panties. They are both sexy and modest at the same time. Is that possible? Anyway, you know what I mean. Joe loves it. He doesn't tell me so; I figure it out because we end up making love two more times.

In the morning, the sun is shining so brightly and I wake up confused as to where I am. As soon as I open my eyes and look around, I smile at the memories of yesterday and last night. No wonder Andrea has a bed out here; it's like a dream. My arms reach over to grab Joe but he's not in bed with me anymore. I wonder what time it is. The sliding glass door opens and I sit up to see Joe coming towards me with a tray. He's brought me breakfast in bed and I have to pinch myself again under the covers.

"Good morning, Angel. You slept in later than Andrea so she got served first. Do you know what time it is?" Joe asks.

"Who cares," I say. "This is wonderful. Thank you so much. Did Andrea leave already?"

I can't believe the spread he's come out here with. There is a cheese omelet with feta cheese, country potatoes, bacon, toast and flowers on the tray. I love that he can cook and that he offers to help do the dishes.

"You're very welcome and Andrea is leaving in about an hour. But you and I need to get a move on after you're done eating if you want to take me to your jewelry store."

I finish eating my breakfast, shower and change in time to say good-bye to Andrea and assure her that I will be here when she gets back. She gives me the spare key and tells me the alarm code so I can go in and out myself. Joe and Andrea embrace for a long time because they know they won't see one another for at least a couple of weeks. I hear him whisper to her to be strong and that he needs her. She gently grabs his face in her hands and kisses him on the lips.

Andrea's limo driver comes to the door and we all walk out together. She leaves for her treatment and Joe and I go to visit Dominic and Vincenzio. It's so nice to leave Andrea's house and not be followed or photographed by the paparazzi. They seem to dig up everything, I'm sure it's only a matter of time before they figure out where Andrea lives, and that she's the one Joe is coming to visit.

As soon as Joe and I enter Pappas Brother's we're given their typical welcome that Joe is not accustomed to.

"Will youse take a fuckin' look at dis," says Dom. "Get out here, Enzo. We got a fuckin' celebrity in our establishment."

I whisper to Joe that they tend to curse a lot and that he'll either learn to get used to it, or he'll have to learn to ignore it. Joe nods his head and approaches Dominic and Vincenzio to shake their hands. They insist on an autograph and pull out their phones to have their picture taken with him. Through all the fuss, they haven't even said hello to me yet.

"Excuse me? What about your best fucking client?" I ask.

They turn their attention to me and start hugging me to help ease the blow. After everything settles down I place my diamond order for *VIP*. Dom and Enzo promise me that what isn't used can be returned. We say our good-byes and leave so I can get Joe to the airport on time. I'm already feeling a little bit sad and I think Joe senses it because we're both quiet on the ride and we hold hands the entire time.

I drop him off outside because he insists that he doesn't want me to park and walk him in. We kiss and hug in my car for about fifteen minutes until the airport security asks me to leave. I surprise myself by not crying as I'm driving away. Instead, I get caught up in an idea that probably won't work, but I think I'm going to try it anyway. I dig through my iPhone contacts until I find Uriah, the rapper slash mover's phone number. He remembers me right away and I ask him when his group is performing next. Looks like I've got someplace to go tonight.

CHAPTER TWENTY-SEVEN

The beginning of the week passes by quickly. Andrea is taking to her treatments really well and I don't think I've ever met someone as brave or dignified in my entire life. I get to know Andrea on a level that is so deep I feel connected to her even more than before. Every day when she leaves for the hospital, I go home and work with Dee. Don called yesterday and said he would be back Thursday, which is tomorrow, so Dee and I make reservations to fly out to Los Angeles tomorrow night.

Since Joe has been gone, we talk on the phone several times each day and FaceTime. Fortunately he's not working fourteen-hour days, so we might get to spend some quality time together while I'm visiting. Both Dee and I will be staying at Joe's house and he's hired a limo to pick us up from the airport. We told *VIP's* agent that we wouldn't be arriving until Monday, so Dee and I will have Friday together and hopefully Joe and I will have the weekend. I warned Dee beforehand that I want to spend as much time with Joe as possible, so she might be partly on her own. Dee told me not to worry about her, and for some reason, I'm not.

On Thursday afternoon, Don arrives back at Andrea's and I say my good-byes. Andrea warns me about the scene in Hollywood and tells me to take absolutely nothing literally. I thank her for the advice and tell her I will call her as soon as I get back. My first stop is home to meet up with Dee and do some work. We're making jackets for Uriah and "The White Boys" for free, as promised. When I get there, Dee has already started and I'm so grateful because we only have a couple of hours before we have to leave. I still have to pack, but Dee is so organized that she packed last night. It's not something I knew about her before. As soon as we're done with the jackets, I finish packing and we're ready to go.

We meet Uriah at the club I saw him rap at on Sunday night. He gives me the demo CD that I asked him for and begs me to tell him who I'm passing it on to. I refuse because I don't want to get his hopes up. I only stayed to watch his group for a couple of songs, but I was really impressed. I don't know why I want to help him, but I do. It might have to do with how I misjudged him upon first meeting him. I don't see any harm in handing *VIP's* agent their demo and asking him to listen. It can't hurt, and the odds of them being discovered otherwise is probably slim to none. Dee and I took a chance on the jackets and wrote "The White Boyz" instead of "The White Boys." Uriah loves both the slight name change and the jackets. I notice Dee is flirting with him unabashedly until I kick her under the table. Now that I know Uriah, I think he is very cute, but way too young for Dee, and she is still seeing Drake.

We're both crazy with excitement on the way to the airport. Neither one of us has ever been to Los Angeles for more than a day or so, and we can't wait. I have a free first class ticket and I treated Dee to one, too. She's really been working her ass off for me and even though I pay her well, it was nice to reward her with something extra. She actually got all of our current orders done before we left so we wouldn't be overwhelmed with work when we came back home. Dominic and Vincenzio are having the diamonds sent over by special high security courier at no extra charge. I wouldn't know what to do if I had to get the diamonds to Los Angeles myself; it was one thing off my mind to know they are taking care of it.

First class is another world. I've never flown first class and now that I'm here, I don't know if I could ever go coach again. Hot towels? Are you kidding me? Dee and I stare at each other and laugh after we're offered free champagne. My one seat seems as wide as a whole row in coach. The entire flight puts Dee and me into fits of giggles over everything and anything. We're just so happy and the other passengers find us contagious. We make friends just ten minutes into the flight, and the great conversation make the hour or so fly by. Get it? Fly by?

Of course we checked bags, because even though we're only here for a week, we both have two large suitcases. Each of us has left half of one of our bags empty because we're anticipating it will get filled from the numerous shopping trips we plan on taking. The limo driver is waiting for us with a sign that has my name on it, and for some reason, Dee and I find it amusing. He helps us with our bags once they come down the carousel and we ask him how long we have him for.

"Mr. Barrick advised me to take you wherever you would like to go and wait for you for as long as you wish." He answers.

"Wahoo!" Dee yells.

I look at the limo driver and say, "Rodeo Drive, baby."

He opens the door and we start looking for a champagne bottle before we're even seated.

"This is so nice of Joe, Mia. It must be expensive."

"Dee, when we were talking about how we were going to make the distance easier for our relationship he offered to buy a private plane. This limo is chump change."

We call Frankie and update her on our trip so far. We feel like we have tons to tell her already even though we just landed a couple of minutes ago. Frankie wanted to come with us but she's in the middle of planning a huge event right now and she couldn't get any time off. We tell her that we'll buy her a present from Rodeo Drive and take lots of pictures. Even though she's still sad that she's missing out, she seems happy that we thought of her enough to call upon landing.

Rodeo Drive is exactly like the movies portray it. Some of the most well-dressed women Dee and I have ever seen are walking around. If I wasn't having so much fun, I might feel out of place. Dee, of course, fits right in. She looks like she belongs here with her amazing looks and wonderful dress style. We hit about five stores and we're shocked by the prices. We end up buying one little thing each at Louis Vuitton. I got a matching key chain to my purse and Dee bought a checkbook cover.

When we get back in the limo it is almost five o'clock and I ask the driver to take us to a specific address. Dee looks at me confused and I tell her it's a surprise. I've made appointments for both of us with a well-known esthetician in Beverley Hills, and we're going to get our eyebrows shaped and waxed. Anastasia is famous for doing all the stars and Dee is ecstatic when we arrive. We both go in together and sit with one another while this amazing woman does wonders with our eyebrows. We're both really pleased when she is done, so I pay and tip generously.

We're meeting Joe at his house at six and the limo takes us to our final destination. I try to tip him also, but he refuses saying that Joe has taken care of everything. Dee and I step out of the limo and both of us gasp. Joe's house is truly a mansion. I remember Frankie and I as teenagers would drive around a very wealthy area called Hillsborough near where we lived. We would pick out which house we wanted to live in once we got rich. None of them came close to what I was looking at now.

"Um, Mia – Your boyfriend lives here." Dee says.

"He couldn't possibly. This isn't a home, it's a compound. How could one person live here alone? Do you really think he's my boyfriend?"

The limo driver is taking our bags out of the trunk and he laughs at what I say. Dee and I look over at him and laugh, too.

"Mr. Barrick advised me I was picking up his girlfriend and her companion, so I would say you are."

Dee looks over and winks at me. I look at the limo driver and he winks at me, too. It seems that people wink at me often and half the time I don't understand their winks. I wink back at the limo driver to see his reaction, but he just keeps on smiling. The driver escorts us to the door with two of our bags and we ring the bell while he goes back to the car to get the other two suitcases. I didn't even realize how much I had missed Joe these last few days until he opens the front door. He's standing there in a white t-shirt and a pair of faded jeans looking as handsome as ever. I practically throw myself on him and I'm overwhelmed by his smell and warmth. After I'm done mauling him, he gives Dee a hug and helps bring our bags inside. We all say goodbye to the driver and Joe closes the front door.

This place is seriously unreal. Joe gives us the grand tour and he was right about having absolutely no furniture yet. The floors are all hardwood and it looks like the only things he got around to buying are beautiful area rugs in almost every room. The ceilings are very high and there are so many windows allowing sunlight to stream through everywhere. Dee and I follow Joe oohing and aahing the entire time. We talk about how we would decorate certain rooms and what colors we would paint everything. The tour is over on the second floor and Joe shows Dee her guest room. You can tell he just purchased the bed, dresser and all the linens. Everything looks brand new. I have to remind myself to thank him for that later. If I was making a list of pros and con's, buying a bed for my best friend to sleep in while we visit is definitely a plus.

We leave Dee to unpack and go to the master bedroom. Words can't describe how beautiful it is. It's similar to Andrea's bedroom in that the majority of the walls are windows. There is a huge balcony and I open the french doors to go outside and take a look. Joe reaches over to embrace me while telling me that the lights and view are really beautiful at nighttime and the main reason he bought the house.

"I missed you, Joe. I had no idea how much until I saw you just now."

"I missed you, too, Angel. I'm so glad you're here. Did you two have a nice time today?" He asks.

"We had a great time. We flew first class and did a little shopping on Rodeo Drive."

"Good. If you want to shop some more tomorrow while I'm working, I'll write down a list of some places you might like to go to. I asked my driver to come back tomorrow for you and Dee so you won't have to drive in the crazy L.A. traffic. If you'd like to drive, you can always use one of my cars."

"Cars? As in more than one? How many cars do you have?" I ask.

"I have twenty cars."

"Holy shit! Why?"

"I'm kidding," he says laughing. "You look so surprised that I'd have more than one car. I have three cars. One is an SUV, one is a convertible and the other is electric."

"Okay, your choices make sense. How do you decide which one to drive?" I ask.

"I usually take the convertible if the weather is nice and I'm not working. I use the SUV a lot during the winter and the electric car I use mostly to get around town."

"Maybe you should get a fourth car for when it rains. And another one that you only drive on Thursdays." I say jokingly.

"Hey, I'm not that bad. I have some friends that have ten or more cars."

I don't have a chance to respond because he starts to kiss me. I forget all about the cars, the mansion, Beverley Hills and Rodeo Drive. I'm just thinking about Joe's mouth on mine and how good it feels.

"I have a present for you. Do you want it now?" He asks.

"Hell yes! Bring on the presents," I yell.

I'm one of the few people I know of that is never shy about receiving gifts. I give Frankie and Dee lists for my birthday and Christmas. Maybe it comes from being an only child. I was always spoiled on holidays because I was the only person my parents had to buy for. They insisted that I write down what I wanted and I always obliged. Then they would buy one special gift that wasn't on my list, which they had picked out together just for me.

Joe comes back and hands me a box that is unmistakable in color. If you know Tiffany's, you know what I mean. I look up at him and he says, "Open it."

"Can we sit down on your bed first?" I ask.

"Yeah, come on."

We go to his bed and both of us sit down next to one another. I start by untying the pretty, white, satin bow on top. I'm doing it carefully because I don't want to ruin it. I open up the box slowly and there is a small, velvet pouch the same color as the box inside. I slowly lift up the flap on the pouch and pour out the contents. Two diamond earrings fall into my hand. They're humongous. They look like the ones that Andrea loaned to me

"Andrea told me you borrowed hers for Star's party and I thought you should have your own." Joe says this while removing one of them from my hand and undoing the screw back.

I still haven't spoken yet because I don't know what to say. How do you thank somebody for something like this?

"Come on, let's get these on you and see how they look."

Joe lifts up my face and I'm crying. I'm so overwhelmed by his thoughtfulness, and without words I'm trying to show him how much I appreciate what he's given to me and why.

"Oh Angel, don't cry. Do you not like them? Are you unhappy?" He asks.

"No," I sniffle. "I'm so happy that I just don't know what to say. How do I thank you for these? It's not just that you bought me diamond earrings, Joe, it's that you bought them because Andrea loaned me hers and you wanted me to have my own. It's so thoughtful and kind. Thank you. From the bottom of my heart, thank you. I love them."

I hug and kiss him and then he helps me put the earrings on. We go into the bathroom so I can look at myself in the mirror and I love them.

"What was that you said before about thanking me?" He asks while standing behind me and wrapping his arms around me.

I look at him grinning behind me in the mirror and break out into a huge smile.

"What are you up to Joe Barrick?"

He leaves the bathroom and I follow him into the bedroom where he pulls out another present. It's a small box and I don't recognize where this one is from.

"Joe, what are you doing? Two presents?"

"Just open it." He says.

We sit down on the bed again and I start to unwrap the gift. I'm not as delicate with this one, mostly because I'm dying to see what is inside. When I finally get the top of the box off I laugh out loud. It's La Perla lingerie.

"A little confident, are we?" I ask.

"Hell, I'd wear that lingerie if somebody gave me those earrings." He jokes.

We both laugh and kiss again. I tell Joe that his thank you will have to wait considering Dee is probably eager for us to go to dinner. Joe leaves the room so I can freshen up, change and unpack some of my things. I go back into the bathroom when he is gone and look at myself in the mirror again. I smile at my reflection, but I'm not sure my reflection is smiling back. Does happiness like this last? I'm so afraid of losing what I have that I never appreciate the moment when something good is happening to me. I throw some water on my face and look back in the mirror.

"I promised myself that I was going in head first," I tell my reflection. "And that's what I intend to do."

CHAPTER TWENTY-EIGHT

Our dinner turns out to be a lot more than we expected. Joe has invited some of his friends and they're almost all famous. Both Dee and I are a little bit star struck at first, but I feel safe because I'm with Joe, and Dee feels safe because she looks just like one of them. She ends up spending most of the evening talking to the co-star of Joe's current film. His name is Jack and he looks a lot like Joe. I grab her hand at one point to drag her into the bathroom with me.

"Dee, what are you doing? You're completely flirting with that guy and Drake is at home waiting for you."

"Drake is at home with his lover, he's not waiting for me."

"What are you talking about? I thought you were his lover." I ask.

"I need a penis for that, Mia. Drake is gay. His parents don't know and he doesn't want them, to so he asked me to pretend to be his girlfriend. In exchange, we go to great parties, hopefully get photographed together and just have a good time."

"Jesus, Dee. Why didn't you tell me before?"

"Because I wanted you to like him and not judge him based on the circumstances. He's a really nice guy and he treats me great, but it's just an arrangement."

"Well, what happens if he finds out you were with somebody else?" I ask.

"Then he tells his parents I cheated on him and at least they get off his back for a while. They're much older and he thinks if he tells them it will kill them. Plus, he's an only child like you and he doesn't want to hurt them."

"Okay, but be careful with that guy, he looks a little shady to me. He's too good looking and he says all the right things. I think he's full of shit."

"You just described Joe, Mia." She laughs.

I laugh, too because on first appearance, that is exactly Joe. The rest of the evening is full of small talk and lots of introductions. We're eating at a place called, "The Nice Guy" and it's apparently the hot spot restaurant in L.A. for celebrities to see and be seen. I had read about it before, and the food is wonderful. I have to admit that the company is, too. Dee and I let out little squeals any time we think we see somebody famous. Joe introduces us to everyone he knows and Dee and I take lots of pictures.

Joe and I find Dee and Jack together drinking coffee in his kitchen the next morning. I can't tell you that I was surprised. Dee is famous for kick starting any relationship in record time. We shop all day Friday for a movie premiere we're going to tomorrow night. Dee told me over breakfast this morning that Jack has invited her to go to the premiere as his date. I'm happy to know that she'll be coming with me and I'll know somebody else there aside from Joe.

We end up at a little high-end boutique that has the cutest things. The owner is working and she tells us most everything here is one of a kind and that she does all the buying. We tell her about the premiere and who our dates are, so she really takes a lot of time helping us find just the right thing to wear. I end up buying a georgette Michael Costello dress that has a sweet pink flower pattern and is casual enough to hopefully wear again. It is asymmetrical with an attached belt and hugs in all the right places.

Dee buys a pair of black slacks that fit her body like a glove and a light blue silk halter-top. We figure if we're going to be photographed together, we might as well stay in the same color family and both get pastels. Dee wears the same shoe size as mine, so she's going to borrow my black Manolo's and I end up buying a pair of high-heeled nude sandals. Both of us are trying to do our shopping quickly because we plan on spending the better part of the afternoon lying out by Joe's pool.

The four of us have a quiet dinner at Joe's house and we end up drinking too much and playing charades. I can't remember the last time I had so much fun. I feel like Joe and I are officially a couple tonight. We let Dee and Jack relax while we cooked dinner together and he helped me set the table. It gave me an idea of what it might be like if we lived together. We talked about our favorite movies and books and I found out that we both love to play tennis. Both of us admitted that we're not very good at it, but we love it anyway.

That night after Joe and I make love, I feel a calmness come over me that I haven't felt in a long time. It feels like contentment and I want to share my feelings with him.

"Have I told you how happy I am to be here?" I ask.

"You have. Have I told you how happy I am to have you here?" He asks back.

"You have." I say giggling. "How many movies do you usually

make a year?"

"Well," he says. "It depends. Sometimes two or three but this year I'm only doing this one. I'm trying to step away a little bit from action movies and get into something different. It's hard, because once people view you as an action star, it's difficult to break out of that role and try new things."

"What is the movie you're making now?" I ask.

"It's a romantic comedy. The director took a big risk on whether or not people would want to see me in a comedy."

"I think you've got the romance part covered." I say smiling.

"Do you really think people would want to see an old man like me in a romance? I'm thirty-five years old now. All those young heart throbs out there, they're practically babies."

"Oh yeah, you're all washed up at thirty-five. Way past your prime. Better call it a day and find something else to do with your life." I say jokingly.

"I love you, Mia Roman."

"I love you, too, Joe Barrick." I say, snuggling closer to him and falling asleep with a smile on my face.

All day Saturday is spent lounging around Joe's pool and drinking Bloody Mary's to help fight our hangovers. The Italian in me has always made my olive skin tan quickly, but I can't say the same for Dee. She spends most of the time in the shade with the highest SPF sun block on. This is truly a vacation for me and the more time I spend with Joe, the more I know that I am falling in love with him.

I haven't shown Dee the earrings yet, but I will today before the party when I wear them. For however comfortable I thought I might be financially, nothing compares to Joe's wealth. He doesn't flaunt his money, but he isn't afraid to spend it and make plans for future purchases. I have to admit that it is a little overwhelming. The other night at dinner a lot of the conversations revolved around flying to Paris for Fashion Week and where to stay the next time you're in St. Barts, it's hard not to be judgmental about what I perceive as excess.

The thing I've noticed the most that money seems to offer people like Joe and his friend Jack, is basically a stress-free lifestyle filled with financial security. They're never worried about monetary things and they want for nothing. I'm trying not to be resentful because I grew up in a family that struggled for money, where money was the core of all stress and worry. I know having money doesn't prevent things, like Andrea getting cancer, but even in that situation you have less to worry about. You can afford the best medical treatment money can buy and you know those you leave behind are taken care of. When my father was going through chemotherapy, we couldn't afford a nurse to come to our house to take care of him. It was my Mother and I by his side when he was throwing up and losing his hair. There were no medical experts that we could summon in the middle of the night; instead there were trips to the emergency room with an ambulance bill left to pay.

I don't want to seem bitter or envious, because I'm not. I came to terms a long time ago with being happy with what I have. I'm also the one staying in this huge mansion and shopping on Rodeo Drive, so as long as I'm staying in this glass house, I can't throw stones. I keep thinking about what Andrea said before I left to come here and I'm not taking anything too literally. I try to relax and forget about the money, at least momentarily so I can enjoy myself and have a good time.

While I'm sunning myself on a lounge chair, I start to come up with some ideas. My phone is inside the house, so I walk in to get out of the sun for a little bit and make some notes. I've made a decision that I want to try and help facilitate Dee and Frankie buying a house, even if they have to do it together. I want them to own some property because as my father always told me, your security is in your land. I also want to look into some charities when I get home and donate a portion of my income. I'm used to making way less money than I have now, I can certainly afford to donate some to a worthy cause. I feel better after writing all of this down and I'm excited to talk about it with Dee and Frankie when I get back home.

CHAPTER TWENTY-NINE

The premiere! Oh my, the premiere! What was I to expect? I went with no expectations and I probably should have set some. Dee nearly passed out when she saw the earrings, and if I do say so myself, we both were looking damn good. Lying out in the sun for me has paid off and I look like I have a very healthy glow. All cameras turned on Dee when her and Jack got out of the limo. Everyone was trying to figure out who she was because she really comes off as somebody famous. Joe and I went last, and the flashes temporarily blinded me. There were so many cameras, people were just screaming questions at Joe and trying to thrust papers and pens in his hand for an autograph.

Joe leaned over and whispered that I would be fine because I was holding his hand so tight it was turning white. On our way inside, they ask you to stop in front of a wall and pose for all of the cameras. Most of the celebrities usually agree to do this because it is the picture that will be used most often. When I walk up to the wall with Joe, they ask me to get out of the way. I walk over to the side and I'm about to start crying my feelings are so hurt. Joe doesn't seem to notice because he just starts posing the way the photographers are asking him to. They start screaming for me to come back in the picture with Joe, so I reluctantly walk back over. He grabs my hand and we pose for a minute or so while they snap more photos.

I feel like punching him in the face and running to the airport, but instead I keep my composure and smile. Next they're asking him questions about me, and one woman even has the nerve to ask him where Olivia is. Joe politely avoids all of their questions, and when he feels like we've stood there long enough, he waves good-bye and thanks everyone.

"Why didn't you answer their questions?" I ask.

"Because they'll just take my words and turn them into something that doesn't resemble what I said at all. Do you understand? I mean, does that make sense?"

"I suppose so." I answer quietly.

Sticking up for me would have been better. I wish he hadn't let me walk to the side when they asked me to. And I wish he would have fielded their questions about who I was and where Olivia was. It made me feel like he was ashamed of me and didn't want these people to know that we were together as more than friends. It puts me in a bad mood for most of the evening and when Dee and I are in the bathroom together at intermission, I tell her what happened.

"Mia, I think he's right. I wouldn't give those people any ammunition at all. They're going to write whatever they want about Joe no matter what answers he gives them. You should trust him; he's been dealing with this kind of thing for a long time. Plus, he's all over you. A blind person can see that you're a couple."

"But it made me feel like he was embarrassed to be with me or something. It's really soured my mood." I know I'm whining, but I can't help it.

"Maybe he is embarrassed to be seen with you. Did you ever

257

think of that?"

Dee and I both whip our necks around to see Olivia coming out of one of the bathroom stalls. This is honestly the last thing I need right now. You would think that girl would know better, especially since I'm with Dee and she appears to be alone. I remember how quickly she wimped out the last time Dee became bold with her. I try to take the kinder route and make amends with her.

"Olivia, I want to tell you something. Joe was planning on ending things with you way before I came into the picture. You need to know that I wasn't the cause for your relationship ending. I'm sorry if you dislike me, but there is no reason why you should. You don't even know me." I'm trying to be as nice as I know how. Dee on the other hand is staring at me like I'm crazy. I'm sure this is not what she thought I was going to say.

"I don't need to know you. I saw *People* Magazine. I know what you did to the shirt that I sent you. Don't tell me I have no reason to dislike you. How dare you call me a bitch and advertise it on a shirt for the whole world to see after you stole my man. Don't worry, Honey, I'm over him. Now you get my sloppy seconds." Olivia is seething while she talks and her face has turned bright red.

"When you say sloppy seconds, Olivia, do you mean that little trick you taught Joe that he used in bed with Mia last night?" Dee asks.

"Bitch!" Olivia says, and walks out of the bathroom.

"She didn't even wash her hands." Says Dee, and we both start laughing.

258

After we've regained control, I ask Dee what she thought Olivia was talking about when she brought up *People* Magazine. I had no idea I was in it and nobody had called to tell me yet. Dee didn't know either. We both grabbed our phones and Googled, but found nothing. We decided we would stop on the way back to Joe's and pick one up.

Luckily, we don't run into Olivia for the rest of the premiere. My mood picks up a little bit after the bathroom incident, but I'm still feeling upset with Joe. We stop to pick up the magazine on the way home under the guise that Dee and I want munchies. Joe keeps offering us caviar and Gouda cheese, but we want chocolate and potato chips, so it's not a complete lie.

We buy two copies because Dee is going home with Jack tonight so Joe and I can have a night alone in his house. We start flipping through the pages right after we walk away from the checkout stand. Dee finds the article first and we both lean over her magazine. There is nothing on the cover, but inside there is a picture of me at the coffee shop we went to after visiting Andrea. It's the one where I'm sitting outside alone and you can see the shirt very clearly. The caption reads: *Could Mia Roman, J.B.'s new love interest, be referring to his jilted ex Olivia Lucas?* There's a second one of Joe and I holding hands and walking back to my car. The caption under that one reads: *Is this plain Jane going to be enough for tomcat J.B.?*

"Oh God, I'm plain Jane! Dee, I'm plain Jane!" I moan.

"Fuck them, Mia. You are so not plain Jane. They just have nothing else to write. Don't pay attention to this shit."

"I'm plain Jane and he is a tomcat. We're Jane and Tom. This is horrible. My Mother is going to see that I'm wearing this shirt and that her daughter is a plain Jane."

"Mia, stop it. Seriously, this is ridiculous. I think it's tame compared to some of the things I've seen them write. Please don't flip out about this." Dee pleads.

"I won't. I promise. We should go; they're outside waiting for us."

The ride to drop Dee and Jack off is a quiet one, and it's deadly silent in the limo when they're gone. I don't know what I'm supposed to say to Joe right now because I'm upset, but I don't have the energy to argue. Joe seems to sense something, but he's not talking either. We thank the limo driver and walk up to Joe's bedroom. I grab my bag and lock myself in the bathroom. I go for the pajamas instead of the lingerie considering the mood between us right now. I leave on the earrings just because I love the way they look. They sparkle so brightly it's almost as blinding as a paparazzo's flash.

Joe knocks on the bathroom door to ask if I'm all right, so I force myself to stand up and walk out.

"Hey, are you okay? You've hardly said ten words to me all night. And why are you all wrapped up in so much clothing? What's up?" He asks.

"If we start to talk about this, Joe, we will argue and I don't want to argue. I'm on vacation."

"That's just not sensible, Mia. My options are arguing with you or the silent treatment? Why don't we talk about whatever it is that's bothering you without the argument?"

"Fine. I'll tell you what it is," I say, taking a seat on his bed. "You let those people, those photographers, push me out of the way and then you wouldn't answer any questions about me or Olivia. You left them to draw their own twisted conclusions. And you have too much money. Do you donate to charity? Do you realize how hard all of this is for me?" I'm crying now and it's not how I wanted this to happen.

Joe comes over and sits next to me on the bed. He grabs my hand and I pull away, leaving me with the memories of my apartment the night I called him a womanizer and he walked out. I change my mind and let him grab my hand.

"Mia, you need to trust me on some things. Those photographers didn't push you away, they asked you to step to the side. It's all part of my job and being in the spotlight at certain times. I already told you why I didn't answer their questions, it wouldn't make a difference. I don't have to justify myself to them. It's none of their business who you are to me or what happened between Olivia and I. That is between us, and we decide when it's appropriate to answer those questions together." He's really getting into speech mode now and I'm enrapt by the animation in his face and hands. It's almost hard to follow what he's saying.

"Secondly, I don't know what constitutes having 'too much money' but I'm doing alright. And I donate a lot of not just my money to charity, but my time as well. Don't judge me because I'm wealthy, Mia. I've earned that money and I have to deal with a lot of shit to have as much money as I do. Money can't buy my privacy, it can't stop people from chasing me down for pictures every time I leave the house, or constantly writing things about me that just aren't true. I told you before that I would give it all back if I had a choice. And lastly, I have an idea of how hard all of this is for you, but I think you make it harder than it has to be. I think you're so afraid something bad is going to ultimately happen, that you can't take time to appreciate the good. You keep delivering up this drama to avoid your real feelings. You keep finding ways to deny your emotions, and I'm here to tell you that I'm in this for the long haul. You're eventually going to have to face the fact that you're in love with me."

I almost want to start clapping.

"Have you ever been nominated for an Academy Award?" I ask flippantly.

Joe looks hurt. "Is that what you thought that was? Acting?" He asks.

"No, no, Joe. I was trying to lighten the situation. I'm sorry." I say feeling guilty now.

"Stay here with me, Mia. Come and live with me. Let's make this our home instead of just my empty house. I love you. I want you to be here with me." Joe drops down on his knees in front of me on the bed and I think for a moment that he's going to propose.

"I can't live here, Joe. My home that I've made for myself is in San Francisco. I love it there. I can't leave my family and friends just like that. My business is there and my life is there. How can you ask me to move in with you when we're in the middle of an argument? It's not going to solve anything."

"Sure it will. You'll only be an hour away from San Francisco by plane. You can fly home as often as you want and your friends can fly here as often as they want. I'll buy you a hundred open ended tickets that you can give out as you please. They can all stay here, the place is big enough."

"Joe? No. It's not just living in Los Angeles; it's all this crap that comes with it. I really like it here, but for visiting purposes only. I could never live here permanently and be surrounded by all of the paparazzi day in and day out. Come to San Francisco. See what it's like to live without all of this for a little while. You say you hate it so much, then get the hell away from it. Andrea did, and she's so much happier. You're already a famous, amazing actor, you don't need to live in Los Angeles to get discovered. You don't even have to live with me if you don't want to."

"The paparazzi are in San Francisco, too." Says Joe.

"Yes, but only because we're a new thing. They'll get used to us as a couple and leave us alone. It's not like here, where your life is filled with eating in famous restaurants and going to movie premieres. You say I deliver up drama, but you do the same by attending all these things you know you will get photographed at." I argue back.

"I need to for my career, Mia. I don't enjoy it. I have to get my face out there and be seen."

"That's bullshit! You're good enough; you don't need to sell

263

yourself out to all this publicity shit to get acting parts. You've already made a name for yourself."

"I don't want to leave, Mia. It's my life and it's what I know, it's what I'm used to. I want to stay here in Los Angeles and I want you to be here with me."

"I don't want to be here, Joe. I'm sorry."

He leaves me sitting there by myself and goes into the bathroom. I hear the lock click and the sound seems amplified in my head. I crawl under the covers and start to quietly cry. I must have fallen asleep because I don't even hear Joe come out of the bathroom, I just wake up the next morning with a headache and a broken heart.

CHAPTER THIRTY

Joe is not laying next to me and the house seems really quiet when I finally manage to pull myself out of bed. I walk downstairs after I wash my face and brush my teeth, but no one is here. The french doors that lead to the back are locked, so I know he's not out there. There's no note, nothing. I grab the phone and call Dee on her cell, but she doesn't answer. I feel uneasy all of a sudden. I have no car, so I can't go anywhere, and I have no idea where Joe is or when he's coming back. I imagine a scenario in my mind where he walks through the front door with a bouquet of roses and tells me he'll come to San Francisco. I even stare at the front door for a moment willing it to happen.

The buzzer for the gate goes off. Damn, I'm good. Actually, Joe probably wouldn't need to ring his own buzzer. I click the button.

"Who is it?" I ask.

"It's Dee."

I click another button to open the gate and peek out the window. She's kissing Jack good-bye and getting out of the car. I open the front door and she looks me up and down.

"What the hell is wrong with you?" She asks.

I tell Dee what happened last night and how I woke up alone this morning.

"I really like Joe, Mia. I mean, I really like him and I can tell that you love him, but what he's asking you to do is wrong. If he hates the spotlight as much as he says he does, he would be dying to get away from it. I'm not buying that it will hurt his career; I think he's already too famous for that. I also think his good looks might have gotten him in the door, but his acting is what has sky rocketed him to where he is now. Where he lives won't change that."

"I'm so glad that you see it the same way I do, Dee. I thought I was going crazy. He keeps telling me that I'm just afraid to be happy and that I won't allow myself to feel emotions. But he's the one who is really afraid. I know that he truly hates all the attention, but he thinks people will lose interest in him if he leaves Los Angeles and doesn't go to a million parties a week."

"What are you going to do?" Dee asks.

"I'd like to go to the hotel that *VIP's* agent said he would pay for. We're starting work tomorrow anyway and I'm just feeling uncomfortable here right now. He could have at least left me a note or something so I didn't wake up alone."

"Okay, whatever you want Sweetie. Let's go pack."

Dee requests an Uber and we both go upstairs to pack our things. The front gate buzzer goes off and Dee and I are ready to go. We check into the Regent Beverly Wilshire and it's a really beautiful hotel. I'm not as depressed as I thought I would be, I know it has a lot to do with Dee being here and me still holding out hope that Joe and I will work this out somehow.

We call room service for lunch and then we call Frankie to update her on everything that has happened. Dee does the majority of the talking and she over dramatizes the Olivia incident, which makes me laugh. While she's still on the phone, my cell rings and I look over and see that it's Joe. I go out onto the balcony and answer the phone.

"Hello."

"Mia? Where are you? Where did you go?" He asks.

"Where did you go? I woke up and you were gone. No note, nothing."

"I had to get out for a while, I was feeling claustrophobic." He answers.

"You live in a mansion, Joe." I'm being sarcastic but there is a ring of truth there.

"Are you going to tell me where you are?" He asks again.

"Dee and I checked into a hotel. We're starting work tomorrow and we just wanted to be closer to the job."

"What hotel?"

"Beverly Wilshire." I say.

"I live five minutes away from there, Mia. Tell me why you really left?"

"Maybe I was feeling a little claustrophobic, too. I was upset last night when I went to bed and I was even more upset this morning when I woke up alone in your house. I felt trapped in a strange place with no car."

"Trapped? I make you feel trapped?"

"That's not what I said, Joe. Please don't take this out of context. Maybe being apart for today will be a good thing. I think we both have a lot to think about."

"But I go back to the set tomorrow and you start working. When are we going to see each other again? How long are you even here for?" He asks.

"It will probably take us two days to do the work, so that means we'll leave around Wednesday. Why don't I call you later tonight and we can make a time to see each other again?" I offer.

"Is this really what you want, Mia? Because it seems to me that you're just running away."

"This is what I want for right now, Joe. I'm not running away, you did that this morning."

Damn. There I go again with those biting remarks. I really have to learn to keep my mouth shut.

"Nice, Mia. Very nice. I'll talk to you later." And with that, he hangs up.

Dee is saying good-bye to Frankie when I walk back into the room. I tell her what just happened with Joe and she thinks the time apart is best right now, too. I'm feeling good about my decision. I really feel Joe is wrong, and some time to think is never a bad thing. We're both afraid, but I let my fears go when I went to him at Andrea's and told him how I really felt. Now he needs to not only recognize what he is afraid of, but let go of some of his fears, too.

After we finish lunch, Dee and I spend the rest of the afternoon at the hotel spa. It's just what the doctor ordered. We both have side-by-side massages that last for an entire hour, and then we have pedicures with a foot massage. It's been a really long time since I last had a deep tissue massage and we're so tired that we end up taking a nap before dinner.

The sun is streaming through the windows when I open my eyes. I reach to turn the clock around that is sitting on the end table and it says 5:30 a.m. Holy shit! I slept the entire night away. I look over at Dee and she is sleeping in the bed next to me. I guess that's what a good massage will do to you. I feel so strange; I haven't gone to bed that early since I was like seven years old.

I take advantage of having the bathroom to myself and soak in a nice, long bath and shave my legs. My purse is in the bathroom, so I grab my phone to check my messages. The display reads five missed calls and several text messages. I hit the voice mail button. The first is from my mom.

"Hi Honey. Hope you're having a nice time in Los Angeles with your friend Joe. Speaking of Joe, Mia – Linda told me about the article in *People* magazine and Daniel went out and got it for me. I can't say I'm too happy with your choice of t-shirts. Daniel tells me you probably have a good explanation. (God bless Daniel, I think.) We're going to drive to Tahoe today and gamble a little bit but we'll be home on Wednesday. Call me when you can."

VIP's agent is the next message and he tells me that a car will pick me up in the lobby of the Beverly Wilshire at 8 a.m. I'm glad I never called him and told him we were going to Joe's, or else I might have to explain how we eventually ended up here.

Uriah leaves a message and him and the other guys in his group take turns thanking me for the jackets and telling me what a hit they were at their show this weekend. I'm really happy for him.

The last two messages are both from Joe. In the first one he seems a little bit upset that I haven't called him yet. I look at the time of the message and it says eight p.m. His second message is at ten p.m. and in this one he sounds really sad. He says that he will be home all night and that I can call any time. He also says that he misses me in his bed and can still smell me on the sheets and that makes me sad, too.

My bath makes me feel refreshed and ready to start what I know will be a long day of work. Dee is so hard to wake up that I practically have to drag her out of bed. Once her eyes finally open and she sees the time, she freaks out.

"We're on vacation! In L.A.! And we fell asleep at five o'clock? I'm getting old. That's what this is, a sign that I'm getting too fucking old to even go on vacation."

"Go get in the shower, you're fine. We had deep tissue massages; they're the equivalent of a horse sedative. You're not getting old." I say.

We're in the lobby at exactly eight a.m. and see the driver is already waiting.

"Hi, are you our limo driver?" I ask him.

"Are you Olivia Lucas?" He asks me back.

I look over at Dee and make a face. Great! She's staying in the same hotel as us? Doesn't she live in Los Angeles? Why is she in a hotel? We tell the driver no and run and hide by the front desk area. I feel like I'm sixteen years old and this is absolutely ridiculous. I'm about to come out of hiding and tell Dee that we have no reason to be afraid to see Olivia, when I hear her voice coming out of the elevator. Dee and I both peek around the corner and she's with Dante, the hairdresser.

"He has a cast on his foot." Dee says.

I stretch to get a better look and we both start laughing. It must have happened at Star's party when he fell on the dance floor. They're approaching where we are, so we stifle our giggles to hear their conversation.

"What the hell do you think she's doing here?" I ask.

"Does Dante live here? Maybe he's visiting and this is where he's staying." Dee answers.

"Excuse me ladies, can I help you?"

Dee and I look up to find a very snooty looking man in a hotel uniform standing above us.

"Do you have an invisibility cloak?" Dee asks.

We start laughing even harder and the man walks away. He looks like he might be on a mission to tell somebody else about us. He doesn't resemble somebody who would just walk away from a situation in a hotel like this. Olivia and Dante are close enough so we can hear what they're saying now. Olivia is telling Dante that she knew it couldn't be truly over between them. Who is them? She also says that seeing him last night reassured her there were feelings between them still and she intended to make a move. Dee and I look at each other with our mouths wide open. Before they walk too far for us to hear anything else, Dee and I catch one final sentence from Dante. He says that he knew J.B. could never fall for a plain Jane like

Mia Roman, and they leave a trail of laughter behind.

"I told you I was a plain Jane. Now everybody is going to be calling me that," I whine. "How could Olivia have seen Joe last night when he left me a message from home at ten thirty?" I ask.

"She didn't talk to him. She's a lying, manipulative bitch. I wouldn't believe one word that comes out of that girl's mouth." Dee yells.

"She said, 'seeing him,' Dee. She didn't say talking to him. She saw him last night." I yell back.

"Stop yelling at me. Come on, we should move before that guy comes back with our cloak. This is the Beverly Wilshire, right? They should have that here."

"Don't joke," I say partly laughing. "This is serious. If he saw her last night, Dee – It's over between us. I'm not kidding." I say.

We both start looking around the lobby for another driver and one walks in. We ask him if he's here from *VIP* and he says that he is. The whole drive over to the job, Dee and I discuss what just happened at the hotel. Dee thinks I should just call him and ask him. She also points out that I did completely flake out last night by not calling him, as she also did to Jack.

"Dee, we fell asleep. It wasn't our fault that we didn't call them last night."

"Who falls asleep that early? We should have gone on vacation to a retirement village in Florida if we're going to go to bed before seven. We'll eat lunch for dinner, play a quick game of Bingo and hit the sack. How does that sound?" Dee asks.

"It sounds like you've completely lost focus on our conversation. Come on, Grammy," I joke. "We're here."

VIP's agent greets us and introduces us to the three members of the group. They're all a little scary looking with tons of tattoos and grills on their teeth, but the moment they start talking and shake our hands, we feel so at ease. We have a meeting to make sure we all know exactly what they're looking for and then we're given the gems that were delivered to them so we can start the job.

Dee and I work the entire day and make incredible progress. It's so much easier working on a large job with a partner. We estimate that we will be done by tomorrow afternoon, which is way ahead of schedule. We stop at around seven o'clock and we're both exhausted. The work is tediously monotonous and it hurts having to hold your arms up all day.

We go to the hotel and get room service for dinner. We also order a bottle of champagne to help us wind down and relax. Dee spoke to Jack during the day today and explained to him about why she didn't call him last night. They're planning on meeting up tomorrow night to have dinner together before she leaves. Their plans make me sad. I haven't called Joe all day and there are no messages from him when I check my phone. Dee is trying to convince me to call him instead of believing what we overheard Olivia say, but I don't want to deal with it.

I really do miss him, but Joe was right about our biggest obstacle being the distance. Who cares if it is one hundred miles or a thousand? When you can't see someone that you love on a daily basis, it's very hard to form a lasting relationship. Especially when the relationship is new and you want to really get to know that person. Just the couple of days that we spent at his house together showed me that we were very compatible in so many ways. Take out all the Hollywood and we would be just fine.

Dee and I are so tired that we go to bed early again. Not as early as last night, but early enough to get a good nights sleep. The next day at our job site, we're both in a really good mood over the work that's almost done. We're both proud of one another and excited at how well the cars have turned out. We call *VIP's* agent to let him know when we've completed the job and he shows up around an hour later with the group. They love it! They really can't say enough nice things about how great it looks and how incredible it's going to be in their video. They also tell Dee and I that they know all of their friends will want similar things done once they see the cars and we can expect to get a lot of referrals.

They have an autographed picture for us, which is very sweet. Dee and I take numerous photos of our work for my web site. Before we leave, I take a deep breath and cross my fingers while I go and thank *VIP's* agent one more time and try my luck with "The White Boyz" demo. I tell him about my experience with "The White Boyz" and speak of Uriah with fondness and appreciation for his music. I hand him the demo and ask him if he'll have a listen when he's got a moment. He agrees, saying there are no promises. I shake his hand and thank him again for the opportunity to work for him.

The ride back to the hotel is a celebration as Dee and I crack a bottle of champagne and toast one another for a job well done. Dee has to start getting ready right away for her last date with Jack. Our plane leaves early tomorrow morning and I can't help but wonder where Joe is and why he hasn't called. After Dee is gone for the night, I get into my pajamas and settle into bed to watch some television. I put on my diamond earrings and it makes me cry. I decide to give in and call Joe. His phone rings once, twice, three times and then his voice mail. I call again and this time it goes straight to voice mail. I leave a message telling him that my flight leaves tomorrow morning, I wanted to say good-bye and apologize for not calling him earlier. I still don't want to hang up the phone yet so I tell him how well the job went for *VIP* and that they were happy with the work. There's nothing else for me to say that will stall my message any longer, so I say good-bye and hang up.

I miss Frankie a lot so I call her next. She's at Charlie's house and I can tell they're having fun together, so I just tell her that I will see her tomorrow. I browse the room service menu and order some ice cream to help chase my blues away. While I wait for my sundae to arrive, I look for sad things to watch on television so it can be my excuse for why I can't stop crying. My patience level is zero and after about a half an hour, I call room service back to complain about not getting my sundae yet. As soon as I'm done griping to the poor, non-English speaking lady who has answered the phone, there is a knock on my door. I apologize quickly and hang up.

"Who is it?" I ask.

"Room Service."

I open the door and Joe is standing there holding my sundae.

"You ordered a hot fudge sundae, ma'am?" He asks.

"Joe! What are you doing here and how did you get my ice-cream?"

"I bribed the room service waiter with an autograph for his girlfriend." He says and winks at me.

Again with the winking. I wink back to gauge his reaction, but he doesn't do anything except keep standing there with my melting sundae in his hand.

"Are you going to invite me in?" He asks.

I motion for him to come in the room, take the dripping sundae from him and put it on the table. I take a seat on the bed and Joe sits next to me.

"What are you doing here?" I ask again.

"I got your message and came right over. I've just been waiting for you to call. I didn't want to push myself on you if you needed some space."

"Oh, is that right?" I ask. "Is that why you went out with Olivia Lucas the other night when you said you missed me in your bed and you would be home?" I kind of surprise myself by saying that. I wish I had been a bit more subtle.

"I did not go out with Olivia Lucas, Mia. I don't know where you're getting your information from, but it's wrong." He looks at me accusingly.

"It can't be wrong. It came straight from her mouth. I heard her say it, Joe."

"You heard her say that she went out with me? Since when do you talk to Olivia?" He asks.

"No, I heard her say that she was with you. I didn't talk to her, Dee and I overheard her and Dante having a conversation when they were walking through the hotel. What is she even doing at this hotel anyway? Doesn't she live here in L.A.?"

"That hair dresser person is staying here for a convention, I suppose she was visiting with him. I was very depressed that night, and Jack called me because he was upset Dee had flaked out on him. We decided to meet for a drink around eleven at night and Olivia was with Dante at the same place we were at. I didn't know she would be there and she came there after Jack and I had already taken a seat."

"Does that mean you had to talk to her about me?"

"She asked me about you, and she seemed genuinely interested in what was happening with us and our relationship. I told her the truth. I needed someone to talk to and she was there. You have Dee and Frankie, I have nobody. I can't talk to Jack, he wanted to play pool and drink beer, not have a heart to heart about our relationships."

"Do you really think Olivia is genuinely interested, Joe? She's only interested in getting the better of me and of you. I can't believe you would share our problems with her. Out of anybody in the whole world, you pick her. Unbelievable!" I yell.

"I didn't pick her, she was just there. I had a couple of drinks and I was depressed. I wanted somebody else's opinion. And stop yelling at me." Joe yells back.

"Okay," I say lowering my voice. "Here's a piece of advice, Joe: don't go to your very recent ex-girlfriend that you dumped to get advice on your current girlfriend who she hates."

"Listen. I came here tonight to try and work things out with you, but you don't want that. I know now that you just want to create more obstacles so that we can't continue to be an 'us.'"

"Leave Hollywood, Joe. I'll show you how much I want this to work out. Leave and come with me to San Francisco. Get away from all this shit so we can find out what can develop between us. We'll never know if you stay here. And it's not like we can't come back to Los Angeles, we can visit here all the time. You'll still have your house and career here, but we'll live in San Francisco."

"Are you giving me an ultimatum?" He asks sadly.

"I wasn't thinking about it that way, but I suppose I am. I'd rather call it a choice."

Joe stands up and it looks like he's going to leave. He leans down and gives me a kiss on the cheek.

"Don't get up and leave, Joe. Leaving doesn't solve anything. You can't keep walking out every time I say something that you don't like." I plead.

"And you can't keep making excuses as to why this relationship won't work. If you want to see what can develop between us, you wouldn't give me ultimatums. Enjoy your sundae." He says, and walks out the door.

CHAPTER THIRTY-ONE

My house is such a welcoming sight. It makes me feel like I've been gone for a month, not just a little under a week. As soon as I walk through the door and put my bags down, my intercom buzzer rings and it's Eleni delivering my new orders. We talk for a little bit, but I'm evasive about Joe because my emotions are just too raw right now. I don't feel like sharing anything just yet. I didn't tell Dee what happened until we were halfway through our flight home. I ended up giving her the day off today so I could catch up on some things around the office.

I take care of inputting and matching up all the new orders that I received from Eleni today and then I go to my website to track all the new orders that were placed. They're still coming in by the hundreds so I call the temporary agency Dee told me about. I tell them that I need two people as soon as possible and what my requirements are. Dee and I are going to have to rework this office space to accommodate two more people. I really don't want all of this spilling into my living room.

My cell phone has been turned off since last night, so I power it up and check my messages. There's only one person I want to hear from and I'm pretty sure Joe hasn't called. Frankie, my mom and Andrea all left messages telling me to let them know as soon as I get in. The last message is from *VIP's* agent. He wants me to know that everyone who sees the cars is going absolutely nuts over them and he also thanks me for the extra business cards I gave him because he's been passing them out like crazy. Normally I would be elated by this news, but it's going to take a lot more to change my disposition today. I'm about to hit save on his message because the man can really talk, when I hear him mention "The White Boyz." He listened to their demo and him and all the *VIP's* think they have a lot of potential. He'd like to speak to Uriah about possible representation and he asks me to pass along his number.

I'm so happy I don't know what to do first. I start scrolling through my contacts to find Uriah's phone number. Should I tell him right away on the phone or should I wait and tell him in person? When he answers, I ask him where he is and he and the guys are actually down the street moving furniture. I tell him I'll be there in fifteen minutes.

Driving is not an option today because my street is so crowded already with cars and it's only one o'clock in the afternoon. I'm not taking the chance of losing my spot; it's not worth it. The walk actually clears my head and I'm disappointed when I spot the "Mambo Mattresses" moving truck. It's one of those times when your endorphins kick in and you feel like you could walk to Canada and back. Uriah is leaning against the truck, taking a break and smoking a cigarette.

"Hi." I say.

"Yo, Mia. How are you? Did you have a nice trip to your secret destination?" He asks.

"I'm good," I say laughing. "It wasn't a secret destination, I told you I just didn't want you to get your hopes up, that's all."

"Can you tell me where you went now that you're back?"

"I can. I went to Los Angeles because I was hired to do a job for *VIP*. They are making a music video and needed me to decorate some cars with gems. They are going to feature the cars in the video."

"Wow! That is the shit! Did you meet them?" He asks.

"We met them and they were very nice. They gave us an autographed picture and let us take some photos posing with them and the cars for my website. Also, I did all of my business dealings with their agent Dave G., and I happened to give him your demo right before I left yesterday." I look at Uriah apprehensively trying to gauge his reaction.

"You are one brave girl. I've heard of Dave G. and no agent like that is gonna listen to our demo."

"I'm sorry you feel that way, Uriah. I walked all the way over here to give you his number. He and the guys think "The White Boyz" have a lot of potential and he'd like to talk to you about representation."

Uriah's eyes widen and his mouth opens up, but he hasn't said anything yet. I keep staring at him waiting for him to respond.

"Uriah? Are you okay?" I ask.

"Yo, Mia, are you for real?"

"I'm for real." I hand him the business card that I've been holding the whole time and I watch him as he reads it again and again and again.

"Do you mind if I run up and tell my boys?" He asks

"Go ahead. I'll talk to you later." I say as I start to turn around and walk back home.

Uriah comes up behind me and gently kisses me on the cheek.

"Thanks Mia. You alright. I'm going to pay you back for this someday."

He turns and runs into the house that they are moving the furniture into. I stand on the sidewalk and listen for a moment until I hear sounds of celebration coming from inside. It makes my heart happy. It also makes me think of Andrea. When I get back to my house, I get in my car, lose my stupid parking space and drive to her house to see her.

Andrea doesn't look well, but her attitude as always, is phenomenal. Don is by her side, doting over her every need and the two of them together make my heart happy for the second time today. Don asks her if she'll be okay by herself for a while and she nods her head yes. I assume he wants to give us some time to catch up and girl talk by ourselves.

"How are you holding up?" I ask.

"I'm doing fine. I've got the best care money can buy and an attitude that money couldn't afford. The toughest part is over, now we just have to wait a little while so I can get some more tests done. I'm really positive, though. Tell me about your trip."

"Joe and I aren't together anymore. He wants me to move to Los Angeles and I want him to come to San Francisco. I did what you said, Andrea and I jumped in head first and let go of all of my fears, but he can't do the same."

"What are his fears, Mia?" She asks.

"I think he's afraid that people will forget about him if he leaves that whole Hollywood scene. He hates it so much yet he's willing to endure it for his career. I believe he is better than that. Don't you?"

"You're probably not going to like what I'm about to tell you, Mia. Joe is different in that the life he hates is also the only one he's ever known. He's got to decide what he wants more, you or his ego constantly stroked. Because no matter how rich and famous he becomes, he's still a little, insecure boy inside dying for attention. You have to let him be now, Mia. Let him make up his own mind."

"I plan to do just that. I will give him time to come to his own conclusions about us and to make his own choices." I say this decidedly and Andrea nods her head.

"Enough about me, how are you and Don doing?" I ask.

"There's something I need to tell you about Don and I."

"Oh God! Please don't tell me something terrible. I just couldn't handle it right now."

"No. Nothing horrible. In fact, quite the opposite. We're getting married!"

"Oh, Andrea. I'm so happy for you!"

I reach over to hug her and I hold on for as long as she'll let me. Never have I met someone so deserving of happiness.

"When?" I ask.

"Soon," she says smiling. "We're thinking of next month. That'll give us about six weeks for me to get myself back together again and to plan a very small, intimate wedding here. I want to get married in my home and Don does, too. Will you help me plan it, Mia?" She asks.

"On one condition." I say.

"You name it, it's yours."

"Can we use the casket to chill the champagne in?" I ask.

Andrea laughs and we hug again. We start to talk about all of the details and we even go so far as to start making a list. I suggest we get Frankie involved to help plan because she's the best at it and Andrea agrees. Don comes back in the room after Andrea calls him in and all of us spend the rest of the afternoon talking, sharing ideas and making arrangements for the upcoming nuptials.

The next couple of weeks pass by in a blur for me. Dee and I have trained the new temps and they're working out great. I put them on a three-month probationary period. If all works out and the orders keep coming in, I will hire them permanently. Dee and I have even thought about getting a workspace somewhere in the city so my house won't be so crowded.

Uriah called me and told me that he has flown to Los Angeles twice to meet with *VIP's* agent and they're going to start recording in a real studio. They can't wait. My mom and Daniel have just celebrated their three-month anniversary and the more I get to know him, the more I like him. In fact, the more I like my Mother because of him.

Dee is still seeing Jack. They fly back and forth almost every other weekend and I like who they are when they're together. Dee sometimes has to face the same thing I did with a little bit of tabloid press, but she's so different than me that she revels in the attention. She doesn't give me updates on Joe and I don't ask for them.

Frankie was going through a slump at work this month, but that worked out perfectly for Andrea and Don. They hired her to plan the wedding. She's still with Charlie and I'm happy to say they have a very normal, regular sex life. She and Dee have been talking seriously about buying a house together and I have told them that I will loan them the money for the down payment with no interest. I hope they take me up on my offer.

Bob and I are doing well. I still ask him on a daily basis where he went off to when he left me, but he never answers. I've filled my life these past few weeks with helping Andrea plan her wedding and working very hard to try and lose myself in my work. I got a call the other day from another agent of a movie star who resides in San Francisco. I'm supposed to meet her at a Pacific Heights address this afternoon to quote her on a job.

I take Uber because the parking is just as bad in Pacific Heights as it is in North Beach. The address her agent gave me has a "For Sale" sign in the front and there is a "SOLD" sign attached to it. Some of the houses in this area can cost millions and this looks like one of them. It's the kind of house I would have chosen on one of Frankie and my drives all those years ago. It's big and beautiful, but it also has a lot of foliage in front and it helps to semi hide the house.

I'm talking to Frankie on the phone when the Uber driver gets buzzed through the security gate. I'm describing the house to her in detail as we pull up to the main entrance. I finally hang up and look up at this huge, white house with pillars in the front and a wrap around porch with a swing on it. It makes you think of ice-cold lemonade and summer days. I get out of the car and walk to the front door slowly, so I can try and sneak a peek through the windows. I knock and wait a while, but nobody answers. I'm thinking I might have the wrong address, so I knock again.

The door opens slowly and Joe is on the inside. He's smiling at me and I don't know what to think. His eyes are so piercing and I feel a sadness rush through me suddenly. He's dressed in a tuxedo and I feel so strange. Is he dating this woman and he didn't know I was coming? I don't know what's going on. He reaches out to hug me and I hug him back. His smell makes me feel almost faint and I can't help myself, but I start to cry. I'm not crying small, sweet tears, I'm full on sobbing and it feels like such a release. I've missed him so much for so long and it feels so good for him to hold me right now. After a very long time, I reluctantly let Joe let go of me.

"Hi Angel." He says.

"What are you doing here, Joe? Where is the woman I'm supposed to meet?" I ask.

"There's no woman. You're meeting me here, I set this up."

"But why? What are you doing in San Francisco? And why are you wearing a tuxedo?"

"Okay, one thing at a time, Angel. I'm in San Francisco because I just moved here. I bought this house. Do you like it?" He asks.

"What are you talking about? You didn't buy this house."

"I did. It's mine. Well, it's actually ours because your name is on the title, too. I just assumed that if we were going to be husband and wife that you would want to live here with me and be part owner of our home."

I can't talk. I do that pinching thing again and it hurts so badly that I yelp out loud. I want to rewind a minute so that I can hear what he has just said again. Instead, he takes my hand and leads me into the house. I'm looking around at how beautiful everything is, how perfect this home is. Joe takes me outside and even though there is no furniture anywhere in the house, there is a picnic set up on the grass in the backyard. Joe places me on the blanket that is spread out and gently pushes my shoulders so that I'm forced to sit down. He starts to bend down on one knee and I'm speechless.

"Mia Roman, I love you. These last couple of weeks have been the worst of my life. I've missed you so badly every single day that it was hard for me to even get up and go to work. Ever since I became famous, I've been searching for someone real and when I finally found you, I let you slip away. The reason I call you Angel is because I feel like you were sent to me. This time apart has made me realize that I can't live without you; I don't want another day to pass that we're apart. I need you. I need you more than anything else in this world. The fame, the attention, the money, all of it – None of it makes me feel the way I feel when I'm with you."

Joe hesitates and starts reaching around in his pocket. Oh God! Oh shit! He pulls out a little box and I let out a sob. When he opens it up, I see the most beautiful diamond engagement ring. It's the one that I could only ever dream of having.

"Will you marry me?"

"Yes! Yes, I'll marry you!"

We embrace for an eternity and fall onto the blanket in laughter. Joe slips the ring on my finger and we sit outside and toast our engagement with champagne. He shows me the rest of the house and leads me back outside to give me a tour of the guesthouse that he thinks is perfect for my business. It is definitely large enough to accommodate the four of us and I can't believe how much he knew about the things I would want in a home.

"I have a confession to make." He says when the tour is over.

"What is that?" I ask smiling.

"Frankie helped me pick out the house. She said she would know the one when she saw it, and she was right. Dee took me to the Pappas Brothers to buy your ring, she said they were the best. Andrea made our picnic basket and I went to meet your Mother and ask her for your hand in marriage. She introduced me to her boyfriend Daniel, and they're the ones that suggested I wear this tuxedo."

The ring that I just can't stop staring at and the house that is so perfect for us. The fact that he asked my friends and family for help makes this moment that much more special. I'm honored that he asked my Mother for my hand in marriage. I feel so blessed by my family and friends.

"How did all of them keep this from me?" I ask.

"They love you, that's how."

At this moment, I feel all of their love.

CHAPTER THIRTY-TWO

Andrea and Don's wedding is held on a beautiful Sunday afternoon. She found out last week that she is in remission. Her dress is a custom made Vera Wang of cream silk with a matching scarf wrapped elegantly around her head. The scarf is hiding her hair that is now almost completely gone and her body is much too thin from her sickness, but those things won't last. That is not what people will remember about this day. Her hair will eventually grow back and she will gain weight and her body will be healthy again. Her smile as she walks down the aisle and sees Don waiting for her. The words they say to one another before they're pronounced man and wife. The amazing people she has invited to share this day with her and Don. That is what people will remember.

Andrea asked me a couple of weeks ago to be her maid of honor and I was flattered. Don asked his son Tony to be his best man. The ceremony is just the right amount of time and the dinner is being served outside with assigned seating. The head table is a small one since the wedding party is only us four plus Joe and Tony's date. The time for the speeches is arriving and I'm more nervous than I thought I would be. I've spent a lot of time preparing mine, and even though I believe it is well written and heartfelt, I'm not much of an orator.

"Can I have everyone's attention, please? Everyone, we'd like to start making the toasts now." I hear Frankie saying this, but it's like I've temporarily checked out I'm so nervous. Then I hear her say that Don's son will go first and I almost collapse in relief. I'm trying to compare his speech to mine, and I'm pretty sure mine is longer. Should I talk for so long? Everyone is clapping and Frankie is handing me the small microphone to take my turn. I reach out to grab it with a shaky hand.

"Most of you here today know that I met Andrea when she asked me to decorate her casket. It now serves as the most expensive champagne cooler in the world," I say this while pointing over to where it is displayed as a beautiful centerpiece next to the buffet table. I'm so grateful when everyone starts to laugh and I wait a moment for it to subside before I continue.

"Andrea, to me, is a combination of every person that I've ever loved in my life. Sometimes I'm drawn to a person because of how brave they are. Others show a kindness of heart that I didn't think was possible. Then, there are the selfless ones who love without condition and give without expectations. While most are fortunate to possess just one of those qualities, as I got to know Andrea, I realized she has them all." I hesitate and look over at Andrea who blows me a kiss.

"It was only fitting that along the road of Andrea's life, she would meet somebody who was her equal. It's not often that a person comes along and changes your mind about your very existence. I once read a quote from Andrea that said, 'When you find true love and you're faced with a decision, love will always make the decision for you.' Don and love made Andrea want to live again, and because of that, I want to celebrate and toast, not just their marriage, but life itself." I raise up my glass and say, "To Andrea and Don, and to a second chance at life and love."

The applause overwhelms me and I take turns kissing both the bride and groom. For the rest of the party Joe and I field questions about when we're going to get married and if we'll have children. We haven't made any decisions yet on either of those things. I am selling my apartment to Dee and Frankie, and I'm already almost all packed up and ready to move into me and Joe's new house. He's almost done filming his movie and we'll have plenty of time to make decisions, start decorating our home and planning the wedding.

There will always be obstacles for Joe and I to overcome, but there is a trust there now that makes things like paparazzi and tabloid rumors easier to handle. It's hard to imagine that only a couple of months ago I felt like I had been abandoned in the worst way and left with nothing. I have no hard feelings left for John, and I only wish him the best in his life. He didn't make my heart happy.

It reminds me of the Post-it note that he left me without any real explanation. I came across it when I was packing earlier in the week and I want to ask Don about it. I seek him out in the crowded house and eventually find him sitting alone on the sofa. He seems to be taking everything and everyone in with a look of pure contentment. I approach him and he looks up and smiles at me.

"Don, I wanted to ask you a question."

"Sure," he says and pats the seat next to him on the couch.

"When Andrea was in the hospital, you quoted Kurt Vonnegut to me. Are you a big fan?"

"I am. I've read everything he's ever written. Why?" He asks.

"Well, this might sound strange, but right before I met Andrea, my boyfriend had left me and all I found was a Post-it note. There was a quote on it and underneath he had written Kurt Vonnegut's name.

"Lay it on me." Don says.

"It read, 'Why you? Why us for that matter? Why anything?'"

"He didn't finish the quote." Don says laughing.

"He didn't?" I ask. "How does it end?"

"Because this moment simply is."

THE END...

Made in the USA
Middletown, DE
19 March 2016